*The Fight
to the Finish*

Also by Richard Hough

The Fleet that Had to Die (Hamish Hamilton)
Admirals in Collision (Hamish Hamilton)
The Potemkin Mutiny (Hamish Hamilton
The Hunting of Force Z (Collins)
Dreadnought (Michael Joseph)
The Big Battleship (Michael Joseph)
First Sea Lord: Admiral Lord Fisher (Allen and Unwin)
The Pursuit of Admiral von Spee (Allen and Unwin)
The Blind Horn's Hate (Hutchinson)
Captain Bligh and Mr Christian (Cassell)
Fighting Ships (Michael Joseph)
Louis and Victoria: The First Mountbattens (Hutchinson)
Advice to a Grand-daughter: Letters from Queen Victoria to
  Princess Victoria of Hesse (Ed.) (Heinemann)
One Boy's War (Autobiography) (Heinemann)
The Great Admirals (Weidenfeld and Nicolson)
The Murder of Captain James Cook (Macmillan)
Man O' War (Dent)
Angels One-Five (Cassell)
The Fight of the Few (Cassell)

Richard Hough

The Fight
to the Finish

CASSELL
LONDON

CASSELL LTD.
35 Red Lion Square, London WC1R 4SG
and at Sydney, Auckland, Toronto, Johannesburg,
an affiliate of
Macmillan Publishing Co., Inc.,
New York.

F
12

First published 1979

ISBN 0 304 30456 5

Typeset by Inforum Ltd, Portsmouth
Printed and bound in Great Britain by
Lowe & Brydone Printers Ltd,
Thetford, Norfolk.

*For Geoffrey
with my thanks*

Contents

Acknowledgements

My thanks are due to Roland Beamont C.B.E., D.S.O., D.F.C., D.L., F.R.Ae.S. of British Aerospace; and to Humphry Wynn at the Ministry of Defence, for their kind help.

R.H.

1

Six Seconds

That blazing light in mid-Channel should not have been there. The darkness should have been complete. Keith kept his eyes turned away from it, fearful for his night vision, and glanced across to his number two on his right. The humped-back shape of the Hurricane was dark black against grey-black, blue-yellow flames from the exhaust stubs the only evidence that this was no ghost at his side.

It was still too dark to make out the figure in the cockpit. But of course it was young Ron Easton. What would young Ron Easton be feeling right now? Sergeant-Pilot Easton on his third ever op, now flying twenty feet above the English Channel, heading for the most strongly defended coast in the world, a pair of 500-pound bombs under his wings? What would he be thinking, damn it?

To hell with that! Keith told himself sharply. This was a time for growing up fast or for ceasing to grow up at all. For the present, all that matters is the following: Is he competent? Is he going to stick with me when the flak starts? Is he going to watch my tail when the 109s come in?

Keith's section had six-second delayed-action bomb fuses; Yellow Section, who would follow hard behind them, had two-second fuses. Not much latitude for mistiming there, the object being to blow up two pairs of 5.9-inch naval guns rather than four of your fellow pilots.

The glow from the blaze on their left was brighter than ever, spreading far over the sea, even touching the white cliffs to the north and south of Dieppe. There was the intermittent pulsing glow of shellfire, too, and tracer was arching across the pre-dawn sky. It looked as if the curtain had gone up before the players were ready; and as confirmation, the C.O.'s voice broke radio silence.

'Sideline Leader calling. The cat's out of the bag now so we'll climb to angels K,' he called, quoting the code altitude.

A comforting, steady voice with its Canadian burr, familiar to them all. A good leader, Jem Maitland. Keith had liked him at once, and now prayed, 'Hope to God he doesn't get the chop.' The C.O.'s section had no bombs. They were going to do the strafing to soften up the target, and 'rather him than me' had been Keith's reaction to this news at the briefing.

Down low, they might have been in a speedboat. Now they were flying again. Keith held the code card to the faint cockpit light. Angels K, three thousand feet. That was better. Climbing at full throttle, visible to one another, Yellow Section outlined against the glow from the burning ship, the C.O.'s section in loose finger of four very faint ahead, and pulling away without the handicap of a thousand pounds of bombs suspended under their wings.

One thousand pounds. They had never had more than two 250s before and there had been a good deal of talk about finally getting off the ground by the time they reached Chichester High Street. The facetious tone had an edge to it, too. To take off in formation in the dark, navigation lights on, with double your customary load, find and dive bomb a gun site behind Dieppe — 'Well, stiffen the snakes!' Range Powell had exclaimed. 'Reaper, sharpen that bloody sickle.'

'Close up, Blue Two,' Keith snapped over the R/T to Sergeant-Pilot Easton.

All except the C.O.'s section were labouring hard to gain height, props in full fine pitch. What a contrast with the Mark V Spitfire he had been flying at the end of his last tour! Even the Hurricanes he had flown in France, two and a half years ago, were nippier than these Hurribombers with their extra load. *Once upon a time I was a fighter pilot, with a respectable score of fourteen by the end of the Battle of Britain. Now I'm just a hunk* of fighter artillery. But even this was better than Training Command....

Here it comes, the first flak. Heavy stuff with yellow hearts, the smoke puffs scarcely visible in this half light, one of them close enough for Keith to hear the c-r-u-m-p of the explosion and feel the shock wave wrench at his stick. He pushed it hard forward and his Hurricane dropped three hundred feet like a stone, his section loosely conforming. Then he pulled up again, not too roughly, remembering the half ton strain of his bombs. It made no difference. As usual the flak gunners read their minds with sixth sense experience. Sweat it out, that's all there was to do, and forget about the T.N.T. eight feet away on either side.

The light stuff joined in when they crossed the coast, the gunners full of fresh early morning zeal for their first customers of the day, Keith noted wryly. There must have been a dozen batteries of 3.7 cm. giving them a colourful reception, the tracer in neat lines arching up gracefully, slowly, then at an increasing pace — or so it seemed — until it flashed by amazingly close, yet harmless until it exploded alongside or just above.

Through the criss-cross pattern of flak, Keith could just make out the twin moles of the harbour entrance and the dark cluster of blacked-out buildings of the town. Most of the batteries firing at them seemed to be on the clifftops east of the town, and Keith could also see the sparkle of muzzle flashes from the face of the cliffs as the heavy artillery opened up on the still distant invasion fleet.

Maitland took them over the centre of the town, and half a minute later transmitted, 'Sideline Leader calling, target in sight and am going in. Blue Section, keep close astern'.

The C.O. flashed his identification light to confirm his position, and the three machines in Keith's section closed in tight on him according to the briefing. He could see the silhouette of the pilots now, Easton on his right, a small hunched figure, and to the left, Watson — a tough veteran if ever there was one — and Brian Walters. The flak had slackened and it was possible to make out areas of woodland and the shapes of fields, the grey reality of the P.R.U. photographs they had studied with such care yesterday afternoon.

Maitland's section had split up, with only the C.O. going in steadily towards the target, a spinney at the corner of a field half-concealing a heavy concrete redoubt. Two of the Hurricanes had twelve .303 machine-guns, two had four 20 mm. Hispano cannons, a lethal combination, and now it seemed there was not even any flak.

Keith found himself singing 'No flak at all, no flak at all,' to the tune of an indecent R.A.F. song.

'Piece of cake!' someone snapped over the R/T.

'Shut up!' It was Maitland's voice, speaking as he must have been lining up on the target.

They were all going in at about 30 degrees with no more than 250 m.p.h. on the A.S.I. dial. Then, as if by simultaneous electric control, the leading Hurricanes and the flak batteries opened up. One of the strafing machines blew up at once, a yellow ball that fused on the eye's retina and then was gone. Keith momentarily lost the target, found it again amidst a tight network of tracer and exploding shells, yelled briefly, 'Close *in*!' and slipped his thumb over the bomb-release button.

The flak strafers were clear — those who had survived — and Keith centred the dot of his reflector sight on the trees, pulled up a shade to allow for drop, and opened fire with his cannon.

That's better! He was doing something at last, and the smell of the cordite wafting back into the cockpit always stimulated the adrenalin satisfactorily. The Hurricane was shaking slightly with the recoil, but not minding it. Relishing it even. This was what she was built for, wasn't it? For fighting. For destroying the enemy. He gave a long five-second burst, then concentrated on his bomb-aiming.

Dive bombing with a Hurricane was an informal sort of hit-or-miss business, using the gunsight. More hit and less miss the closer and lower you dared go. Keith went very low indeed, identified the long barrels of the guns through the camouflage netting, took no evasive action against the flak tearing past, steadied his machine, and pressed hard with his thumb as the trees seemed to fill his screen.

From the corner of his eye he saw Easton's machine, fifty feet higher than he was, unsteady in the flak, but who could blame him? At least he wasn't lagging behind, getting mixed up with Yellow Section.

Then Keith blacked out, both hands hauling back on the stick, and his Hurricane shot up like a swerving mallard facing the guns, relieved of its weight and a proper fighter again. Keith's vision came back almost at once, and what he saw — scattered machines diving, climbing, aileroning wildly in the deluge of flak — caused him to jam forward his stick and seek the comfort of the ground again.

But that was never the full answer, not now, with northern France bristling with flak towers that shot *down* at you when you went daisy-cutting. They had coned someone in Yellow Section who was skidding his machine right, left, left again, but was followed through every evasion. When bits began to tear off, a panel here, then the canopy, and white glycol streamed behind, Keith turned all his attention to his own survival. He knew the sequence of what would follow in the next seconds so well now that the manner in which the Hurricane went in — maybe blowing up, perhaps slamming the ground and disintegrating — was of academic interest. At this sort of height, under these conditions, you did not, definitely did *not*, survive....

The speed of events was recorded by the eruption of the bomb blasts off Keith's port wingtip: six seconds'-worth of time had embraced, for a start, his climb and dive and evasion, and the death of at least one more of his squadron. Six seconds. The near-simultaneous exploding of sixteen 500-pounders nudged Keith's Hurricane sideways, and he saw the columns of smoke and debris reaching high into the grey sky, the whole target area quivering with the concussion like a movie shot taken with a shaking hand. Several of the blasts were off target but enough were dead centre on the now crushed spinney to signal the end of that gun site.

'Rendezvous four miles west of Westham.' It was Maitland's voice, calm and crisp, as if they had completed a routine exercise. Keith had learned by heart the principal code place-names for the day and set course south-west at 100 feet above the fields of northern France, glancing right, left, above and behind continuously in search of Hurricanes or enemy fighters.

There was a lot of tracer light flak going up over Fécamp, and Keith steered towards it, identifying several Hurricanes dodging and circling very low over the fields just inland.

'Blue One joining you,' Keith transmitted, and saw Maitland's T-Toc passing fast behind some trees, with Easton's Hurricane close behind. There were five in all at the rendezvous, and when

5

the C.O. spotted Keith he called up:

'Sideline Leader calling. We'll return to base now. Form pairs and steer 355.'

Easton tucked in beside Keith. He had a shell hole in his fuselage five feet aft of the cockpit, slap in the middle of the roundel, the torn canvas revealing the wooden criss-cross framework that helped give the machine its remarkable structural strength. Keith had seen much worse during the Battle of Britain, but this would be sufficient to impress the inexperienced sergeant-pilot when he got home. If he got home. For the flak had not finished with them yet. A lot of 20mm. hosed them when they flashed out over the sand dunes, ruddering and jinking hard down over the wave tops.

When they were at last clear, Maitland took them to 2,000 feet. The sun was not yet up but visibility was good, and they could see a mass of shipping closing the coast off Dieppe — medium-sized transports, small and large landing craft, some R-boats, destroyers etching curving white wakes on the sea. Above the gun flashes from ships and shore there was a rising cloud of drifting smoke, and above this again, Keith could just make out the dots of covering fighters, Spitfires from Ford and Hawkinge and Manston, on the look-out for Focke-Wulf 190s and Messerschmitt 109s from Abbeville and St Omer.

Operation Jubilee was on, and 727 Squadron, now short on fuel and ammunition (and pilots, too, it seemed) could do no more. Half-way across the Channel, the six Hurricanes were diverted from Ford to a small satellite airfield, Southdean, near Brighton. Keith had not landed here since they had been detached to it in the heat of the Summer '40 fighting when it seemed that half the 11 Group Sector stations were unserviceable and some squadrons were operating from emergency grass strips.

Now as they slipped into the circuit, awaiting the first green light from the watch office, Keith found himself recalling the fatigue that had seized them all at this temporary station two years before, when the Luftwaffe came over in ever-increasing numbers, regardless of the daily fighting and destruction, when life hung in the balance between your gunsight and a German gunsight, and the vapour trails of aerial armadas patterned the sky like surrealist ceiling paper. And Jenny lay smashed up in hospital. And Mike, bitter from the loss of Eileen, had been seized with the fanatical zeal of some violent prophet to get at the enemy. And Keith himself had fought on, day after day, in a stupor of weariness and sickness at the death that lurked in the clouds and scarred the fields of Sussex and Kent.

There, just below Keith's starboard wing, were those dreadful little holiday huts which had been their sleeping quarters, for Polo Satterthwaite and Range Powell (still miraculously alive), for a dozen more now dead, like that steady New Zealander, Kiwi Robinson, and 'Halfpenny' Farthing and that crank and curious Fleet Air Arm officer, whose end had been as strange and violent as his character....

All two years — or a million years — ago. So many ops and prangs, roadsteads and rhubarbs, circuses and ramrods, so bloody many scraps, and always the flak. And they had still not yet begun to win the war. Things were bad in North Africa, in Russia, and the fortress of Europe was intact, today's Operation Jubilee being only a probing operation. Half the Pacific was in the hands of the Japanese, and we had been thrown out of Greece and Crete, Singapore and Malaysia, Hong Kong and a hundred other places. No one was even *talking about* victory. And here am I, Keith Stewart, going through the old ritual once again, and after a very shaky do indeed, of putting down a Hurricane on a strip of grass.

Check mixture, pitch fine, flaps down, undercart fully locked down with green light showing, tighten straps, back with hood with the cool air slapping your face. O.K. to pancake, the C.O. already taxi-ing fast towards the dispersal. A touch of sideslip, then line up, long nose obstructing the view ahead. Back with the stick, gently jiggle the rudder bars, hold her steady at 75, 70, then feel the gentle stall like an unresisting woman, and let her sit. A touch more ruddering, then off the runway to make way for your number two already on the final approach.

Oh, but it was good to unclip that mask, slip off the helmet, feel the breeze against the sweat, release the hands and fingers from the discipline of the gauntlets, stand up in the cockpit to stretch, and then onto the port wing, and jump to the grass below. Solid English *terra firma*.

Keith Stewart ran his fingers through his corn-coloured hair and cast his eyes over his Hurricane. A couple of 7.9 mm. bullets in the rudder, some more in the canvas length of the fuselage, and

7

one 20 mm. shell hole in the port wing, turning up the aluminium like a badly opened can. He wondered fleetingly why he had not felt the shell hit. But then, there had been a lot going on.

He called Easton over, and while the sergeant-pilot was walking towards him, Keith heard the deep boom of Merlin engines, a sound that would be in his ears for the rest of his life — for what that was worth. Three Hurricanes came in from the south-east in ragged vic formation, the centre machine with one of its wheels down and clearly being nursed along by the other two.

The damaged Hurricane came straight in without a preliminary circuit, and without flaps. Easton, now at Keith's side, asked, 'What's he going to do, sir?'

'The best he can, I suppose. I'd rather brolly-hop myself.'

The Hurricane skimmed the perimeter fence very fast, the single wheel and tail wheel held just above the grass for the first 100 yards. Keith could not see the identity letter but it was clear that this crippled machine was in the hands of a veteran. The pilot held it on its single wheel for some two hundred yards before the loss of speed caused the port wing to fall and the Hurricane went into a series of ground loops, churning up the grass and coming to rest beneath a cloud of dust.

A figure detached itself from the wreck before the crash wagon and ambulance could reach it, a tall, lanky figure running fast in their direction.

'Thank God, it's Range!' exclaimed Keith. 'What's the hurry, old boy?'

The answer to Keith's question came in a sheet of flame and a simultaneous whoof as the Hurricane's tanks caught fire and exploded. Keith dragged Easton to the ground beside him, waiting for the ammunition to go up. Instead, he heard Range's harsh Australian voice, panting from his run: 'Relax, cobber. I put the last of my bloody ammo into a 190.'

They squatted on the grass in the early morning sun, the two flight commanders and the green young sergeant-pilot, who refused a cigarette he badly wanted because he knew his hands were still shaking, talking over the op while the ground crews set about refuelling, rearming and patching the small holes with red dope.

Three out of twelve had failed to return, and all had been killed, there was no doubt of that. Tim Brooks, a farmer's son

8

from Devonshire, had blown up alongside the C.O. on the strafing run, the pilot Keith had seen being torn apart by the flak had
been Pierre Armand, a Free Frenchman who had played poker
like a demon and whose hatred of the Germans was limitless.

'The bloody Abbeville boys arrived over Fécamp just after you
left,' said Range. 'And, stone the crows, there were bloody
millions of them. Two of them shot down Mike Henry, on his first
bloody trip, poor old cobber. Then we had our hands full until
some bloody Spits arrived and then we skipped off after I did my
block and put three seconds'-worth into that 190. Bloody nice
little blaze, she made, I'll tell you.'

Range Powell, from Paddington, Sydney, and back now from
the Far East, had two remarkable attributes. One was surviving,
the second seducing. It was more than two years since Keith had
found him alone on an airfield at the height of the French retreat
— alone except for his smashed Hurricane and a French farmer's
daughter in his arms. The day before he had shot a Frenchman
who had refused him petrol from a bowser. Since then he had
shot his way out of more corners, and shot into more beds, than
Keith could remember. Keith loved him — his foul tongue, his
appalling ruthlessness with women and in combat, his carelessness about details like washing and manners. What else could
you do but love a man who had fought alongside you for so long,
and had risked his life so often protecting young sprogs who
panicked when the flak or the fighting hotted up? Tonight,
Range Powell would drink himself into a haze of remorse and
gloom over young Sergeant-Pilot Henry and try to kid everyone
it was over a sheila.

Now, Flight Lieutenant Powell D.F.C., five feet eleven, rumpled dark hair, rumpled black moustache which he chewed
ruminatively, in oil-stained Mae West over oil-stained battledress blouse, dragged himself to his feet, cursed the loss of his
favourite Hurricane, and announced he was going to eat three
eggs and bacon before he was going to favour the bloody Intelligence Officer with a bloody word of report.

* * *

James Maitland was one of the oldest Squadron Commanders in
Fighter Command. He made 'Bull' Rowbotham, Keith's previous Squadron Leader, seem a mere stripling by comparison. Jem

9

was thirty, a regular Royal Canadian Air Force officer from Vancouver. He had been off flying for eighteen months, commanding one of the early Empire Air Training Schools in Saskatchewan, when he was posted to England and to 727 Squadron, where he had been viewed with some dismay by many of the veteran pilots, including Keith and Range Powell. Tall, austere, with the bearing more of a civil servant than a fighter pilot, Jem Maitland was at first taken to be the new Squadron Leader Admin. He spoke slowly in his mild Canadian drawl, weighing his words carefully, drove his staff car as if there were precious farm eggs on the back seat, and drank no more than a pint of beer in the evenings.

Within three days he had proved his worth. He was seen to be shy rather than reserved, began to reveal a puckish sense of humour, and was firm and just on the ground. But it was in the air where his great qualities revealed themselves. 727 had been having a rough time carting 250-pound bombs across the Channel on rhubarbs, mostly in pairs or fours and without fighter escort. It was highly dangerous precision work against pin-point targets, nipping into cloud when you met trouble, or getting below tree-top height.

The Hurricane had been too slow in 1940. In 1942 she was completely outclassed as a fighter, but her strength and carrying power made her useful as a fighter-bomber. It was also the most dangerous work in Fighter Command, and pilots came and went missing or were killed so frequently that Keith found it difficult to remember the names of everyone in his Flight.

Jem Maitland could not make the Hurricane fly faster any more than he could reduce the accuracy of German flak. But he put new heart into the squadron by making Group always provide Spitfire fighter cover in clear weather, and by limiting operations against very heavily defended targets to dirty conditions, when his pilots could at least dodge back quickly into cloud if things became really hot. He always insisted on leading the worst ops, and his calm steadiness— quick, precise orders, marvellous, un-showy flying—filled everyone with new confidence.

Just before lunch, Jem Maitland ordered Flight Commanders and all pilots to the tent he had commandeered as a temporary office for the day. It was hot in there, and almost everyone was smoking. A hundred yards away, a Merlin was being run up, and when the cut-out was pulled, they could hear instead as a background chorus the murmur of many distant engines of more Spitfires going out on the standing patrol they were keeping over the Dieppe beaches all day.

'Group tell me the troops are having a rough time of it,' Maitland told them. 'If they were all British it would be bad enough. But they're mostly 2nd Canadian Division. That means we've got to give them special support.'

There was muted laughter in the tent. After the dawn casualty rate of 25 per cent no one felt like going further than that.

'The Hun's bringing in reinforcements along all the roads south of Dieppe. We'll be going out in pairs with two 250-pounders, blasting up everything we can find. O.K.?' Then, in answer to a Flying Officer's question — 'Oh sure, there'll be fighter cover over the whole area. Keep your eyes open just the same. Yellow Section got bounced this morning, and we don't want that again.'

Maitland called Keith and Range to sort out the pairs and times of take-off. Then they made for the old clubhouse where, in peace-time, chaps had flirted with their popsies and given them too many white ladies, and then taken them up in their Tiger Moths. Instead, on this hot, eventful August day, eight Hurricane bomber pilots settled down to an austere makeshift meal, several with too much fear in their hearts for the good of their digestion. No one ate much, but a lot of tea was drunk over deeply inhaled cigarettes.

* * *

122 miles south-south-east of Southdean, a Churchill tank, stalled on the steep shingle below the cliffs on White Beach, received a direct hit from a German 88 mm. shell. In five seconds the crew had been burnt to death. Very few Canadians on the beach observed the shot and its consequences because they were nearly all dead already. Smoke from burning buildings in the town and from wrecked landing craft drifted over the scene of carnage like a funeral pall. At Dieppe it was all blood and suffering.

* * *

Sometimes the pre-war Keith Stewart was a remote stranger to Flight Lieutenant Keith Stewart D.F.C., R.A.F., or a figure he

11

had once met so many years ago that the face was scarcely recognizable, and certainly not recognizable as his own twenty-three-year-old face. It had changed from puppy-fat fair cheeks with soft down on the chin, innocent of a razor, to the gaunt, bony face with lines about the eyes. And the eyes themselves, once innocent blue, now steel-grey blue, wary, worldly, darting eyes that had seen so much slow death and quick death, and death just avoided. The soft blue eyes that once reluctantly and hesitantly followed a pheasant with the sights of his side-lock Churchill ('Young fellow, how *could* you have missed that!'), could now hold a wildly jinking 109F clear down to the deck and put sharp half-second bursts into the cockpit area or the glycol tank of its Daimler-Benz engine. These were the eyes that had stared up into the sun from 15,000 feet through the Battle of Britain, had spotted the massed Luftwaffe formations, had seen the Messerschmitts coming in head-on at a closing speed of 650 m.p.h., when the survival margin of reaction was not one tenth but one hundredth of a second.

But the contrast was neither so simple nor definite as that. There were still times of introspection, dangerous though he knew them to be. He knew in the depth of his heart that the boy of 1937, with doubts and a conscience, had not been completely corrupted and destroyed by the war. In the early fighting it had been brute survival that had kept him going, and he often wondered at the luck that had got him safely through those first combats, when his shooting was so weak and the boyhood doubts about the ethics of killing still filled his mind like lumbering, obstructive barrage balloons filling the sky over London.

Keith remembered waking up at three in the morning, an hour before he was due to go on immediate readiness, back in July '40 — a precious lost hour of sleep — and his mind's eye was filled with the image of the twin-engined, twin-finned 110 going down the previous afternoon. He had shot with sublime accuracy, killing the rear gunner with the first burst with a full deflection shot. The pilot was still alive, though, fighting to recover from the high-speed stall the poor stupid bugger had got himself into. And then the flames had, one second, begun to lick tentatively, and the next second it was as if the Messerschmitt's nose was the head of a striking match, and the dead gunner and burning pilot had gone down together on their three-mile-long vertical journey to a

Kent hop-field, where their flying coffin had dug their shared grave for them.

That was the drinking time, and Keith had reached under his bed for the bottle of Haig, and had another stiff one in his tooth mug before dragging on his flying boots, throwing cold water at his unshaven face, and stumbling in the dark to the mess.

Yes, the two Keith Stewarts did sometimes meet, usually in the dark, like shy, half-recognizing old acquaintances who then continue on their own way.

They were certainly a long way apart and complete strangers at 3.27 p.m. on 19 August 1942, when the old war-worn Keith Stewart was racing down the length of a German military convoy three miles south of Torcy-le-Petit releasing a pair of two-second-fused H.E. bombs on a column of tank carriers heading for Dieppe. And the shooting that followed, with blue-grey troops leaping from the open trucks and hurling themselves into the ditch or behind the poplar trees, was far removed from the hesitant, uncertain shooting at Rising Hall when the beaters put up a couple of dozen young pheasants, and Keith was so preoccupied with the beauty of their colour and their flight that he was too late picking his bird. Or was it that he did not want to see his spaniel, Sheila, tail wagging triumphantly, bringing in the blood-dripping warm corpse?

Now he did not even turn to see what destruction he had committed, not from any fastidious motive but because his first concern — his only concern, for God's sake — was to get out of the place fast. Over Dieppe he caught the whiff of the fires on the seafront, and his Hurricane bounced in the heat above the roof-tops. He briefly saw huddled figures through the smoke, a dozen tanks with their broken tracks about them on the beach, like dying Mastodons at their last prehistoric moment of extinction. The grey sea was streaked with oil slicks and littered with drifting, burning boats, yellow life-rafts and the debris of military catastrophe.

The flak followed him out to sea relentlessly and with customary precision. 'Speeding the parting guest!' Keith shouted bitterly, soundlessly into his mask, ruddering right, right, then right again (that sometimes foxed the buggers). Then a British destroyer joined in, and with Easton still gamely with him, Keith hauled back the stick, pulled the plug for ultimate boost, and skid-climbed at full throttle for the shelter of the afternoon clouds that were forming over the Channel.

The two Hurricanes emerged into total sun at 4,000 feet, and Keith was relieved to see Easton searching the sky with the speed and care essential under these circumstances. If he survived a dozen more ops he might stand a fifty-fifty chance of completing his first tour. He seemed quick to learn, and that was the prime need for survival.

Nothing to be seen except a distant squadron of Spitfires patrolling in three sections of four to the north-east. Keith decided to transmit for a fix and get a course home. It was not until he began speaking that the thought crossed his mind that it might, by incredible, glorious chance, be Jenny. After all, she had been at sector for a week now, and sometime ...

' ... six, five, four, three, two, one, zero. Sideline Blue One, over.'

The pause was no longer than five seconds, and then the woman's voice, crisp, deep, incisive, came over the ether from the Ops Room.

'Sideline Blue One, steer 292, steer 292, over.'

Yes, it was. My God, it really was. The old joke they had shared had become reality, and Keith could not resist throwing over the transmission switch. 'Thanks, love,' he said. No more and there would be no reply. But that would be enough. She would know that 727 had been deeply engaged in Operation Jubilee, and had suffered grievously. But now she would also know that he was O.K., at the cost of some embarrassing glances from the W.A.A.F.s in shirtsleeves and headsets around the ops table, and maybe some giggles too.

Keith turned onto the course that would take him above cloud back to Southdean, checked the sky again, set weak mixture and economic cruising revs, and the compass. He kept Jenny out of his head when he was flying. Women and flying are a disastrous mixture when airborne — that had been a very early lesson at Eldergrove. But considering the unlikelihood of the Luftwaffe's bothering about them now when they were fully stretched over Dieppe, and the unlikelihood of their getting no R.D.F. warning; and considering the strenuousness of the day as well as the beguiling tone of Jenny's voice, Keith, somewhere about twenty miles south of Beachy Head, did allow his mind to wander momentarily; although, with canopy thrown back, he checked the sky continuously above, below, to right and left, and in front and behind, without a pause....

Jenny, mid-July, a month ago, on forty-eight hours' leave. Her snug little flat in Half Moon Street, mercifully preserved through the Blitz. Jenny, in a dress at Keith's insistence while she complained of its out-of-fashionness, dancing in his arms at Hatchetts, dining late, and with the double-British Summertime clocks, they were still able to stroll through the Mayfair streets in the black-out with light in the sky touching the plane trees in Berkeley Square and the gaunt skeletons of burned-out buildings.

Later, Jenny said, 'Certainly not. It's a ridiculous idea. We are both far too busy for that sort of nonsense. Yes, you can buy me a ring if you like, darling.' She laughed. 'Plain and austere, as befits the times. And your bank balance.'

With what Keith considered a correct sense of priority, she moved his right hand onto her breast, and kissed him lingeringly with her dark hair falling about his face.

'But as for marriage — not with this horrible war. Marriage is something different and special— too special to be influenced by bombs and shootings and tanks and U-boats and rationing and beastly black-outs and ... and.' She was breathlessly running out of words, and let herself fall onto him, holding him tightly, rolling a little from side to side and whispering into his ear. 'I love you, my darling Keith. But let's keep it like this, living in lovely sin, as your friend Moira puts it so sweetly.'

They made love for the second time with not a sound, not a glimmer of light now, coming through the open window. When they were lying side by side, Keith said practically, 'You'll get a lovely widow's pension. Especially if I can make it to Squadron Leader first.'

'I don't want any beastly pension. And you're not to talk like that. I am going to control you from my Ops Room with a rod of iron. I'm going to vector you away from the slightest risk of meeting any beastly German Geschwader.'

They had first met just round the corner from this flat nearly four years ago now, during the Munich Crisis of '38, and had many times laughed at the circumstances: Keith, tight as a tic at the Caledonia, and angry and miserable in the mistaken belief that his old friend Mike had left him adrift and was seducing his

Eileen. And then the chance meeting with Jenny, dumped by her escort. So they had cheered one another up, in this very flat. And, through the rigours of total war, from the Western Front before the fall of France, to the north of Scotland, through Jenny's own savage wounding when on duty, their love had endured.

Keith knew that, without it, he would long since have been dead— probably before the Battle of Britain had really warmed up. People who said love and war did not mix were liars and fools. There had been times when his nerves and endurance were so stretched, his physical capacity so reduced, that only Jenny, and his love for her, had given him the stamina to fight on because defeat would mean the severance of the last thread of tenderness in his life.

That other peace-time Keith Stewart had suffered a parallel experience when his parents had been killed and, at thirteen, there had seemed to be nothing left except his calf love for Eileen, the only child of the Barretts who had unofficially adopted him after this catastrophe.

Now, Keith and Jenny met Mike briefly as he passed through London. Jenny suggested a drink in her flat before luncheon at the Ritz a hundred yards away. 'Come on. Yes, silly, of course it's all right,' she said on the telephone. 'Keith's *here*, don't you realize!'

Keith smiled as he heard the whoop at the other end of the line, imagining Mike's face screwed up with delight, the lines on his forehead accentuated as they always were by excitement, his wide-set brown eyes sparkling. And five minutes later, there was the reality, bouncing out of the little lift as if on springs, arms wide to embrace Jenny. 'Gee, it's good to see you— it really is. And Keith— goddam it, you're looking swell.'

Jenny had wheedled a bottle of Gordons out of Fortnums and they drank vast pink gins without ice as her refrigerator had packed up. 'You're getting back your old accent, Mike,' Jenny said as she topped up his glass. 'I suppose it's being among all those Yanks again.'

Mike Browning, scion of a New York banking family, had joined the R.A.F. at the same time as Keith, but after the entry of America into the war eight months ago, had taken over command of one of the American Eagle Squadrons which operated with British machines under the R.A.F. The fact that he was now

16

one rank ahead of Keith made absolutely no difference between them.

'How *are* all those Yanks?' Keith asked.

'They're coming on. Not bad at all. I've got some good guys.'

'Got your new Spits?'

Mike shook his head. 'No sign of them, and it's sure tough going against the 190. Boy, do they go!'

Keith laughed. '*You're* complaining! You try dealing with the 190 in a Hurricane. At least you've moved forward to Mark Vs since the Battle of Britain. We might as well be in Gauntlets.'

Jenny put her glass down with a bang on the Heal's table. 'Enough of this shop talk, fellows. I'm hungry and you can both buy me lunch.'

Over the coffee and brandy Mike said, 'I've been invited to Rising Hall for a couple of nights next week. Any message for Eileen?'

'My love, of course,' said Keith. 'I just hope you find her a bit stronger. What a slow business it's been!'

A slow business, and before that, a bad business. After a catastrophic period in the W.R.N.S., Eileen Barrett had been at death's door for weeks, and then, physically recovered, had had a nervous breakdown and had been convalescing at Rising Hall for almost a year, looked after by a full-time nurse and her mother. Her engagement to Mike had never been formally broken off and he always said he was prepared to wait for ever for her recovery.

'I'll let you know how she is.' Mike glanced at his watch. 'I've got to get back. We're busy tomorrow unless the weather clamps down.' He kissed Jenny lightly on the cheek, touched Keith on the shoulder and walked quickly out of the grill room, pausing to pay the waiter on the way.

Jenny said, 'Nice boy.' Then, after a pause, 'Why do I call him "boy"? He's twenty-three like you. And you're not a boy.'

'His looks. That messy hair and the freckles. And those lines on his forehead.'

'Boyish and vulnerable. Like that other pilot, Lindbergh. Mike was never built for worries.' Jenny drained the last of her brandy and Keith noted with pleasure the delicate line of her neck, the sympathetic, slightly one-sided smile when she put down her balloon. 'Mike was built for playing,' she went on. 'He should have been a lovely rich playboy. With an open supercharged Auburn and a different heiress every night. Parties. Tennis matches. Like a Scott Fitzgerald character without the fuss and drama.'

'That's just what he was afraid of becoming,' said Keith. 'He would have made a lousy playboy. He's got a man-sized conscience and would have hated himself. That's why he crashed his way into the R.A.F. after seeing what was happening to Spain and Germany.'

Then Keith remembered Mike at his lowest and most desperate, almost suicidal with grief over Eileen and at the same time ferociously hating the Germans as they blasted England in 1940, poised for invasion. He had had a giant share of the danger and suffering of this damnable war — 'this goddam war', as he always called it. But then he had a giant heart to cope with it. And that was why Keith had liked him so much and for so long....

Jenny said, 'Goodness, I'm feeling a bit tiddly!'

'I'm not surprised. So am I.'

'Do you think we ought to go back to my flat?'

'Emphatically.'

'What time's your train?' Jenny asked, as if she did not know.

'Half past five. Plenty of time. I think we ought to go now. It's lovely tasting of brandy at a quarter past three.'

'Deliciously decadent,' said Jenny. 'Yes, now.'

2

The Eagle Fights Back

'This hut's a goddam disgrace!' Mike stood at the doorway looking at the Mae Wests and parachutes on the floor, Irvine jackets draped over the backs of cane and wooden-armed chairs, torn copies of *Look* and *Life* mixed with gauntlets and helmets and oxygen masks on the tables. A poker school was in full swing in one corner. 'And stand to attention when your commanding officer comes in, goddam it.'

The British were already calling them 'Oversexed, overpaid, and over here.' But at least the regular American forces in the UK had been given a taste of discipline before they left for overseas. Mike's Number 10 (Eagle) Squadron of volunteers had long ago reverted to the relative anarchy from which most of them had come. Adventuring playboys they were, from the same privileged and wealthy background as Mike himself, or leathery cropdusters with thousands of hours on Wacos and Stearmans, bruised and battered circus pilots, stunt pilots from Hollywood and one or two idealist individualists.

This motley crowd were all shuffling to their feet now, some with cigars in their mouths, others holding playing cards and chewing gum. They were Mike's first squadron and he liked the lot of them, and he thought that he attracted their respect, as much as any of them respected anyone. But you had to know them in the air before you could claim to know them at all. In the air it was different — a transformation — and every one was a fine

19

pilot, one or two of them superb. Here, on the ground, they were impossible, as he now told them with some relish.

'You're the scruffiest bunch of flying hoodlums the world has ever seen. Get this place into order. Then I'll give you some news that will shake the weevils and nits out of your foul, unwashed skin. But not before.'

They wore uniform, of a sort. R.A.F. officers' blue, with the deep, buttoned side pockets, R.A.F. wings on the left breast, and the distinctive emblem on the shoulder, the letters E.S. above a bald-headed eagle. And now, fired by curiosity, they all made an attempt to create some sort of order out of the chaos, and then stood by their chairs, cigars extinguished but with jaws still working at gum.

Mike sat on the orderly's table by the telephone and told them to sit down. 'Here's the gen. We've got a dawn shipping strike tomorrow unless the goddam weather's duff.' There were groans from the pilots. 'And it's the last ever.' This time a thin cheer came from Mike's men. 'Because,' he went on, stabbing a finger towards them and pushing his hat characteristically onto the back of his head, 'because as of the next day, twenty-ninth day of September in the Year of our Lord 1942, we shall no longer be in the R.A.F. We shall be in what is now called the U.S. Army Air Force, 4th Fighter Group. Get it? New command, new uniform and new discipline under a new C.O. who's a West Point martinet, let me tell you.'

This time the sounds of outrage were long and noisy, and as they faded, Mike became the target of angry questions. 'Why the hell?' 'I want nothin' to do with the cocksuckin' Army Air Force.' 'I'm resigning my commission, right now.'

Mike held up a hand and shouted for quiet. 'As the goddam Limeys say, "Don't you know there's a war on?" You're under military discipline, believe it or not, and if any of you deserts you'll be shot. What's more, fellows, I'll do it myself, personally. And you know my shooting ...'

'Lousy,' interjected Flying Officer Lew Hickory from South Bend, Indiana, who had had a private 'plane as a boy, soloing unofficially at sixteen from a field beside his father's ranch.

The slack attitude among 10 Squadron disappeared on the arrival of the British Intelligence Officer, a small ginger-haired Scot with a limp from an accident which had finished his flying

20

days before the war. The I.O. represented ops, and ops was the one thing they all took seriously. Those who had not in the past, were now in the past — just a name under the bald-headed eagle on the wooden memorial board in the mess.

The I.O. put his big map of the south-east corner of England, the coast of East Anglia and the French, Belgian and Dutch coasts up to the German frontier, on the briefing board. It was covered with heavy cellophane upon which chinagraph lines had been drawn, indicating their course out and back on tomorrow's shipping strike.

The red line stretched from Savile Farm to Ludham at the eastern tip of Norfolk, where they were to top up their tanks, then across the North Sea to the Hook of Holland. Here they were to rendezvous with a squadron of bomb-carrying Coastal Command Beaufighters, their track marked with a dotted line from their Norfolk base.

They were then to sweep north up the coast to Den Helder in the hope of picking up one of the numerous German convoys that hugged the coast from the river Scheldt estuary. If they did not, it would be a waste of time, just part of the mammoth waste of war, and they would probably be attacked anyway. If they did, there would be a flakship or two as escort, the shore batteries would join in, and the fighters from Schipol and elsewhere would almost certainly come out.

'Take-off time, 05.45,' ended the I.O. 'Do you want to add anything, sir?'

Mike, standing on the other side of the board, told them a dozen Spits would probably be available, and that the pilot list would be posted before 8 o'clock that evening.

'If you think this is a dicey do,' he told them, 'then spare a goddam thought for the Beaufighter guys. They're doing the dirty work. All we've got to do is look after them, and if any one of them is pranged by a Jerry fighter, I'll regard it as a personal slur on the squadron — and on its last R.A.F. op at that. O.K.?'

Silence. No caustic comments. This was ops. And the poker school remained dead until every pilot in 10 Squadron had marked his map, checked his equipment and his personal armoury (one Texan carried no fewer than three guns, a Browning, a Colt and a Smith and Wesson) and had gone out to his plane to talk to his rigger and fitter, with a word to Chiefy and the

21

Engineer Officer to double-check.

* * *

A rendezvous between two converging squadrons flying at about 240 m.p.h. at a point above the North Sea off an enemy coast, called for special skills. It needed a bit of luck as well, especially as both squadrons were at nought feet in order to 'keep under' the German R.D.F. Mike remembered one op when they never even saw the machines they were supposed to escort.

On this morning, everything went well. Mike caught sight of the twin-engined Beaufighters ten miles off the Dutch coast. With their big radial engines and thick, dark fuselage they looked like a dozen Havana cigars skimming the grey wave tops, half lost in the mist that always seemed to cling to this sea.

Mike called up his opposite number, 'Hullo Rangoon Leader, this is Medway. We are at three o'clock to you, same height. In 90 seconds we are going to angels three and will conform with your course. Over.'

The Beaufighter C.O. replied, and, having broken radio silence, Mike took his Spitfires up to the prearranged height, the dark line of the Dutch coast at once appearing ahead, sand dunes first, rising higher, then flat farmland, green pastures alternating with light brown recently harvested fields. It was a trim, geometrical landscape, friendly-seeming until the first heavy flak spat out from gunposts among the dunes and the grey puffs spotted the sky about them.

The Germans had seen the Beaufighters, too, and as the guns, at full depression, marked their course with heavy bursts, and the 3.7s joined in with parabolas of tracer, the big machines began jinking and the Beaufighters' C.O. led them out farther from the shore.

'Convoy twelve o'clock. Seven ships. Medway Red One out.'

Mike at once recognized Milt Scheller's voice and noted with amusement that the thirty-year-old veteran from Kansas City had kept his almost unbroken record of first sightings to his squadron's last op. Grizzled old eagle-eye, Milt, of the 10th Eagle. It was another second or two before Mike could make out the smudges on the sea ahead of them, half a dozen small coasters and what looked like the inevitable flakship in the centre of them. Their smoke drifted lazily on the westerly wind towards the shore. Below, the Beaufighters were splitting up into sections of four, one turning to attack from the landward side, a second wheeling to port, for the simultaneous attack from three sides. This was an evolution they had practised many times and no orders were necessary.

Mike snapped out, 'Medway, to angels five,' and at once pushed his throttle open side, ruddering sharply and varying his rate of climb when the heavy flak started to get in amongst them again. There was no need to alert his boys to the risk of being jumped. They knew their job as well as the Beaufighter pilots, and if he glanced at any of his machines he would see the pilot constantly turning his head to search the sky above and on all sides.

The attack was rapidly developing now, and three words from the Beaufighters' leader started off the final run as if a fuse had been lit: 'Going in now!'

The Beaufighters had all gained height and were jinking and weaving in the flak that was coming out at them like percussion blows. And, inevitably, it was making its mark. One Beaufighter was streaming smoke from an engine, and was turning back, jettisoning its bombs, which exploded in tall waterspouts 2,000 feet below.

The flakship had joined the shore batteries now, with heavy, medium and light guns dividing their fire between the three groups of fighter-bombers. Mike glanced down and took his squadron in a wide circle above the convoy, and saw the culmination of the attack, like some *pas de trois* carried out amidst fireworks and confetti, the C.O.'s stern section slightly closer than the flank machines. He would be using his nose cannon, four 20mm. Hispanos, raking the decks of the sternmost vessel at over 300 m.p.h. in a shallow dive. Then the bombs began spewing up either white spouts, or the litter of wreckage from the bright glow of a direct hit.

The scene of seven quietly steaming vessels in a calm sea had been transformed into a maelstrom of smoke and flame, of high explosive and screaming metal. Men were dying down there, some instantly and without pain, others in slow agony with disbelieving eyes recording their obscene wounds. Mike caught a glimpse of a Beaufighter, mortally stricken, turning back and, with flames tearing it apart, diving straight at the centre of the flakship. The other attackers were scattered about the sky at every angle and altitude as if they were additional debris, trying by evasion and full power to rid themselves of the whiplash of shellfire.

This was the moment — the very second — when the fighters liked to come in; and with predictable precision the warning cry came from — who else? — Milt Scheller: 'Bandits, boss, four o'clock high'.

'Chee — rist!' shouted another voice; and Mike at once threw over his switch, 'Medway Leader — shut that mouth.' Then: 'Buster!' for full emergency boost, and finally, 'Medway aircraft, take them as they go down and wait till you can count the rivets before you press the tit'.

They did not need the advice, and Mike knew it. 10th Eagle knew exactly what to do, and there was not a squadron on either side with higher shooting standards than these Americans. But he also knew that they liked a few encouraging words of incitement, like a cavalry regiment's bugle call or a mariner's drum riffle before combat.

They were Messerschmitt 109Fs, faster than the 109s Mike had fought against so often in the Battle of Britain, with a strutless tail and retractable tailwheel which gave a smoother configuration. They might be faster than the earlier mark, but so was his Spitfire V with the clipped wings, especially when they were low down like this. There was little or nothing to choose between them.

There were at least forty 109s, probably three *Jagdeswaden* from Schipol, hardened by experience like 10 Squadron, tough antagonists every one of them. They came down like plummeting lapwings, aileroning over onto their backs and streaking after the fleeing Beaufighters.

Mike turned his section to meet them and when the Germans went through without firing, threw his Spitfire into a vertical dive that quickly built up past the 400 m.p.h. mark on his A.S.I., the rev counter needle spinning as swiftly round the dial.

As Admiral Lord Nelson claimed that the word 'Frigate' would be engraved upon his heart, Mike knew that the shape of a 109 would be etched upon the retina of his eye for all time — that arrow-like, villainous-looking, lethal little fighter which had

24

killed so many of his friends. He hated the 109s with a cold, controlled fury and fought them with the knowledge that both his antagonist and his weapons were as good as he and his Spitfire were, and that therefore only consuming concentration would result in the destruction of his foe and his own survival. Once, long ago, it had not been like this, when the fury was white hot, and he knew that he had not deserved to survive then.

Not now. Now he reduced the angle of his dive, with the mottled sea coming up fast to meet him, half-rolled onto his back and chose his target, the third from the left of a *Schwarm* of four, hoping the pilot was the leader.

Little high-set tail, arrogant black cross on the fuselage, radio aerial just aft of the cockpit, the black dot in the cockpit — the pilot's head ... What was going on in that head? He really thought he could get at that Beaufighter skimming the sea a mile ahead and below before the Spits could get at him? When a glance in his mirror would show Mike at 800 yards and fast catching up. And this was one of the feared Schipol *Jagdeswaden*.

Then, the sight bars told Mike that the range was 600 yards and it was worth a short 10 degree deflection shot. The whole *Schwarm* began to jink evasively, with that incredibly fast up and down motion which made shooting so difficult. But the German made no attempt to turn into the attack, and Mike let him pulsate for several more seconds, the gap closing fast as the 109 lost more speed.

It was nearer five degrees when Mike squeezed the cannon button with his thumb, and the shells — high explosive, armour piercing, tracer, in that order — linked the two racing machines.

Mike had had his first gun at six, and had been shooting ever since — quail, coyotes, roe deer and stags, buck rabbit and elegant pheasant; and, more recently, German airmen, how many he would never know.

Mike added one to his score now, at 0825 precisely on this 28th day of September, 1942. He was twenty-year-old Hauptmann Hans Flecker from Ingolstadt in Bayern, and he experienced no alarm nor pain beyond the searing, instantaneous heat blast that utterly destroyed his chest after the 20 mm. A.P. shell thrust through the armour plate behind his seat as if it did not exist. His 109F continued its flight with dead hands and feet on the controls, little damaged and as if nothing had happened.

25

Mike did not see it crash, but two of his section watched the fighter steepen its dive as if seeking concealment in its shame, and go straight in, the spume falling back like a shroud.

The fighting, as the communiqués blandly put it, then became general; which, in this context, meant that twelve Spitfires fought thirty-nine 109s, none of which wanted to fight them, their priority target being the Beaufighters. This stretch of sky, from ten feet to 5,000 feet out to sea off the little Dutch town of Egmond, was for several minutes a tumult of whirling, twisting single-engine fighters, all closely matched in skill and fighting power, struggling to get in a burst on target and avoid the machine-gun and cannon fire that filled the air in brief, lethal bursts.

10 (Eagle) Squadron's youngest pilot, Paul Willensky from Chicago, made strikes on the tail of one 109 but could only claim it as damaged. But Sam Potterton, a New England boy with smart schooling behind him like Mike himself, got a long burst into the engine of a 109 with a bright yellow spinner and a Mickey Mouse emblem on its fuselage. Like Mike again, he never saw the result, but his number two watched the machine throw out, first white glycol, then ever darker smoke. And, a fifth of a second later, the 109 exploded. The debris was still falling when Sam's number two had to rudder like a rugby footballer kicking for touch as tracer whipped past his cockpit.

Only one of the 109s got near a Beaufighter. The pilot was firing at it from dead astern while the Beaufighter twitched right and left so that the gunner could fire the Vickers gas-operated .303 from his station half-way along the fuselage. Flying Officer Kurt Walkowsky, who had crashed more stunt planes for Hollywood studios than (like his injuries) he cared to count, but had never scored against the enemy, caught this 109 in the nick of time. He swore aloud with his transmitter on as panels of alloy, the undercarriage unit, and finally the engine, tore past him as if in final defiant revenge. Only a small piece hit the leading edge of his port wing. He shouted 'Shit!' to the world at the top of his voice, then realized that he was live on the air and switched off.

Mike called out, 'I am at angels four, rocking my wings. All Medway aircraft form up on me.'

Five of them succeeded in finding him, which was just as well in view of what was shortly to take place. Meanwhile, the Beau-

26

fighter leader called up the Eagles. It was brief but did not need to be any longer. Just 'Thanks, Yanks.'

Ten minutes later, Mike's engine turned rough. His screen was soon covered with oil, the pressure gauge fell, the temperature gauge rose swiftly, sure signs that he would very soon be without power.

Mike transmitted a Mayday to Coltishall, and instructed his number two to give a long transmission for a fix in case his own radio packed up. Then he prepared for the inevitable. Third time unlucky?

The first time he had brolly-hopped was in the heat of the Battle of Britain, over Portsmouth, and it had been an uncomfortable experience in several ways. Then the second time. Well, that had been over enemy territory a year ago, and he reckoned that he preferred that to the middle of the North Sea in late September.

The engine was getting very hot now. He could feel the heat coming back at him through the baffle-plate, and he turned off the switches and fuel cocks, pulled the cut-out, and ejected his canopy. A quick thumbs-up to his number two, and Mike tore off his helmet, pulled the pin of his harness, and went out the classic way — a quick flick of the stick to throw the machine upside down, and leave the rest to gravity.

He was at two thousand feet, and he pulled the ring at once. The opening jerk came quicker than he remembered from last time, and he had about thirty seconds of peace and idleness, swinging gently in the warm air before he prepared for splashing down. He hated water up his nose, and shut his eyes and held his nostrils with one hand before turning and banging the quick-release box to release the parachute. Then he was deep under the water, remaining submerged (he thought with alarm) for much too long.

He felt a fool being so quickly panic-stricken and told himself that, of course, with his boots and flying gear, and his saturated clothing, it was not surprising that he was unbuoyant. Then he succeeded in pulling the tag to inflate his Mae West and in a few seconds had his head clear. His dinghy was floating a few feet away, connected like an umbilical cord to his waist, and he drew it towards him, surprised at the roughness of the sea which had looked so calm from above, and affronted at the amount of water

27

he had swallowed and he was constantly getting in his eyes.

It was all right when he had scrambled into the dinghy, which had inflated itself. Most of the water in the bottom was what he had brought in with him, and more spilled out of his boots when he pulled them off. Then he lay back, panting and feeling calmer now. His number two was still circling at a couple of hundred feet, canopy thrown back. Mike waved and gave the thumbs-up sign, glad of the company but knowing that the pilot should go back to base now. So he waved again with both hands and pointed away from the morning sun.

The Spitfire came down very low, unmistakably American with its bosomy female painted on the engine cowling, skimming the wave tops, the pilot waving and rocking his wings. And then he climbed away to the west. Good guy, Mike reflected. Jimmy Kennedy from West Virginia, just twenty-one. Paid for his own flying lessons and then bullied his way into the Canadian Air Force. Hope he gets through O.K.

In spite of the late summer sun, Mike was chilled through when the Walrus turned up at mid-day, escorted by a pair of Mark IX Spitfires, which circled comfortingly at 3,000 feet while the amphibian touched down and taxied close enough alongside for one of the crew to get a boat hook to the dinghy and pull him alongside. He was a middle-aged cockney with a broken nose and a comfortingly matter-of-fact manner.

'Glad you hain't a 'un,' he greeted Mike. 'Carn't stand pickin' up 'uns.'

Then he gave him a half-tumbler of ragingly powerful Navy rum which sent Mike to sleep on the long, bumpy flight to Felixstowe....

* * *

'Greetings and congratulations to all 10th Eagle pilots in their conversion from R.A.F. to U.S.A.A.F. and may you continue to knock them out of the sky. Sorry not to be with you today, goddam it. From your old chief. Mike Browning. Squadron Leader, R.A.F.'

Inadequate. Banal. But it would have to do. Perhaps Air Chief Marshal Sholto Douglas or Major General Carl Spaatz would read it out at the change-over review up at Debden, and he imagined 'his' pilots, the whole scruffy gang of them, lined up and

28

to attention as the C-in-C Fighter Command and the newly appointed American chief inspected them. Surely to God, for this occasion at least, Mike prayed, they would have got their batmen to smarten up their uniforms and polish their shoes.

He would miss them all right. A good bunch of guys. And he was relieved to have the news that they had all got back from their last operation, with a score of three including his own. But it would be good to see the States again. And it would be good to get out of this hospital after his statutory twenty-four hours for 'observation'. There had been none of that goddam rubbish back in the Battle of Britain days, as he told the outraged nursing sister who had tucked him into bed with a hot water bottle. 'Wring out your pants and back into the goddam cockpit ...'

* * *

'I've never cracked myself up as any sort of a teacher, no sir,' Mike said, and laughed ruefully. 'But I've been told that I've got to lecture these young rookies. The bearded veteran, too old for the fightin' line, passing on his hard-won experience. That sort of crap. And testing. I'll be out in Southern California testing some new crates. They seem to think I know a bit by now ...'

Sir Richard Barrett, stoutish now in his mid-fifties, thick grey hair, grey moustache, every inch an English country gentleman, knocked his pipe out into the log fire, and poured them both a whisky and soda from the tray. 'So you must know a bit, my boy. A great deal. It's almost three years since you knocked down that first Heinkel with Keith. And someone told me you got your fifteenth the other day. Congratulations, my boy. You must be what we used to call an "ace" in the Great War.'

Sir Richard walked with a limp from a Mauser bullet he had picked up on the first day of the Somme, 1 July, 1916. Then he had been invalided out of the army, like Keith's father, who had been his platoon sergeant before coming to Rising Hall as estate manager. Mike loved the old man, loved shooting over the estate with him, or just chatting late into the evening like this.

Rising Hall had become his English home, ever since he had fallen in love with Eileen, and he had become very close to both her parents, first when they had agreed to their engagement, and then all through Eileen's crisis in the W.R.N.S. and her subsequent breakdown. Now she was recovering, but still very slowly.

29

Mike had walked with her for an hour round the grounds that afternoon, and an hour had been enough. They had kissed for the first time for so many months, gently and tenderly, out of sight of the hall and by the lake. He had cupped her face in his hands and looked into her marvellous green eyes, and seen clear signs of renewed life in them where for so long they had seemed listless and incurious.

'I hate the idea of your going away,' she had said, and really meaning it. Not with the old verve and passion which had so fascinated him when he first met her. But better. Much better.

Now Sir Richard said gruffly, 'Don't like the idea of you testin'. Nasty business testin'. Never know what the damn machine'll do.'

'Oh, they're not experimental kites, sir,' Mike reassured him. 'Prototype test flying's a very special skill. Not many pilots can do that. They call this combat appraisal testing. Some R.A.F. pilots are already doing it. They don't know much about European conditions over there, and certainly not combat conditions.'

They continued to talk shop and war late into the evening. Barrett felt out of things up here in Leicestershire, unwanted and becoming boring, without the stimulus of his London clubs or the House of Commons of which he had been a member for many years. With the receding of the risk of invasion even his Home Guard work seemed less important, and that left him with only his 'Dig for Victory' work to exercise his natural zeal and patriotism. He looked forward to these occasional days of leave when Mike or Keith would arrive at Rising Hall.

Lady Barrett came into the study to listen to the nine o'clock news with them. She had the same soft, fair-touched-with-auburn hair as Eileen, and Constance Barrett's figure was still good, though squared off a little in her middle age. She was a kind, quick-thinking, orderly and authoritative woman, and Mike was fond of her and still hoped that one day— if he survived — he might be her son-in-law.

She smiled at Mike and offered him a cigarette from the heavy silver box. 'You two have been w-w-winning the war, h-h-have you?' she asked lightly, with the slight stutter Mike found rather attractive.

Mike lit their cigarettes in turn and sat down beside her on the sofa. 'Eileen seems so much b-b-better. I do wish you were

30

staying longer, Mike dear.'

'I wish so, too, m'am. I really do. But the *Queen Mary* sails — oh, I'm not supposed to say! Anyway, soon, and I must leave tomorrow.'

Sir Richard switched on the wireless, and the familiar voice spoke of the tremendous battle for Stalingrad, and of yet another American bombing raid on France. It was less than a year since they had all listened to this same wireless announcing the Japanese attack on Pearl Harbour, and Mike had then experienced a deep sense of relief that his own country was, willy-nilly, now in the war, and Sir Richard had given a toast to Britain's new ally.... And now this new ally, his own homeland and the most powerful industrial nation in the world, was flexing her muscles and demonstrating to the Axis powers of Germany, Italy and Japan that she meant business.

At the end of the bulletin, Constance Barrett glanced across at her husband, whose eyes had closed and whose chin had fallen to his chest. 'Poor darling,' she said softly. 'All this open air and riding about persuading people to plant their winter v-v-vegetables is too much for him.' She put away her sewing and woke him up. 'Come along, you'll be more comfortable in bed.'

They left Mike by the dying fire. He was in a contemplative mood, wondering about an immediate future without the danger and the fighting that had seemingly become a permanent way of life for him. He lit another cigarette, poured himself another whisky and soda and put his feet up on the sofa, thinking with mixed feelings of the weeks stretching ahead, without scrambles or ramrods or dogfights or circuses or rhubarbs, without the ever-present threat in the air of being bounced by 109s or Focke-Wulf 190s, or peppered by German flak. Also, without the comradeship engendered by shared risks and triumphs, the satisfaction of leaping down from a Spitfire's wing, discarding helmet and mask, parachute and boots, and just simply lying on the grass, staring up at the sky which had again spared him, and deeply inhaling the cigarette, which tasted so especially good after breathing oxygen.

Before going to bed, Mike wrote a letter to Keith, telling him of the utter peace and beauty of Rising Hall in the early autumn. 'I still can't believe how marvellous it must have been to *grow up here*! Jeepers, Keith, what a place! Eileen is really much stronger and she is set on remaining engaged, and that sure suits me! Now I'm off to the good old USA — what a contrast! Steaks, cold beer, giant automobiles ... Look after yourself until I come back.' And he finished with the half-ironic song they used to sing during the Battle of Britain when they were very drunk in the mess —

> 'To tell the tale
> Watch your tail
> Or the Hun
> In the sun
> Will getcher'

Accompanied by a rattle of simulated gunfire....

* * *

America's capacity to surprise was as limitless as ever, Mike decided at the end of his first day in New York. The *Queen Mary* had taken him across the Atlantic in less than five days, unescorted and relying on her great speed to avoid U-boat attack. Inevitably, the New York skyline was the first surprise, as it had been for millions before him. The fact that he had lived in or near this city for the first eighteen years of his life made no difference. After such a long time away, the contrast between this brash, vertical city erected precariously on a chunk of rock in the middle of the Hudson River, and the ancient, maze-like cities of Europe, still took your breath away when you came on deck as the great liner was chivvied in towards the lower east side docks.

The next surprise was the reception. There were several senior diplomats, an emissary of the Free French government, and a number of senior officers of all three British services on board, and Mike had come to know them and play bridge and other games with them on the voyage. The reporters and photographers, almost all in trilby hats and raincoats, arrived like boarding pirates as soon as the gangway was down. Then, to Mike's amazement and embarrassment, he found that he was their first target — the returning hero, the ace pilot who had fought through the Battle of Britain, the adventuring hero-volunteer of the socially well-known Wall Street and Long Island Browning family.

Mike cowered and tried to escape when he discovered too late that they were after him rather than General Sir Edward Piers or the last Ambassador in Vienna.

'How many Nazi planes have you downed, Squadron Leader?' 'What was your worst experience during the Battle of Britain?' 'How're the Eagle Squadron boys getting on in England?' 'Did you ever have to bail out, sir?' 'Did the King of England pin that decoration on you?' The questions came from all sides, and so fast that Mike could scarcely answer them even if he had wanted to, and the flash-bulbs were popping continuously.

At length, he shouted, 'My worst experience is right now, this very goddam moment. And this,' he added, shielding his face from the flashes with his elbow, 'is worse than any German flak.'

This started them laughing. It was just what they wanted, and the questions now came in more disciplined sequence — 'I'm from the *New York World*, sir. You must have lost a lot of buddies in the battle ...'

'Yeah, quite a few. Good guys, French, New Zealanders, Canadians as well as British.'

'*New York Times*, Squadron Leader— will you tell us how our B17 boys are doing in their bombing raids?'

It was Mike's father, Ralph Browning, tall, courteous and firm, who put an end to the press questioning. He and his wife, Suzy, had hurried up the gangway immediately after the pressmen came on board and had witnessed impatiently their son's ordeal.

'Right, fellows, you've had your ration of my boy. You go back and write your stories.' Many of the reporters recognized the well-known banker, friend of the rich and influential, and they backed away grumbling good-naturedly in the face of his intervention.

Then his mother was holding him tightly in her arms, fighting off the tears, and he followed them down the gangway to the waiting Lincoln. Lunch in the apartment overlooking Central Park, the old negro butler, Ephraim, openly and unashamedly in tears. Talk, talk, endless talk through the afternoon. A few old friends in for cocktails. Then Mike had to suffer being taken out to dinner with a small party— 'In your uniform, darling, please,' his mother had begged. 'Let's show you off just for once.'

At the table a girl brushed the eagle on his shoulder as she passed; another, rather high, kissed him on the cheek and asked him to dance. It was a nightmare of an evening, as if he had suddenly and undeservingly been thrust into the role of a famous dance band singer. The next day he slipped thankfully into an old suit, took a bus from Fifth Avenue, ordered some underwear and shoes from Brooks' Brothers, bought some books at Scribners' bookstore and had a long, relaxed lunch with his father at the Century — all anonymously, all without a glance of curiosity or admiration. Once or twice, he even thought he detected a look of disapproval that such a vigorous young man should not be serving his country, and that gave him great satisfaction.

Three days later, shortly before he was due to fly out to Los Angeles, his father said at breakfast, 'It's back into best uniform for you tomorrow. And a haircut.'

Mike, still relishing the thinly-sliced, crinkly American bacon with his eggs, asked, 'What's up, Pop?'

'It's a summons. F.D.R. wants you to dine with us at the White House. He wants what one of his staff calls "hearing it from the horse's mouth".'

'Jeepers!' exclaimed Mike, and could think of nothing more to say.

* * *

The Braniff DC3 descended to 5,000 feet over the stark, dusty, brown hills separating the Mojave and Colorado deserts from the lush coastal strip upon which Los Angeles extravagantly sprawls. It was six years since Mike had been here, as an eager boy stunned by the brash vulgarity and pretentiousness of Hollywood and Beverly Hills. Where his father's friend, Cecil B. de Mille, had introduced him to Clark Gable and Myrna Loy and Barbara Stanwyck and the Marx Brothers, until he was stunned into awesome silence. A girl from the Follies had tried to seduce him in the back seat of an enormous Packard. So had an ageing star of the silent screen who was rapidly declining into alcoholism. He had resisted both efforts out of sheer fright and embarrassment rather than from moral propriety, and had not told a soul.

The Douglas banked steeply over the suburb of Glendale. Even some quite small backyards sported a swimming pool now, and between the rows of white frame houses, traffic like nowhere else in the world ran like colourful necklaces along the broad boulevards. Gas rationing did not seem to have interfered with the Californians' love affair with the automobile.

And, my goodness, in '36 Ginger Rogers had taught him the

first principles of tap-dancing and a well-known agent had bought him a pair of tap shoes. Ah, days of innocence, Mike reflected! A million years ago. Harvard had loomed then. Debs and parties. A trip to Hawaii.... Then that sudden, irrational urge to see Europe — a Europe, he had read, that was tormented with political strife and impending revolution and civil war. So it had been. And so....

Here he was, in the false war climate of late 1942, a national hero (the press cuttings his mother had collected!) summoned to the West Coast flying schools to tell young rookies about air fighting. And to fly what these pilots would be fighting with until Japan and Germany were beaten at last.

The DC3 touched down gently on the long concrete runway of the big airport. There were machines everywhere, on the ground and in the air — Lockheed Electras, DC2s, some old Ford trimotors, a big four-engine job Mike did not recognize, and a number of military aircraft, too, with the familiar five-pointed-star insignia. He had heard that the California aircraft industry — Lockheed, Douglas, North American — was pouring out planes in thousands for the needs of the war. Military planes and war movies were bringing a new prosperity to California.

* * *

A few days later, Mike was standing on the tarmac in the mellow Californian winter sun. Flanking him were Major Jerry Hawkins of the U.S.A.A.F., and Carlos Ricardo of North American Aviation. The major had escaped from the Philippines with General Douglas MacArthur after flying P40s against hopeless odds until there were none left. His language was lurid, and to Mike he had described the Japanese Mitsubishi Zero-Sen as 'a shit-arsed little bastard that can outrun, out-turn and out-fight any fuckin' ship you've seen'. And then had added with a nod, 'Except this'.

Ricardo was a senior designer for the company, a flying veteran whose log book went back to the early 1920s and included almost every type of machine produced in the USA during the 1930s.

The object of their attention was a fighter in glistening silver, a satisfactory but not greatly impressive-looking machine, which in his mind Mike likened to a modernized Hurricane without the British plane's aesthetic balance. Its one unusual characteristic was its deep belly, caused by the positioning of the radiator far back in the fuselage with another small carburettor intake directly behind the four-bladed airscrew. The laminar flow wings were clipped square, like those of the Mark V Spitfire Mike had been flying, which did not add to the machine's beauty. The three pilots walked round it slowly, the major and the designer saying little and giving their attention to Mike's reaction.

Mike had seen the Mustang on the ground and in the air in England. It was reputed to be fast low down, a good ground attack machine with nice handling but inadequate armament. The prototype had been turned out in the incredible time of 117 days, and had flown just two years ago. The Americans had been unimpressed, but the R.A.F. had ordered it.

'Yes,' Mike commented at length, 'a nice clean fuselage, and a friend of mine told me its aileron control's impressive. But it's no good high up.'

Major Hawkins said, 'So you know about the Mustang?'

'Oh sure. There're quite a few in England. They did well on the Dieppe raid back in August.'

'I guess we'll quit teasing you,' said Mr Ricardo good humouredly. 'This is not the Mustang you've seen fly. This is an Anglo-American hermaphrodite.'

The major tapped the engine cowling. 'That ain't no Allison in there. That's a Rolls-Royce engine, built by the Packard automobile people under licence, a Merlin 61 pushing out more than 1,500 fuckin' horsepower.'

'And what does that do to it?'

'It makes it *go*. Brother, you ain't been that fuckin' fast in any goddam Spitfire,' said the major.

Mike looked at the Mustang with a fresh eye, his head on one side. 'I guess I'd better get into that cockpit,' he said. 'And fly the thing, if it's all that hot.'

'Sure. That's why you've come 6,000 miles, buddy.' Carlos Ricardo nodded towards the cockpit. 'It's all ready for you. Chute. Helmet, the lot. We lay on everything for our customers, except the Messerschmitts to shoot down.'

Mike sat in the Mustang's cockpit for more than half an hour, teaching himself the position of everything so that he could have flown it blindfold. He liked the layout of instruments and controls, but did not approve of the hood, which badly restricted vision and was much inferior to the Spitfire's.

Ricardo, standing on the wing beside him, answered Mike's questions, warned him of the severe torque swing on take-off, and also of the density of the air traffic in the Los Angeles area. 'Get away over the hills to the desert,' he suggested. 'You've got gas for two hours.'

Starting the Merlin was no problem. It caught first time, and he let it idle, relishing the deep familiar growl before opening up and releasing the brakes. Mike set full opposite rudder trim to offset the torque, but even so, as soon as the airscrew began to bite and the Mustang began to accelerate, he was forced to use strong rudder to keep the machine steady down the long runway.

As soon as he had lifted off, Mike knew that he had a thoroughbred in his hands. He kept her low after retracting the undercarriage, and then pulled hard back on the stick at the airfield's perimeter, climbing at a steady 200 m.p.h. with the rate needle showing almost 4,000 feet per minute. He shut the hood, reduced revs and mixture, and climbed more steadily to 12,000 feet over Pomona. With the 10,000 feet snow-capped peak of San Antonio on his right, he kept the Mustang on a northerly bearing over the San Gabriel mountains, the Mojave Desert stretching limitlessly beyond. Only on a rare, crisp winter day would you get visibility like this in northern Europe, where for weeks on end you might be lucky to see a few miles, and impenetrable fogs could close down in minutes.

Mike revelled in the clean, clear air, the sight of half southern California, from San Diego in the south to far north of Santa Monica, laid out below him; and above all, in this keen, super-fast, wonderful fighter— surely the shape of things to come in the European war. At 20,000 feet, Mike pushed the throttle wide open and, flying straight and level, watched the needle move round the A.S.I. In no time, he was travelling faster than the Spitfire he had been flying in September, and in five minutes his speed was close to 400 m.p.h. Not satisfied with that, the needle swung farther, more slowly now, but steadily towards a true air speed close on 440.

Mike sang out with joy into his oxygen mask. Not even the latest Focke-Wulf could get near him at this speed. In this Rolls-Royce engined Mustang you could choose your time and place of combat to your advantage, and leave when you chose to do so.

Then Mike tested the aileron response — as good as a Spit's; dropped the nose slightly, pulled her up, aileroned her through a slow roll, keeping the stick hard forward when upside down, and came out with another 2,000 feet on the altimeter. Perfect.

Right — three 109s coming in fast from above. Break — now!

Mike went into a fierce right-hand turn, imagined the Messerschmitts flashing past, threw the Mustang onto its back, and dived flat out, aileroning gently all the way down to 8,000 feet, the speed building up to 500 m.p.h. No wing flutter. And she came out steady as an arrow after a hard pull on the stick. Some AT6 advanced trainers from Muroc were practising formation half a mile to the right, and the Mustang went past them as if they were standing still. That, Mike told himself with satisfaction, will inspire these guys on to finish their course and get into a real kite!

Down low she felt good too, though not so relatively faster than the Mark V Spitfire. Mike skimmed the hard, dusty desert soil, spotted here and there with cacti and shrubs that raced past his wingtips. By contrast, he returned to Los Angeles at over 30,000 feet with Catalina Island and the endless blue of the Pacific stretching ahead before he turned through 180 degrees, lost height at high speed again until he was in the Inglewood circuit and could lower flaps and undercarriage.

'O.K.?' asked Ricardo.

'O.K.'

'Every department?'

Mike confirmed — yes, every department. 'Not at her best low down. But she'll be the best escort fighter in the world — bar none. You want to get a couple of thousand of those to the 4th Fighter Group in England next week.'

Ricardo laughed. 'Give us till next month, will ya?'

Later in the week, Mike went over to the Lockheed plant where the first P38Fs were rolling off the line. He had seen this twin-boom, twin-engined fighter in European skies, too, and had heard pilots talk about it, but not very flatteringly. It certainly looked futuristic and spectacular on its tricycle undercarriage, with the pilot set into a pod between the two Allison engines, with the guns massed in the nose and protruding forward like an insect's antennae.

He found it a curious experience to fly this big twin, with a wheel instead of a stick, which seemed to confirm the impression that he was handling a light bomber rather than a fighter. The P38 felt like a tugboat after the sensitive little Mustang, and visibility that should have been spectacularly good from the perspex-hooded cockpit was ruined below to port and starboard by the massive engines.

These engines gave the machine a good turn of speed, especially in the dive and zoom, but Mike decided that he would not wish to get into close combat with 109s with this clumsy-feeling great airplane.

He also got his hands onto a Republic P47 Thunderbolt, 'the man-made monster' as this massive 15,000-pound machine was nicknamed. He did not care much for this brutish fighter, either, and likened flying it to driving a fifty-ton truck with slow and unassisted steering. The 2,000 horsepower radial engine gave it a good turn of speed, she dived like a stone, and there were no special vices to contend with. But again, Mike felt that he would not have liked to dogfight the beast. One diving pass and away, that would be the best tactical policy with the P47.

At the end of October, after a week of flying from a number of fields in the Los Angeles area, Mike faced the prospect of lecturing student pilots with increasing dread. He was twenty-four years old now, had travelled the world, brushed against death more often than most people in a lifetime, had the support of wealth and position, but remained shy and uncertain of himself socially. The adulation with which he was met everywhere in the States was an embarrassment and he hated it. The thought of facing boys a year or two younger who would hang onto his every word filled him with dismay. (At a dinner party a few evenings earlier, sitting next to a well-known movie star, he alone was asked for his autograph by a stranger; and the star's smile when Mike apologized had been a stiff one!)

He visited the North American plant again a day before he was due to visit a number of American schools and a British school in the desert.

'Mr Ricardo,' he said in the designer's office, 'I think you've got the greatest fighter plane in the world out there.'

'Flattery will get you nowhere, Squadron Leader,' the man had answered smartly.

'I thought it might get me one of your prototypes again— your

39

XP-51Bs as you call them. Just for a few days.'

Ricardo took the cigar out of his mouth and threw it into the standing ashtray. 'You want to show off to those kids, right?'

'I sure do. And think of the order I'll make the British Air Ministry give you.'

* * *

Mike flew the little silver bullet above the Polaris Flight Academy in the Antelope Valley at 5,000 feet and at over 400 m.p.h. He turned once through 180 degrees, came back again slow rolling steadily, finishing with a loop from straight and level.

Below, he could see the British training field buzzing with planes like bees round a hive — Stearman biplane primary trainers, looking like something out of World War I, Vultee Basic Trainers with fixed undercarriages, and the sleeker AT6s, or Harvards as they were known in England. Circuits and bumps, cross-country flying, elementary aerobatics and simulated forced landings — every process and stage of flying training seemed to be taking place within a few miles of this field outside the little town of Lancaster.

Mike did a wide, cautious circuit at 2,000 feet, wheels and flaps down, while instructors or pupils cleared the approach, and he could receive the green light from the watch office.

The flying school consisted of small bungalows, lecture halls and a canteen set round a grass square. The Stars and Stripes and R.A.F. flags fluttered from a flagpole outside the administrative headquarters, signifying the close interlink between the services of the two allies. The R.A.F. commanding officer led Mike to one of the lecture halls where they drank coffee with some of the instructors. They were rather like his own boys on 10 (Eagle) Squadron, only ten to twenty years older — hard, scarred and polyglot, survivors of stunting, dare-devilry for Hollywood studios, crop-dusting or flying the pioneer mail and passenger lines when a closed cockpit was considered effete.

They looked at Mike with curiosity. 'What's that ship you brought in, son?' one lined and scarred veteran asked.

Mike told him, but when another instructor asked about its speed, he had to shake his head. 'Just fast. Believe me, real fast. Faster than anything in Europe.'

40

A bald, stout instructor, with deep furrows set about his keen grey eyes, said, 'I'd give six months' salary to fly that ship. I sure would. How about it, young fellow?'

Mike shook his head again and laughed. 'No deal, I'm afraid. But join the Air Force and you might find yourself fighting the Japs in one.'

'Christ, not at my age! No, I'm condemned for life to teaching spotty Limeys circuits and bumps in Stearmans.'

The cadets filed into the lecture hall when flying for the day had finished, looking younger in Mike's eyes than he had seemed to appear to the instructors. And it was odd to find these massed R.A.F. uniforms, smart white flashes in their caps, far out here in the California desert, the most distant of training stations.

Mike stood up reluctantly and climbed with characteristic springing steps onto the platform with the blackboard behind. He looked at the sea of faces filling the hall. They were all still and silent and respectful. Mike smiled at them, though he felt that it was more of a grimace. They were waiting for him, and he did not know how to begin. Goddam it, I'm going to desert....

Then he pulled himself together, undid his jacket and took it off, and said in a loud voice, 'O.K. fellows, I'm not used to this. Give me a *Jagdeswader* of 109s any day. But let's smoke and talk and strip off what makes you comfortable — I'm not used to this California heat either ...'

It was all right from then on. The questions came fast, and in answering them Mike found himself lucidly explaining the development of fighter tactics since they had first gone into action in tight vics of three, changing to line ahead with a tail-end-Charlie just before meeting the enemy; the dangers and deficiencies of this inflexible formation; the imitation of the German finger-four 'Schwarm' which the Luftwaffe had evolved during the Spanish Civil War.

Then some personal anecdotes, how to get out of a Spitfire in a hurry, the importance of synchronizing your guns personally, keeping your screen spotless, and a hundred more tips.

At the end of two hours, he realized how much the years had taught him. He had been five years in the R.A.F., learning all the time, often under the urgency and heat of combat. If he had been five years at Harvard studying the Dark Age of Greek history, he would know a thing or two about that now, too, he reckoned.

The whole station turned out to see him off in his Mustang, and as he taxied out and cadets and instructors and lecturers waved their caps and cheered, he thought feelingly, 'This, buddy, had better be a damn neat take-off!'

It was all right. The lovely little silver Mustang did its usual torque trick, but was soon airborne, and Mike came back low over the runway at full throttle and then pulled up into a series of climbing slow rolls.

It was Muroc that evening, the same sea of faces, this time the cadets in neat khaki, very short haircuts, typical American young faces, eyes set wide apart, many with snub noses, some with spots, more with freckles, all so innocent and eager. Then to Bakersfield. They sent a team out from Inglefield to service the Merlin, and for three more days Mike continued his Southern California tour, finding it increasingly rewarding and also exhausting.

Late in November, he began to work his way back across the continent, flying himself whenever he could lay his hands on an acceptable machine, or using local airlines, talking to more flying schools in Arizona and New Mexico, Texas, Mississippi and Georgia, and back via Washington to New York.

Since he had left Britain, the Allies had invaded North Africa, and General Montgomery had roundly defeated the Germans at Alamein, and now the two armies were slowly, implacably, squeezing the enemy out of Africa altogether. The Germans had moved into Vichy France as a defensive measure, had failed to take Stalingrad, just as the Japanese had failed to take Guadalcanal. At last, the news seemed heartening. Winston Churchill, Mike read, had recently told the British House of Commons, 'This is not the end. It is not even the beginning of the end. But it is, perhaps, the end of the beginning.' The old warrior had, as usual, got it right.

On Christmas Eve Mike and his parents travelled out to the estate on Long Island. It was very traditional, with all the family there, and Mike sent a cable to Eileen three thousand miles away at Rising Hall. 'Back quicker than you think,' it ended. And that was right, too.

While in Washington, Mike had wangled a P38 for himself for the return trip to Britain. 'Goddam it — sir,' he had said, 'I'm no more valuable than any other delivery pilot, and they're doing the hop all the time. Why waste good flying skill in a damn boat—sir.'

The major-general had yielded, and on 27 December 1942 Mike took off from a field in upper New York State in the Lockheed with big drop tanks, and with refuelling stops at Newfoundland, Greenland, Iceland and Lossiemouth in Scotland, crossed the Atlantic and delivered the machine, with 'no more trouble than a sore ass,' as he put it, to East Anglia.

From there he telephoned Rising Hall and got Eileen on the line. 'I told you I was a fast mover,' he told her. 'Christmas on Long Island, New Year at Rising Hall. O.K.? And, darling, I warn you. I'm pure Yank now. Khaki uniform, U.S.A.A.F. wings. And call me "Major"...'

3

Randall's Tiffy

Keith Stewart peered out of the watch office window at the disenchanting scene, a North Yorkshire airfield suffering an early winter snow squall, with a bitter east wind driving the flakes horizontally across the runway. He could just make out some of the nearer Hurricanes in their blast pens, looking like hunch-backed old men sheltering from the elements. The ground crew were attending to the engine of one of them. The panels lay on the ground and an engine fitter on a ladder, wearing wool bala-clava, blue overalls and gumboots, was probing the Merlin.

The great hangar beyond loomed like the place of worship for this community of aviation set in an exposed and inhospitable land, and airmen and W.A.A.F.s on bicycles and wearing capes, headed towards it like worshippers, heads bent low. The build-ings beyond — the airmen's mess block, the tall parachute store, station headquarters with flag stretched taut on the staff, and the admin and domestic blocks — were dimly-seen silhouettes. The Wing Commander's Hillman staff car was heading towards the watch office, leaving a twin trail in the snow that formed into four curving lines as Maitland's driver turned and drew up outside.

The only sounds Keith could hear were the whisper of snow on the glass and the murmurs from the ambulance and crash tender crews playing pontoon in the little room below. It was 11 November 1942, Armistice Day of an earlier great war. This one was more than three years old and looked as if it would last for ever. The day was also Keith's birthday.

The voice came sharply and harshly from the loudspeaker above the controller's desk, causing Keith to start and turn to the duty pilot. 'Hullo Eastover, this is Delivery 27. Am approaching circuit. Permission to pancake. Over.'

Keith seized the microphone and threw over the transmission switch. The man must be mad.

'Delivery 27, this is Eastover. Visibility 400 yards. We're Harry clampers. I will give you a course to Hutton Cranswick where they have 1,000 yards.'

But before Keith could give him the vector, the pilot broke in. 'Thank you, Eastover. Coming in now.'

At the same time there was a sound like a strip of cloth being torn apart close to Keith's ear and through the glass he glimpsed a dark shape passing rapidly overhead.

'Who in God's name is that?' Jem Maitland, now promoted to Wing Commander, burst into the watch office and ran towards the window overlooking the runway.

'I believe it was the first of our Typhoons. But now we'll never know.'

Keith was quite wrong, and would not have made such a rash prediction if he had known who was at the controls. 727 Squadron was re-equipping with these secret new fighters, and the first had been due for delivery at North Rigby that day, but they had not been notified of its departure, and there had been no flying in this area of North Yorkshire since dawn. Harry clampers, as Keith had told the pilot.

The Typhoon emerged through the snowstorm like some giant predatory bird, the wide-set undercarriage its claws, deep-set air intake beneath the spinner its beak. It touched down in the dead centre of the runway and exactly opposite the watch office in a gesture of defiance, the tyres sending up fountains of slush. Anyone who could accomplish a landing at all in these conditions would also have to be skilful enough to make a perfect three-pointer, and this is what he did. Keith saw the machine snaking slightly from harsh braking before it disappeared into the murk. Then, three minutes later, it re-emerged on the perimeter track taxi-ing fast towards the watch office, ruddering from side to side for clear visibility ahead.

Maitland said, 'I'll have that guy on a charge. He must be crazy, risking a brand new kite like that.'

'I'm not sure we have any disciplinary control over A.T.A. pilots, Jem,' Keith suggested.

But Keith was wrong again. The Typhoon came to a halt beside the watch office, received by a surprised standby ground crew, who ran out with chocks to the strange machine. Before they could accomplish anything useful, the pilot had switched off, the massive three-bladed prop coming to a stop with much smoke from the stub exhausts, and the pilot in R.A.F. uniform had opened the door and jumped down from the wing to the tarmac.

It was the jump and the jaunty walk that gave Keith the first clue. He had witnessed so often the way that figure had walked away from aircraft — Avro Tutors back in early 1938, Hurricanes during the Battle of Britain— as if to indicate, 'that's that — now for some jars of beer at the mess ...'

Flight Lieutenant Randall had been forty when he had taught Keith to fly at Eldergrove, a scruffy ruffian of an officer with no ambitions towards promotion and total ambition towards flying. He had knocked down a dozen or more Spads and Fokkers in the Great War, and had ended that conflict in a shell hole amidst the wreckage of his S.E.5a in 1918: thus the great scar across his forehead. Beneath his grimy wings was a D.F.C. ribbon, the early and rare horizontally striped type. Keith had heard that he would have been asked to resign his commission on a number of occasions but for his exceptional skill as a pilot, and as one of the mainstays in the spectaculars at the annual Hendon Air Display. The R.A.F. put up with Flight Lieutenant Randall as a husband puts up with a tiresome wife who is also a brilliant *cordon bleu* cook.

Now he came up the steps two at a time and pushed open the door of the watch office with an ancient flying boot stuffed with maps. 'Morning, all,' he said cheerfully. 'Not quite sunbathin' weather but it'll soon be summer.'

Wing Commander Maitland looked at him bleakly. 'You landed without permission,' he said.

What a contrast there was, Keith reflected, between the Canadian in greatcoat and highly polished black shoes, two ranks higher, sixteen years younger, and the hard-bitten, hard drinking, hard flying Randall!

'No alternative,' said Randall, lighting a cigarette from a crumpled paper packet and adding 'Sir' only as an afterthought. 'Once I'd spotted the runway I knew you wouldn't have wanted me to go off again into all that fuckin' filth, risking your lovely new Typhoon. And there she is, the whore. And a proper old handful you'll find her, with a kick that'll have you clutchin' your crutch.'

Keith looked through the snow, coming down faster than ever, at the Hurricane's successor, bigger, bulkier, heavier, faster — much faster— than the earlier Hawker machine which Keith had first flown three years ago. Crouching, menacing, with thick canted wings from which four Hispano cannon protruded aggressively, and long, bulky nose containing the most powerful and complicated aero engine in the world. The Typhoon had been pressed into service, before a full test programme had been half completed, to offset the superiority of the Focke-Wulf 190 over the latest Marks of Spitfire.

But its reputation was already a black one, and it had killed many more British than German pilots. At the bar before lunch, Randall made light of the Typhoon's supposed vices, but Keith could read the truth between his expletive-spotted comments.

'Lateral stability's not bad,' he said over a second pint. 'Some of these pilots around today aren't fit for Tiger Moths — make a soddin' fuss about everything. It's a wonder they ever get near the fuckin' Hun.'

He reassured Keith about the tailplane, too. Briefly in the snowstorm, the two pilots had walked round the machine together and Randall had pointed out the heavy fishplates which reinforced the aft end of the fuselage at a point where so many early Typhoons had shed their tails at high speed.

'Yes, I don't mind if I do. Ta, very much.' Keith pushed another mug towards his old instructor and asked him about the engine.

'Goes all right. Makes the old Hurricane seem like a push-bike. I did Christ-knows-what straight and level, and more still in a dive on the way here. That soddin' Sabre pushes out the horses, you see.' Randall wiped the froth from his mouth with the back of his hand, and glanced down at the two-and-a-half rings on Keith's sleeve.

'Glad to see me old protégé's doin' all right,' he said, his lined, battered face set in a good-hearted grin. 'No more than average as a pupil, I seem to remember.'

Keith laughed, remembering the invective that would come down the Gosport tube as he struggled with rate three climbing turns. 'Lucky,' he said. 'Two things the Battle of Britain did to you. It either killed you or promoted you.'

'Same in '18. I went up to Major from Second Lieutenant in eight months. Faute de bloody mieux, as the Froggies say. No one else left.'

They walked into the dining-room together, the short, bandy-legged veteran of forty-five and Keith Stewart, twenty-four today and under the same strain as Randall must once have experienced in another war.

Randall said, 'You'll be adding to your score now — you see. As soon as you're worked up with the sods, you'll be chasin' 190s and swattin' em down like fuckin' flies.'

Keith had a quiet word with the catering officer, and champagne in a bucket was brought to their table by a W.A.A.F. waitress, who did not know how to cope with the unfamiliar bottle.

'Used to put down three or four a night of these at Marquise,' Randall said with a wink at the girl. 'And that was before you were a twinkle in your father's eye.'

They got very drunk that night and organized a party and mess rugger match.

'Not quite like Savile Farm in the Battle of Britain,' Keith said at one point, jacket undone and swaying dizzily.

'Nor soddin' Marquise back in '18,' Randall agreed. 'Better than nothin' though.' And he made a flying leap at Keith's legs and they went down together on the mess floor, which was awash with beer.

*　*　*

The whole squadron, including the adjutant, engineer officer, I.O., Flight-Sergeant 'Chiefy' Norton, and all the ground crew— the 'troops', the 'erks' — assembled at 0900 to study 727's new acquisition, the hush-hush Typhoon. Chiefy and two of the corporal engine fitters had been on a Sabre course, but none of them had seen the machine in the air or on the ground before.

The Typhoon stood where Randall had parked her, her engine

covered with a tarpaulin, which two airmen now removed, revealing the sleek lines. She might have been a famed new acquisition by a racing stable showing off her fetlocks and fine neck to the jockeys who were to ride her, and the stable boys who were to care for her.

The pilots paced round the big machine, studying every feature from the sturdy retractable tail wheel to the tip of the Rotol prop boss cover.

'What looks good must be good,' Keith commented.

'What about not being allowed to fly out to sea, sir?' asked a sergeant-pilot. 'Is that because the engine's unreliable?'

'The engine's had some teething troubles,' the engineer officer said. 'So would you if you had twenty-four cylinders, sleeve valves and a two-stage supercharger.'

'A chap I was trained with just disappeared in a Typhoon — just went missing,' a young pilot officer added. 'There've been quite a lot, I hear.'

Keith recognized that it was time he exerted his authority. He climbed up by the retractable step onto the Typhoon's starboard wing and called for silence. He looked down at the group of men below him, his first squadron. He had inherited a good team from Maitland, a cheerful ground crew in their thick sweaters and balaclavas and gumboots, and a bunch of pilots who, with few exceptions, had worked well together. As usual, the pilots were wearing a motley collection of clothes against the cold, from Polo Satterthwaite's inevitable once-white polo-neck sweater, to Titch Brambell who had somehow succeeded in getting on two Irvine jackets, the outer one reaching almost to his knees.

'Chaps, this is what we're flying from now on,' Keith began. 'It's a bloody good kite, the fastest thing we've got, and 190 pilots are going L.M.F. [lack of moral fibre] at the sight of a Tiffy on their tail. Those who don't get the chop.'

They were grinning now, the whole lot of them. He had got them all right. 'Anything as good as this needs special treatment. It's twelve-hour inspections from now on so the fitters are going to be busy — eh Chiefy?' Flight-Sergeant Norton nodded, and Keith continued, raising his voice now. 'But I'm not having any defeatist talk. Do you get that, loud and clear? I want pride in these new kites, not criticism.'

Keith cast his eyes over the faces of his pilots — his two flight commanders, Polo and Range Powell, old chums from way back; Watson with his two D.F.M.s, now, reluctantly, a pilot officer; Brian Walters; Inch Samuel from South Africa; little Brambell; Ron Easton, who was getting better every day; and the rest. They were all watching him with serious expressions, and several of them nodded when they saw him looking at them.

'And to show you what a bloody good kite the Tiffy is, I am now going to take off.' Keith grinned down at them again. 'And I'd bloody well better not prang her ...'

Keith and Randall, groaning with their hangovers, had emerged from the officers' quarters at dawn so that Keith could learn the cockpit drill from his old instructor. It was all part of the act, and he now opened the forward-hinged door and climbed speedily into the cockpit as if settling down in his office for a morning's routine work.

His regular rigger, the waggish cockney Bertie Silver, helped him on with his 'chute harness and straps, wound open the window for him and shut the door and canopy lid. 'Give 'em hell, boss,' he said with a grin, thumb raised, and jumped down to the tarmac to push the step into the fuselage.

Keith completed his cockpit drill rapidly and nodded to the engine fitter standing below with a fire extinguisher at the ready in case of a blow back from the 2,200 horsepower engine, selected the first of the six Coffman cartridges, and pulled a handle to detonate it. The prop jerked into motion as the engine fired, caught, and expired. Keith cursed. There was not a murmur from the crowd watching him. The second cartridge was no more successful, and Keith thought, 'My God, the thing *must* start! After that speech, it *can't* fail me.'

He set the throttle marginally further open and when the third cartridge fired, joggled the lever to and fro, caught the first detonations, nursed the engine for a couple of seconds longer. And suddenly it was all right. The Sabre burst into full deep song amidst gouts of black exhaust smoke, and the vibration in the cockpit was like physical ecstasy.

Keith turned on the oxygen, which you were instructed to breathe regardless of altitude as a precaution against carbon monoxide poisoning (sufficient of it to cause unconsciousness had been found in the liver of one dead Typhoon pilot). Then, chocks away, ease off the brake, and taxi straight onto the perimeter track.

'I'm feeling self-confident,' he kept telling himself. 'Of course I am, of course I am. Got to show 'em there's nothing to it.' He swung the tail right, left, right, left all the way. A petrol bowser drove off onto the rough to let him pass. There were two W.A.A.F.s in the cabin. He knew them both by sight. Pretty, capable girls they were, now watching him curiously, just as half the station would be watching the big, crouching secret-list fighter.

At 90 degrees to the end of the runway he ran up the engine to 1500 revs, checked rev drop on the two magnetos, and completed the rest of the take-off drill: air intake open, 15 degrees of flaps, full rich mixture, full fine pitch ... O.K.? Channel D on the R/T. 'Hello Eastover, Moorland Leader calling. Permission to scramble.'

'O.K. to scramble, Moorland Leader. Out.'

It was Maitland himself, up there in the watch office, as keen as the rest of them to see how he got on.

Keith turned onto the runway, opened the throttle against the brakes, released the grip, and at once felt the full flow of power pressing against his back. It was like nothing he had experienced before, thrusting the six tons of metal down the runway — and, my God, almost off it! Keith had set full opposite rudder tab but the torque was so ferocious that he had to press with all his strength on the left rudder pedal to keep the Typhoon straight.

But she came off nicely enough, and quickly too. The moment she was off the ground Keith corrected rudder and lifted up the undercart lever. One, two, the wheels retracted into the wings, setting up strong vibrations until he remembered to squeeze the brake lever momentarily to stop the wheels spinning. The Typhoon sank slightly as he raised the flaps and closed the air intake at 1,000 feet, and eased back throttle and mixture.

There was a thin layer of cloud at 3,000 feet, and Keith slipped through it gratefully. He wanted to get acquainted with the beast in private. And this he now proceeded to do, liking the quick aileron response, very like the Hurricane's, and appreciating the sturdy feel. Nothing dainty about this machine, which was so far removed from the Mark V Spitfire. But no nonsense, and if need be, she would take the punishment all right.

But it was the sheer power that you had to love. It was the first merit, the one characteristic that was unforgettable. You might lose 2,000 feet in a slow roll if you were not very firm with the Typhoon. You might not have the tightest turning circle. Flick rolls could be cumbersome. But you could not fault the power, nor deny the sheer speed, Keith decided.

At 5,000 feet, he could not resist putting the machine onto her back and pulling back the stick. The Typhoon dropped into a dive as if kicked down by some superhuman power. He was still in a steep dive when he went through the cloud, hauling hard back on the stick, anxious now. By chance he came out over North Rigby, smack over the runway, still pulling back with all his strength.

He had not intended to show off, nor break regulations by diving into the circuit. But Keith had no alternative. It was all he could do to bring the Typhoon out straight and level a thousand feet above his own base. He caught one glimpse of the figures still assembled around the watch office before blacking out. Then he was climbing again, still at an immense speed, clean through the cloud layer into the winter sunshine, over onto his back, full port aileron. And there he was, having completed the fastest, deepest Immelmann in his life; besides almost ending his life on his first Tiffy trip.

Chastened and sweating, Keith told himself he was a fool. Squadron Leader, veteran, decorated, survivor of countless ops, and you start taking liberties with this kite before you've even got to know her! Idiot!

For forty more minutes, Keith did what he should have done at first more thoroughly, feeling his way with the machine, trying out different rates of turn with and without rudder assistance, stalling her gently, and then, at 12,000 feet, putting her into a spin and bringing her out again at 9,000 without any drama. Finally, at her best height of 8,000 on the first stage of her supercharger, Keith eased the throttle wide open, and felt again that comforting thrust in the armour-plated back of his seat. The A.S.I. needle followed the boost indicator round the dial, up into the mid 300s, more slowly after 375 m.p.h., and finally indicating a true 400 m.p.h. without going through the emergency boost throttle gate.

He kept the throttle at this setting for five minutes. The cloud layer had cleared below, and to his astonishment, he found himself approaching the Tyneside balloons. Arriving sooner than expected was something else he would have to adjust to. . . .

After that he did a dummy cloud landing near to his base, and was glad he had done so because the Typhoon dropped very fast once the power was off, and when he got back into North Rigby's circuit, he could make appropriate allowance for this characteristic. Otherwise, no special skill was required, so long as there was plenty of runway. The landing speed was far higher than the Hurricane's, and when the wheels touched there was a shriek of protest from the tyres.

Taxi-ing in, Keith wound down both windows and took his helmet off, allowing the cold wind to play against his sweating face. That was another thing about the Typhoon. She was a hot machine and you did not need an Irvine, even in the dead of winter. And she threw oil. During the full boost run, the Sabre had thrown a lot of oil back onto the screen. Always carry a cloth — and mind how you put your hand out into that slipstream. He was learning.

Fifteen minutes later, he had all his pilots together down at the dispersal hut, passing on his findings while they were still fresh. 'About that low pass,' he began, determined to talk straight to his own men, 'well, I didn't intend it. I bloody nearly *did* prang her. And here's the reason ...'

The next day, two more Typhoons arrived at North Rigby, one flown in by a chit of an A.T.A. girl, which partly outraged and partly inspired them with further confidence. In a week, A Flight had five of them, and Range Powell, who loved the brute already, was heard to comment, 'Stone the bloody crows, we're in bloody business, cobber.'

* * *

They had reached the bottom of St James's Street in the Old Steine. They had passed the Royal Pavilion and ahead of them was the Palace Pier, closed for the duration and with rolled barbed wire across the esplanade. Keith had always loved Brighton, and relished the first whiff of sea air. In a few seconds they would hear the crash of the waves on the pebble beach. But they heard another sound first, harsh, staccato, threatening.

Polo, at the wheel, shouted, 'Get out!' as he stamped on the brake pedal.

Keith just had time to throw open the Hillman's door and leap onto the road. He intended to reach the gutter and throw himself into it. But the 190s were too fast for him.

The ground was shuddering to the impact of bombs bursting in Kemp Town, and the Bofors along the sea front were pumping out their shells like steady deep drum riffles against the chorus of 20 mm. and machine-gun bursts from the ground and in the air. People were running for the shelters with no chance of reaching them before the raiders were overhead. A double-decker bus had halted outside the Royal Albion Hotel and several of the passengers had got out and were running, bent double, for the hotel porch when the gunfire began skating hysterically across the tarmac, kicking up gouts of smoke and rubble and then hammering into the hotel and the rear of the bus.

Keith watched it all — all the two-second-long bloody catastrophe: the annihilation of the bus, the shattering effect of shells and bullets tearing it apart, the explosion of the fuel tank that was no more than a glare of yellow and blue, the wide scattering of steel and wood, limbs and torsos, the first of the little stubby-nose 190s racing past at roof-top height, a deadly flicker of sound and sight — black cross, swastika and muzzle flash from its cannon. Then another, and another a shade higher, a fourth with its 500 kg. bomb still in its rack. There must have been eight in all, the last one trailing a thin line of black smoke.

Keith and Polo began running. Everyone else in the broad, open Old Steine, among the gardens, on the road or pavements, appeared to have been frozen, and all the traffic remained stationary, stunned into immobility.

'The bloody bastards!' yelled Polo, pronouncing it 'blooody' in his thick Yorkshire accent.

The air raid sirens groaned into action, the warning rise and fall of their unsynchronized notes from all over the town a mockery to the dead and maimed. The sound of the 190s' engines had been cut off at once beyond the line of sea front hotels, and the *thud — thud — thud* of Bofors fire faded into the distance. The planes would be out at sea by now, streaking back to France right on the deck, the pilots preening themselves with satisfaction at their handiwork.

A scream shrilled above the sirens' cry, continuing inexhaustibly for an unnatural length of time, its note still steady, its

54

location mysterious, when Keith and Polo reached the scene of the massacre.

What was there to do? What could you do? Keith asked himself, except to fight off the nausea and pray that an ambulance would soon arrive. What was left of the main body of the bus was smouldering, inside a dozen or more corpses (impossible to count), black and obscene in their nakedness and distorted attitude. Young, old, fat, thin, female, male — who was to tell without a long and close examination? And that was beyond contemplation.

A dozen yards away, one of the bus's seats had been thrown clear and, unlike the woman sitting on it, seemed intact. Keith was not sure because he could not bear to look, but he thought she had probably lost both her legs although she had retained her shopping bag. She was in her fifties, Keith reckoned, with wiry grey hair. She was moaning softly, and when Keith put his hand on her head as some sort of gesture of comfort, her grey eyes lifted in the cataclysm of death and she said in an everyday sounding voice, 'I've lost my hat, dear.'

He turned and there was Polo among the wounded and dead in the hotel porch. To his shame, Keith saw that he was actually doing something, tearing a shirt from a dead man and tying it as a tourniquet high up on the thigh of a woman with a gaping bullet wound in her leg. Keith ran to join him, across the road with the scattered smoking fragments of bus, of mysterious lumps of clothing and baskets and jagged lengths of steel. And he followed the ragged line of big nicks and smaller raw nicks in the road surface from the 20 mm. and 13 mm. gunfire, like a footpath to hell.

The ambulances began to arrive before Keith could do more than utter a few words of reassurance and comfort to the sprawled wounded lying in the blood of the dead and the dying in this pocket of suffering. Keith saw one middle-aged man sitting on the seat beside the smashed glass doors of the hotel, well wrapped up with a woollen scarf and gloves as if he were a winter holidaymaker taking a rest. Keith, by now distrusting innocent appearances, wondered for a moment if he was dead or grievously wounded. Nothing of the sort. As he was about to go over to him, the man got up and walked briskly out into the street, looking neither to right nor left, keen only for a constitutional with a breath of sea air.

The ambulances' bells died in turn as they halted beside the pavement. Suddenly the privacy of the holocaust was shattered by bustling figures in blue uniforms, hard professionals with soft voices, wielding stretchers and instruments.

A hundred yards away from where they were no longer needed, Keith said, 'I think I'm going to be sick'. And was. Polo held his head, and said, 'That's O.K., lad. That'll do you champion.'

Nobody else saw his shame, except a Bofors gun crew near the Aquarium who were too busy clearing up empty shell cases and talking excitedly among themselves to care. When Keith was able to stand again, and walk back to the car, he saw smoke rising above Kemp Town. The paralysis of shock was over. A.R.P. vehicles of all kinds from heavy rescue to fire engines were in the streets, travelling fast towards the incidents. Everyone was in a hurry and there was much shouting. The police had roped off a wide area about the remains of the bus and the hotel entrance. The processes of healing, recovery and authority were again in command.

As they were getting back into the car, a bus pulled up alongside and the driver slid back his window and began shouting at them. He was a man in his mid-forties, Keith guessed, perhaps a survivor of the last German push in 1918, perhaps wounded in 'the war to end wars' and now experiencing the same thing all over again. He had a small waxed moustache and angry light blue eyes. 'You're supposed to stop them buggers,' he shouted. 'That might've been me and my passengers,' and he waved in the direction of the crowd gathered about the smouldering bus. 'Why don't you do something?'

There was no sensible answer and Keith dropped into the passenger seat without a word. 'Let's get the hell out of here.'

Driving along the Marine Parade past the hotels with windows boarded up or criss-crossed with bomb blast tape, past the sandbag gun sites and the rolled barbed wire with its complement of captive litter and the West Pier with its missing mid-section as an invasion precaution — past the closed ice cream kiosks and the dummy concrete new ones concealing anti-invasion guns, Polo drove thoughtfully and in silence.

There were naval cadets doing exercises on the lawns by the

56

Prince Alfred training headquarters. Beyond, the sea that would claim many of them, was grey and without hope. Polo said, 'Well lad, it's time we came down here'.

Keith threw his cigarette out of the window and lit another. 'There's nothing like seeing the tip-and-run business from the muzzle end.' He knew that, however hard he tried, he would never delete that scene of the piled burned corpses from his memory. 'I'd have liked all my pilots to see what a few 190s can do to a town.'

* * *

Before they were fully worked up, before all 727 pilots had mastered the Typhoon and carried out sufficient gunnery practice, before the necessary confidence in their massive and fast machine had developed, Keith had been ordered to bring his squadron down to the south coast. Morale of the citizens of Brighton, Eastbourne, Worthing, Seaford, Folkestone, Dover and Margate, and their trust in the R.A.F., had both waned seriously. Tip-and-run raids had become a political as well as a security and compassionate issue. Churchill had ordered positive counter action, and 727's move from North Rigby to Southdean was one of them. Where a Spitfire V pilot would watch helplessly as a Focke-Wulf pulled quickly away out of range, a Typhoon could catch a 190 straight and level and blow it to pieces with its four Hispano cannon. There were pilots along at Manston to the east already doing this with great success. Now it was the turn of Keith's squadron.

Polo and Keith were acting as the forward reconnaissance party, and the squadron would fly in the next day. Keith had been appalled at the idea of operating patrols from Southdean. This pre-war private flying field had served its emergency purpose during the Battle of Britain when 140 Squadron used it briefly. Nothing had changed when Keith had landed here after the Dieppe raid. Now he had been told that it had been transformed.

Polo drew the car to a halt beside the perimeter fence and Keith got out. It had all been changed beyond recognition. The area had been doubled, three tarmac runways laid down, a new brick watch office built on the site of the old club-house, and several Bessoneur hangars erected beside the dispersals. Blast pens, dispersal huts, admin and domestic blocks were all new.

At the main gate a smart R.A.F. police corporal in puttees and blancoed webbing belt stepped from the guard house and saluted and asked for papers. Behind, the R.A.F. flag fluttered from the pole.

Polo Satterthwaite summed it all up. 'Well, lad, this is reet champion. New bloody kites and new bloody airfield. Can't wait to get at those buggers now ...'

* * *

The hunch hit Keith like a hammer blow to his head, jerking him out of deep sleep. There was no rational reason why the Luftwaffe should send over tip-and-runners at pre-dawn on this particular day but the hunch was too strong to be thrust aside. He got out of bed, drew the black-out curtains and switched on the light. It was 5.15. A quarter past five on ... Then he remembered. It was the first day of the year. 1 January 1943. Yes, it made sense after all. Some German planning officer had calculated that the whole of Fighter Command would be suffering from a hangover after last night's parties, and they could slip in safely and be away before even the gun crews had dragged themselves out of their hangovers.

But there had been no parties at Southdean. A few drinks before dinner. Some singing in the Officers' Mess when the sergeants were invited in after dinner; and everyone in their rooms by 10 p.m. That was the rule Keith had instituted three weeks ago when the strain of standing patrols first became evident. And they had not yet intercepted a single raid....

Keith grabbed an apple from the fruit bowl in the mess, got into his car and drove off. There was not a glimmer of light in the sky down at the dispersal. It was one of those neutral winter nights, cold but not very cold, no stars, no moon, ten-tenths cloud but not very low, he guessed. Met. confirmed: a layer of cloud at 1,500 feet along the Channel coast, clear above, Force 2 wind from west-south-west. Perfect tip-and-run weather.

'I'm going to take off in about ten minutes,' he told the sleepy duty officer on the phone in the watch office. 'Give me the Drems when I call up. And ring ops as soon as I'm airborne and tell them I'm keeping radio silence. I'll be patrolling Beachy Head to Brighton.'

He got his flying gear from his office and woke up the duty

58

orderly. 'O.K. — I'm not a ghost. I'm doing a solo early patrol and I'll need your help. Oh — and happy New Year.'

The corporal threw off the blankets. 'Thank you, sir. Would you like a cup of tea?'

'No, I want to get airborne, so extract your digit, corporal.'

There was just the faintest glimmer of light in the east when he went outside again, but there was no illumination from it and Keith had to use a torch to find his way to the blast pen where his H-Harry was parked. His mind went back momentarily to his boyhood when, always attracted to this hour of mystery and silence, he would saddle up one of the Rising Hall hunters and go for a hack through the fields and along the bridle paths, always ending with a stirring gallop. And now here was his wartime mount. No wide-eyed start of surprise and indignant toss of the head from his Tiffy.

The corporal had got himself an extinguisher, and Keith showed him how to push home the step after he had got into the cockpit, and to take away the chocks as soon as the engine was running.

The blast of the Sabre crashed out across the airfield, and Keith switched on his landing lights intermittently to find his way along the perimeter track to the runway. Then he was racing down the runway, guided by the Drem lights on his port side. He could imagine Chiefy sitting up in bed at the sound, wondering what lunatic pilot was getting airborne without his authority, and Polo and Range wondering which of their pilots had gone berserk, roaring twenty feet over their heads at 5.40 in the morning.

Above the cloud sheet the stars shone dimly above him. The dawn was a glow of faint salmon pink spread from one eastern horizon to the other, broken by a few flecks of high cloud like far-distant airships. Keith felt the tug of expectation as strongly as ever. They *were* going to come — they were! And he even knew the place. They were usually circumspect about Newhaven with its heavy ack-ack defences and had not been there for months in spite of the temptation of shipping and docks as well as plenty of flimsy houses to blow apart. That's where they would go — you see!

Keith flew east for four minutes, relishing the loneliness of the sky and sensing the tingle of expectation when he dropped down through the cloud again into the dark world below. He could just make out the configuration of the coastline, with the high white cliffs west of Newhaven dropping to the estuary of the River Ouse, which snaked back through the Sussex countryside. The town was a small irregular spread of deeper black against the darkness of the land, the sea now a distinct shade lighter. He headed for Seaford and Beachy Head just below cloud-base and adjusted the rheostat on his reflector sight and the range bars for the 34-feet wingspan of the 190. At the outskirts of Eastbourne, he turned through 180 degrees, and doubled back on his patrol line.

By 6.15 he could see more detail — the line of the railway to Seaford, the farm-houses north of the Downs, the glow from the shaded lights of a car. Keith remained confident. The hunch that had startled him from sleep, and the practical realization that had followed. Oh yes, the buggers would be coming. He even knew that they would come in from the east, across the flat estuary land.

It was no more than a manifestation of the inevitable when his eyes were drawn to a riot of flashes from Seaford. They rapidly spread west along the coast, like a fuse that also marked the course of the raiders racing invisibly towards their target.

Right. At last. They would be in loose line ahead. They always were. He would start at the rear and work his way through them. Sitting sodding ducks.

The faint crackle in his ears was broken by an excited voice. 'Moorland Leader, Moorland Leader, many bandits approaching Whipstaff, angels zero ...'

'I have them,' Keith cut in. He had already slammed forward the throttle. He put his Typhoon into a steep dive, the speed building up very quickly.

Now he could just make out the faint cross shapes of three of the leading machines, and then more behind — twenty maybe — flashing across the fields a mile from Newhaven at what seemed an unmatchable speed. Already the harbour guns were opening up, and more heavies on the cliff above the town. He would have to chance his luck with them. It was all a part of this rough-and-tough tip-and-run game.

The last 190 was exactly over the railway line, no more than twenty feet above the telephone poles that ran alongside it, when

Keith came within range and had to throttle back to avoid overshooting. Just five degrees deflection, the little hunched shape filling the sight. A real bounce, a real old-fashioned bounce! And Keith's first-ever 190....

His thumb pressed the round button on his spade grip. And it was as if he had fired a three-second burst into his own engine because his Sabre chose that split second to cease to operate. U/S. Dud. Just like that. He never even saw whether he had hit the Focke-Wulf.

The suddenly dead engine and stationary prop reduced his speed so rapidly that he felt himself pressed hard against his straps. With tracer 40 mm. ack-ack following him remorselessly, Keith turned hard to the right and gained what height he could with his remaining momentum and looked for a place to put down.

Out of the corner of his eye he saw the flashes of the 500 kg. bombs in Newhaven and the docks, and the ether was full of voices giving warning cries and information as it came in from the Observer Corps and the radar on Beachy Head. Amongst them he heard the sector controller ask, 'Moorland Leader— any joy?'

'Like hell!' Keith snapped. 'Putting down north-east Whipstaff.' And that was all he had time for. Belly-landing a Typhoon was not something you did in mid-conversation, it was not a game for amateurs, especially in this light. He could see a field along-side the main road, big enough but criss-crossed with drainage ditches. He would have to chance them. He was at 300 feet and sodding beggars can't be sodding choosers, he told himself grimly.

O.K. Fuel cock off. Jettison canopy— and a blast of icy air hit him. Tighten straps. Switches off. Was that all?

Without any hydraulics, it was no use selecting flaps. He managed to hand-pump down a few degrees, but in this still air he would hit the ground fast anyway.

And he did, bouncing up fifteen feet and slamming down again. 'Oh, for God's sake don't flip — not at this speed!'

And he didn't. Amidst a holocaust of torn earth, the Typhoon cut its way at 100 m.p.h., 90, 75, along the grass. Stop, you brute!

But still she went on. At 50 he carved through a hedge as if it were not there, then he saw the first ditch, and the big machine went over it like the leading horse at Aintree, but casting adrift

61

half the air intake and some of the side panelling, too. At the end, she ground looped twice on a swampy bit of ground, and came to rest at right angles to the long dark groove she had cut across 500 yards of farming land.

When Keith tore off his helmet he heard a faint chorus of dripping sounds, a steady hiss and a sigh like the last breath of a wounded old warrior. But that was for only a moment, for Keith knew the potential dangers from a forced landing and wanted to be gone.

So, straps off, a turn and bang on the parachute box, and he was out, leaping onto the wing, then onto the torn-up ground, and he was running clumsily through the water from recent heavy rain. At fifty yards he turned. Poor old H-Harry seemed to be eyeing him reproachfully, a wreck of a machine half-flattened into the ground, most of the tail gone, the three blades of the prop bent right back against the panel covers of the engine that had failed him — failed him when he wanted it most.

'Oh shit!' exclaimed Keith, who was not much of a swearer as a rule. 'Oh God, what a waste! Whoever invented this 24-cylinder monster of an engine should be strung up in front of those four cannon, and I will personally press the tit.'

Then, remembering that he had not switched off the safety shield, he walked back cautiously and more realistically to the Typhoon and did so. After that, feeling cold, miserable and angry, he sat on his salvaged parachute and took out a cigarette. He was surprised to discover that he had some difficulty in lighting it.

Across the flat valley, there were fires burning, and in the still dawn air he could hear the faint sound of ambulance and fire engine bells. More smashed bodies, more armless, headless little children, more old men lying in agony under the rubble of the homes they had lived in all their lives. What a filthy, rotten, sneaky game!

Keith had appreciated, even before the end of the Battle of Britain, how lucky he was. Lucky Keith! It had followed him ever since, had wonderfully given him Jenny, hadn't it? Was it going to fail him now, when he needed it most, with his own squadron, and charged with the task of destroying this tip-and-run menace? And with the machine to accomplish this task. So long as it works, he added as a postscript. Tiresome Tiffy!

But we are going to catch these devils incarnate who machine-gun buses, and even people on bicycles — there had been a case of that only last week. We are going to win....

And this was his conviction, the promise he was making to himself, when the army arrived. A dozen of them in a Morris truck, rifles, bayonets fixed, and other evidence of hostility. 'It's all right,' he said wearily to the corporal who was running towards him, and pointed in the full daylight that now filled the sky, at poor old H-Harry. 'That's got roundels on it. And I'll make you a present of it.'

* * *

They had the meeting in the annexe to the officers' mess lounge at Southdean, eight of them in all, three from Sector H.Q., the Station Commander, Keith's I.O., and his two Flight Commanders — Polo actually wearing a collar and tie.

The Group Captain, a burly, grey-haired man who smoked a pipe almost as pungent as Polo's, said in a voice gravelly from heavy smoking, 'I've asked one of our best people from ops to come along too, to help with the radar side'.

There was a knock on the door as he spoke and Jenny walked in, saluted, took off her hat and shook out her dark hair. After the first glance of mixed delight and confusion, Keith kept his eyes off her until she had taken her place at the table between Polo and Range Powell. Then he allowed himself one flicker of a wink, and turned his attention to the Group Captain.

'I think we ought to get you to summarize the problem, Stewart,' he said.

Keith did so, lucidly and frankly, without any hint of excuse-making for 727's failure to engage the tip-and-runners along this length of the coast. 'Lack of kites is the worst part, sir. With only twelve hours between services, we're lucky to have eight Tiffies ready at any one time. We try and put up patrols at dawn and dusk, but that's not always possible. And we've lost three from forced landings in the last month.'

Keith took a cigarette from the Wing Commander's silver case, and while he was lighting it, Range said, 'Tell 'em about yours last week, cobber.'

Keith did so, silently congratulating the Australian on avoiding the word 'bloody'. He saw Jenny look up sharply from the

63

paper she had been studying when he recounted how the ack-ack had followed him all the way. 'We're used to that, sir,' he added. 'And we can even put up with engine failures. But we must have the machines.'

'I'll have a word with the C-in-C,' the Group Captain said. 'There's a squadron working up in 13 Group, and we could pinch their kites for a few weeks. If we can really hit them hard on one raid, I think it might discourage them enough to stop them altogether for a while.' He turned to Jenny then and asked, 'Flight Officer Simpson, when's that new bag of tricks starting work?'

'Next week, with any luck, sir.'

For a fleeting second, Keith remembered the Jenny of 1938, bored, spoilt, rich, unhappy, with a cruelly unhappy marriage and a divorce behind her. And now this crisp-talking, self-confident, responsible W.A.A.F. officer. But as lovely and desirable as ever. His eyes fell to her hands, clasped on the table, and he remembered their touch. And now the voice that could whisper absurdities in his ear was saying, in response to the Group Captain's request for details, 'The T.R.16, as you know, sir, possesses an ultra high frequency wavelength. The days of the goniometer are now past ...'

Keith allowed himself a fleeting moment of amused wonder at the contrast, and then gave her exposition his full attention.

'I'll be running the team there myself for the first few weeks, until I feel they can cope,' she ended, and smiled a business-like smile in response to the Group Captain's thanks.

Outside, it was a crystal clear winter's day. A light blue unarmed P.R.U. Spitfire was touching down, no doubt hungry for fuel, and a Sabre on an engine check was being run up in the hangar.

'Well, good luck, Stewart.' The Group Captain shook Keith's hand and answered his salute before getting into his car.

'Can I take you anywhere, Flight Officer?' he asked Jenny through the open window.

'No thank you, sir. I've got to get to Bentley Priory for a meeting.'

Keith intervened swiftly. 'I'll see she gets transport, sir.'

As the car drove away, Range said urgently, out of the corner of his mouth, 'That's my sheila.' Keith had seen how the

Australian had never taken his eyes off Jenny, and Keith was for once thankful for his two-and-a-half rings.

'I'm flying up to Hendon to pick up a couple of engine fitters we need urgently,' Keith said to Jenny, his face expressionless. 'I'll be glad to take you.' And to Range, he said firmly, 'You'll please take over the squadron until I get back.'

Keith loved flying the little Dominie he had wangled for his squadron in the autumn.

'This is highly irresponsible behaviour,' Jenny said as she settled in the co-pilot's seat of the little twin-engine biplane. 'As for these mythical fitters!'

Keith started the engines in turn and signalled chocks away. 'Of course, if you're scared of flying. Or don't trust me ...'

'Don't be a fool, Keith.' She had to shout to make herself heard. 'It's all very well when we're on leave, but ...'

Keith opened the throttles wide and her voice was lost in the roar. The Dominie lifted off in the first quarter of the runway, and they climbed up into the chill blue winter sky. There were patches of snow in sheltered combes on the Downs and the dew ponds were covered with ice.

Keith throttled back at 5,000 feet and called up sector. Then he turned to Jenny and said, 'O.K.?'

This time she smiled, that slightly uneven smile that had caused the first flutters of desire all those years ago. More than four years ago. Four years, and the only way they could be private together was at 5,000 feet in a Dominie.

'Do you want to take over?' he asked.

Jenny seized the co-pilot's controls and hesitantly pushed the wheel backwards and forwards, and turned it left and right.

'Don't be frightened of it. Put it in a steep bank — like this,' and he helped her. 'A little back now, and some gentle rudder ...'

The Dominie, with little help from Keith, went into a rate three turn clear through 360 degrees.

'Now a dive, trim forward ...'

After a few minutes he took over again, and Jenny said, 'That seems easy enough. And what fun!'

'Talking of fun,' said Keith, throttling back. 'I could set the trim for straight and level and we could make love in the back there,' he added, pointing to the cabin. 'Very aphrodisiacal, this vibration. That would be something for the log book. "Seduced

Flight Officer J. Simpson at angels five over — " ' he glanced down and at the map '— "the Hogs Back. On her back." '

Jenny laughed. 'You're a disgrace to your service. You're supposed to be shooting down 190s, not playing the fool over Surrey.'

'Even Drake was allowed to finish his bowls,' Keith said, undoing his straps. 'You hold the controls then.' And he got up and leant over Jenny, undoing the buttons first of her greatcoat and then her tunic.

'Keith, you're mad.'

'Just sex mad. Steady now, a bit back on the wheel.' He put his left hand over her naked breast, feeling the nipple hard against his palm as he gently caressed her and kissed her, brushing her lips, for a long time.

Jenny at length took a hand off the wheel and pushed him away, saying chokingly, 'You'll kill us. Look!'

They were in a dive, but not a very steep one, and Keith returned to his seat, laughing triumphantly. 'Well, that was the next best thing.'

The London balloons were on the starboard quarter, a mass of silver spots like Christmas glitter stretching far into the distance where the Thames Estuary spread out in a wide, uneven V. Keith called up Hendon and asked for a car to take Jenny to Bentley Priory. She had buttoned her coat up, combed her hair, and was now putting on some lipstick — just the regulation touch, no more.

Keith said, 'Back to the stern world of duty, eh?'

'Yes, Squadron Leader Stewart. And back to a world of well-behaved officers and gentlemen.'

She settled her hat on her dark curls and Keith said, 'You look rather fetching in that.'

Back in the mess at Southdean that night, Keith had to endure a great deal of mockery and stand a round of drinks. But he hugged to himself with satisfaction the occurrence over the Hogs Back. That was his own private world, and one day it would be his only world, if this war ever ended, and if....

* * *

The next time he heard Jenny's voice it was just seven days later. And this time it really was from the stern world of duty — the

66

world of the Ops Room in the nissen hut alongside the steadily rotating aerial of the new T.R.16. She had picked up the faint blips moving fast across the screen in front of her from Calais on a course of 264 degrees. Swiftly she drew a line with a chinagraph on the glass, calculating at the same time the distance south of Dungeness they would be in three minutes, and where and when they would make landfall on the present bearing.

Keith was on the end of the runway at Southdean, strapped in, helmet on his lap, reading a magazine, when Jenny picked up the plot. It took fifteen seconds, the 190s travelling just $1\frac{1}{2}$ miles, for the call to get through on the direct landline to Southdean's watch office, and another five seconds for the duty pilot to seize the Very pistol and fire it through the open window. It was answered by a handbell from the dispersal, but its sound was drowned by the simultaneous crash of two Sabres bursting into life.

Keith and Pilot Officer Watson were already moving by the time the red Very cartridge had fallen to the ground, and the slipstream was scattering the pages of the magazine as far as the perimeter fence.

Keith was trying to secure the clip of his mask and cope with the manful task of getting his Typhoon into the air at the same time. It was a rough take-off, but that steady veteran Watson was tucked in nicely beside him as they lifted over the bungalows at the end of the runway.

'Moorland Leader airborne,' snapped Keith.

'Steer zero-eight-seven,' Jenny said into the mouthpiece of her headset. And those four words were enough for Keith. They were all he needed. She was going to bring them luck. Jenny and her new 'bag of tricks' as the Group Captain had called the new radar. This was not going to be another abortive scramble, of which they had had so many. This was going to be the real thing. Must be....

As well as the instant cockpit readiness, another of the decisions reached at the conference was to use informal R/T and, for additional clarity, to dispense with code-names. Now Jenny pumped out the information as she followed the course of the raiders on her ultra low-seeing set which permitted the Luftwaffe no more secrets.

'About twenty bandits. Speed 310. Course is now 240. Position twenty-four miles south of Bexhill.... They have altered course to 340. This will bring them over Eastbourne in exactly four minutes ...'

Keith and Bill Watson had gone through the throttle gate, and Keith's A.S.I. was registering 415, a higher speed than he had ever experienced straight and level, r.p.m. 3,900. A glance at the map on his knee showed him that it was possible to make an interception before they reached Eastbourne, with luck, and if their Sabres stood up to this ferocious boost. Keith cursed the oil that was already spraying back on the screen, and transmitted, 'Tell the gunners at Brighton to keep their trigger fingers under control, I don't want to waste time going inland.'

'Roger.' Jenny was not wasting words.

727's immediate-readiness pair were already airborne. Keith heard, with relief, Titch Brambell acknowledging Jenny's course to steer. He and Watson would need all the support they could get. Back at Southdean there would be a great deal of running and frantic bicycling as the rest of the squadron on various stages of readiness attempted to get into the air in time to join in the imminent scrap. The only risk now was that the German monitors would pick up this R/T talk and translate and transmit it as a warning to the fighter-bombers before they reached their target. But for the present, as Jenny calmly, crisply snapped out the figures, it was clear that they were still closing in fast on the English coast.

There was scattered cloud at 3,000 feet, and Keith indicated to Bill Watson with a pointed finger that they would go up into it. They were off Newhaven, seconds later off Seaford. The undulating white cliffs — the Seven Sisters — were behind them, and there was Beachy Head.

At 10.26 precisely, 6½ minutes after take-off, Jenny said, 'They are one mile ahead of you, course 340.'

Keith saw them while she was still transmitting, in five loose groups of four — twenty Focke-Wulf 190A-4s, stubby-nosed, with the beefy B.M.W. radial engine, with, no doubt (you could not tell for sure from above), a 250 or 500 kg. bomb under each wing, tearing in towards Eastbourne, so low they were hugging their own shadows on the rippled surface of the sea.

Keith did not bother to say 'Tally Ho'. He just threw his Typhoon on its back, and Watson followed at once, transmitting in his strong cockney voice, 'Ain't science bloody wonderful!'

It was not to be the bounce Keith had hoped for, out of this patchy cloud and taking the rearmost *Schwarm*. The pattern was confused as he and Watson came down, although with the experience of so much combat now, the scene was imprinted instantly and imperishably on his mind, and he reacted with snap reflexes. The five *Schwarms* were breaking into rough line ahead, the leading 190s no doubt with delayed action fuses on their bombs, and the foremost group were about one mile out to sea from Eastbourne, already receiving the attention of heavy ack-ack from the guns along the esplanade.

But either a sharp-eyed pilot had spotted the two Typhoons, or base control had warned them of likely trouble, because before Keith could get within range of the last 190, it turned sharply to port, jettisoning its bombs and attempting to gain height. All but the first *Schwarm* followed in different directions so that in seconds this patch of sky became a mêlée of twisting, turning, climbing dark-camouflaged Focke-Wulfs, and the sea below was torn apart by more than thirty jettisoned exploding bombs, water spouts rising high above their circular shock waves.

Keith saw Watson making a head-on attack on one of the climbing 190s, and he got in one brief full deflection shot at another just before it went into the sharpest aileron turn he had ever seen. Another flashed past only feet above him, and he glimpsed the black cross, the empty bomb rack and the project-ing cannon, a stubby nose and bright-painted spinner. They were going to stay awhile and fight it out, and who could blame them with odds at twenty to one?

Speed— that was the one vital factor in their favour, and Keith took advantage of the momentum of his dive and the huge power of the Sabre to take himself above the whirling mass of planes. Smoke was billowing up from bomb blasts in the town, and those four would now be turning through 180 degrees to join in. Keith saw one of them crossing out over the coast just east of the town and decided that was his. He angled his dive to come out behind him on the starboard side, lost him momentarily beneath a fleck of cloud, saw him again as he edged slightly to the west, the light catching the long Plexiglass canopy.

Keith glanced behind and above, saw to his relief the heavy-jawed silhouette of two more of his squadron diving down, and gave his attention to the 190 that was now no more than 1,000 yards ahead and below, and growing fast in his screen.

The first burst was with 5 degrees deflection, and it was good shooting. At once the 190 began jinking like a March hare, kicking rudder one way then the other. He was not going to turn. This one did not want to fight sixty-five miles from his base — not against an ever-increasing number of Typhoons with their four cannon and superior speed....

It was difficult shooting and Keith used half-second bursts, throttling back to avoid overtaking him, keeping both hands on the spade grip and striving to keep the centre dot steady on his jerking target. He saw the flash of strikes on his fourth burst, just forward of the tailplane. The 190 suddenly climbed as if kicked. Keith thought he had killed the pilot, and he was wrong. The pilot was alive and seemed to have changed his mind and his tactics, because the Focke-Wulf went into a very sharp aileron climbing turn, and came down on Keith almost at right angles, ripples of gun flash from the wings as he opened up at extreme deflection and almost on his side.

Keith wrenched back the stick, blacking out, white trails at wingtips, slammed the throttle wide open again, and came down on the 190 as it dived for the sea. His Typhoon was hard to hold, very hard, the port wing wanted to drop and was only held by a firm grip on the stick. A large lump of alloy wing had been torn up just forward of the aileron by a shell. What more damage had the 190 done? For the moment, Keith did not care. He was pouring with sweat, very angry with himself, very determined to get his adversary — and to hell with the oil-smeared screen and smashed wing.

And he did. Five seconds later, dead behind and a shade below the little fighter — half-retracted tailwheel, thin rudder topped by radio aerial, faint glint from the rear of the canopy — Keith put in a long burst. The pilot could not have known the danger he was in, and was dead as the first shells struck, tearing off the tailplane, pounding into the cockpit, incendiaries in the fuel tanks, armour-piercing shells turning that beautiful 14-cylinder radial engine into a shambles of hot steel and copper tubing. The explosion was like some terrible celebration of death and destruction, and Keith had to jerk his damaged Typhoon up and out of the way of the fragments that streamed back towards him.

Now he was aware of the shouts and interjections, the cries of warning and triumph, on the R/T. Inch Samuel seemed to have got one. His 'sweet' South African accent was immediately identifiable. And Watson broke in once to say laconically, 'Got that bugger!' That was no surprise to Keith. Then a voice he did not recognize shouted, 'Break Red Two!' Silence. And Keith hoped the pilot did as he had been told in time....

But the fight was dying. It had moved far out in the Channel, and every yard gained would be to the advantage of the German pilots and the disadvantage of 727. Distantly he heard a voice — was it Ron Easton's? — transmitting for a fix, and then calling 'Mayday!' repeatedly. Air Sea Rescue would cope with him, with luck.

'Moorland aircraft, rendezvous over Beachy Head, angels three,' Keith transmitted. 'Return direct to base if you're low on fuel.' Now Jenny would know that he was safe. But, like the good controller she was, who had completed her part with the intersection, she remained silent in her nissen hut, watching the fading blips of the surviving 190s.

Keith did not stay for the rendezvous after all, leaving Range to bring home the squadron. His machine neither felt nor smelt right, and he cruised back to Southdean at sufficient height to bail out if things started falling off.

After he had landed, fast without flaps, and arm aching from holding up the damaged wing, Bertie Silver had a quick look over his machine. 'That's five cannon and a dozen machine-gun strikes, sir.' He was circling the holes with a piece of chalk. 'That's not like you. I'll 'ave to make this Cat B damaged and get you another one from Chiefy.'

They all agreed that the experience with the 190s was a shaking one. They were not like 109Fs at all — much faster and with that incredible aileron response, a very tough adversary. No wonder Spitfire Vs were unable to cope. But they had got four of them, all confirmed by cine camera, with final odds of twenty against the eight of 727 who had managed to get there in time. And Ron Easton, fulfilling his earlier promise, was back that night, very full of Navy rum and unfit to celebrate his first victory.

After giving their reports to the I.O., the phone rang. Keith listened to the gravelly voice of the Group Captain. 'I hear you caught them at last, Stewart.'

'Yes, sir. And a hell of a donny it was.'

'Four? Is that right? That's more like it. The Hun doesn't like twenty per cent casualties. The controller on the new bag of tricks did well, too.'

Keith agreed warmly. 'Couldn't have done it without her, sir. Hope she gets a decoration...'

4

The Direct Hit

The B17's starboard outer engine caught fire. Mike saw the flames jet from it, and almost at the same time the wing creased just inboard of the flames, fell to 90 degrees and broke away. Like a model. Like a goddam model plane when the wing glue gives. As a boy, he had had one like that; always falling apart until he threw the thing away in a rage.

The result for the B17 was inevitable. The big machine tipped as if violently kicked, fell on its side, and dropped in long swings to right and left, a swinging gondola of death, through the broken cloud at 8,000 feet and was lost to view in the mist of lower altitudes. No one got out.

Mike pulled his P47 into a starboard climbing turn — how sluggish she was compared with the P51! — and called out to his number two to rejoin him. The 190s and 109s had completed their attacks and gone home to refuel and rearm. But there would be more. Like in the Battle of Britain, there were always more. And how goddam difficult they were to deal with!

It had gone well at first, and they had given the Germans the shock of their lives. Mike's Group Commander had got his hands on a dozen 200-gallon long-range tanks, and Mike, first to hear the news, had secured them for his own squadron. So, when the rest of the Group turned back soon after crossing the Dutch coast, leaving the B17 Fortresses, Mike was able to continue for at least another hour's penetration into *Festung Europa* with his squadron spread out into four groups of four above the bombers.

The red-nosed 190s had swarmed round the B17s ten minutes later, with confident radar reports that the escort had left. Instead, Mike had led his squadron down from 30,000 feet. The P47 was wonderful in a dive, and they were in among the Focke-Wulfs before they could complete their first pass. For a moment, Mike's heart had lifted, the adrenalin had flowed, his eye felt as steady, his concentration as total, as if he were still at the height of his powers. He had even made some strikes on a 190's fuselage before it flicked away in an aileron roll as if it had been electrocuted. Young Luke had made a kill. Mike saw it, fifty feet above him, and had to turn smartly to avoid the bailing out pilot who flipped past his wingtip.

The 190s were thoroughly though only temporarily demoralized at this first appearance of the tubby Thunderbolts — the 'Jugs', for juggernauts — deep inside the Third Reich. They had no business to be here. Later, the pilots would learn of big drop tanks being picked up by farm labourers in the fields of Westfalen, and they knew then that life would never again be as easy for them.

But later on the raid, a dozen P47s were insufficient to provide the big formations of bombers with proper protection. Three more had gone down before they had reached their target — a machine tools plant — and now, on the return leg at last, the big twins started coming in, heavily armed Ju.88s and Me.110Gs.

Milt Bowley, one of Mike's Flight Commanders, was the first to spot them against the dark green of the German countryside, climbing fast. Mike knew what they would do, clever Krauts. They would make belly passes and drop down again to around 15,000 where the Thunderbolts lost so much of their performance.

Mike's squadron could drop on them, and did, but their rate of climb was so poor that it seemed to take forever to regain a superiority above the great lumbering dark bombers. Mike saw one of the 88s climbing up very fast at a straggler, undeterred by the fire from the ball and rear gunners of the bomber. The Junkers was a C variant with a massive mixed armament firing forward and a couple of machine-guns firing to the rear, a consideration in close combat, for fighter and bomber alike.

Mike called up angrily again for his number two. (Why did he always sound so petulant on the R/T now?) Then he went down on the 88. It was a badly timed interception. He had twice to kick rudder to adjust his course, sank too deeply out of his dive, and managed to get in only a single two-second burst with his eight .5s at extreme range. And that was after the 88 had torn a line of shell holes like a crazy zip-fastener along the length of the bomber's belly.

The 88 dropped away vertically, confident that his victim would never get back. (It did not. It belly-landed very roughly in a vineyard just outside the village of Rheinegholt, seven of its ten crew dead, two wounded. The bombardier who had taken over was thankful when a bunch of German engineers cut their way into his foetid, bloody cockpit and dragged him out.)

Then the guns took over, and there was nothing they could do about that. Mike could see the B17s far ahead in tight-packed vics of three, making contrails of geometric exactitude, in contrast with the multitude of grey puffs of flak that were spattering the summer sky about them. It appeared to be arbitrarily careless, this flak, but Mike knew what it was really. It was, as usual, lethally accurate.

'We'll get above them,' Mike told his squadron sharply. 'Milt, take your Flight to thirty and the rest of you stay with me at twenty-eight. We'll maybe draw some of the fire. Out.'

They did. German gunners six miles below could not resist throwing up shells among the Thunderbolts, and Mike did not have to order his pilots to spread out and jink. One shell exploded close enough to Mike for him to hear the whoomph, and almost instantly he was flying through the smoke so that Milt called up, 'You O.K., Chief?'

Mike confirmed, and Milt, 2,000 feet above, skidding and dropping his burly Jug, said, 'Jeez, get a load of that flak! They could get out and walk on it.'

The B17s were really going through the fire now, the puffs like paint drops from a flicked brush, so close that as they dispersed they formed a short-lived layer of cloud. There had to be casualties. The laws of chance would not permit sixty B17s to get through that wall of high explosive and flying steel unscathed. And as he watched, way out in front, black smoke began streaming from a starboard outer engine. The pilot put it in a steep dive in an effort to put out the fire. For another at the rear of the formation, the end came quickly, with a direct hit on the tail — a flash, a puff, a scattering of minute fragments. The bomber was thrown over onto its back and hurled into an inverted dive. The tail gunner would by now be no more than a contribution to the fragments. And Mike could imagine the desperate efforts of the surviving crew members to get out, struggling in their heavy flying gear, their flak suits, their encumbering gauntlets and helmets and oxygen masks. Struggling, too, against the pressure of negative G and the roaring gale that would be sweeping the shattered fuselage from end to end. This was not what they had dreamed of when they bravely signed on for the Air Corps. Not this panic and pain.

One — thank God. Then another, and two more distant white circles, no more than dots, spread out below. And that was all. Prayers of thankfulness. Prayers of grief.

They were crossing the Dutch frontier, and this would inevitably mean a renewal of fighter attack, this time from the JGs at Schipol. It should also mean some relief for Mike's handful of Thunderbolts. And the good news came first, a British voice — so British after these hours of sharp American voices with their urgent and cryptic comments: 'Hullo, Highstrip Leader, this is Bandsman Leader,' it said, as if announcing some Royal levée. 'Please give me your position. Over.'

These were the Spit IXs they had been told to expect, come to help them over the last leg. Mike caught sight of them, canopies glinting in the sun, at 25,000, twelve of them.

'That's not all, chief.' It was Milt's voice again. 'Take a look eleven o'clock high.'

Keen-eyed Milt Bowley had seen the Jerries, the faintest of dots almost directly in the late afternoon sun.

'Nice timing, Bandsman.'

Then the English voice again: 'Thanks. I have them. Bandits five o'clock above, all Bandsman aircraft. Ready to break. Out.'

For a few seconds — and it was only seconds — Mike was able to witness the mêlée slightly below them and still to the west. But the German fighters, greedy for the slow, fat Fortresses, broke free from the Spitfires as soon as they could.

'Shall I take the starboard, chief?' It was Milt's voice again, reminding Mike he was the leader and should be giving orders.

The chief was getting slow, that's what he was getting. Slow.

'Sure.'

They were mixed 190s and 109s, the Schipol crowd they had tangled with so often, scattered, careless, untidy, innocent even you might think them, if you did not know their methods. They had things worked out, though, these tough veterans. With the Spits hanging on as best they could, the German came tearing head on at the block of B17s.

Milt's flight was getting in their way. Mike saw Milt himself in a very tight turn boring in on a 190 and opening fire with a full deflection burst. But, head-on, you had to be quick, damn quick, attacking or defending. And the B17 nose gunners were never too discriminating either, and who could blame them? Some of the crews had extemporized additional .5s and .3s in the nose and you might be within the range of three, or even four, machines when you were on the tail of a 190.

The German fighters tore in like hurled missiles, on their back, weaving and jinking crazily, then steadying for their single burst of fire that could tear a 50,000-pound Boeing B17 to shreds.

Mike took four of his men down after the fighters as they pulled away from their passes. His number two was very close to a 190 when he last glimpsed him, but he lost his own target in a thin cloud layer, and cursed himself (and how often he cursed himself now!) as he pulled up and struggled for height again. The B17, which had lost an engine earlier to the flak, had regained height after putting out the fire but was straggling, and Mike positioned himself above and behind, rocking his wings to establish his identity and encourage the crew.

The Spitfires, fresh to the battle, seemed to be having a field day. It was like being back in the R.A.F. for Mike to hear the clipped accents, exclaiming or warning — 'I'll finish him off, Sammy!' 'He's gone for a Burton. Don't waste your ammo!' or 'Break Red One — break now!' Gradually the voices faded with distance, and Mike brought his squadron together. There were only eleven now. Someone was missing but he could not yet see who it was.

'Anyone go down, Milt?'

'I thought I saw Charlie Schwartz in trouble, chief. But I was too damn busy myself.'

As there was no call from Schwartz, Mike presumed he must

have gone down. Their first casualty for a couple of weeks. But that was nothing compared to the bomber crews. They must have lost nearer 15 per cent than 10 per cent. And they still had the North Sea to cross. Mike sent four of his squadron to nurse along two more stragglers and to give a clear fix for them if they splashed. Then he closed in on the survivors of the bomber group now streaming with less discipline at 16,000 feet. The cannon holes in the fuselage and tall, sweeping tailplane of the nearest bomber told of the fury of the ordeal it had been through — ball turret gone (did the poor devil get out?) leaving a hole that must be letting in a freezing gale, rudder ripped in the centre at the hinge which would almost certainly mean a belly-landing .... And way up front, behind the plexiglass nose, the painted giant-bosomed blonde with Veronica Lake hair, 'Nebraska Nell' in extravagantly rounded writing below, and below that a 20 mm. shell hole with turned-up silver edges against the camouflage paint. That had probably killed the bombardier.

And yet the Group Commander could still call up Mike, and with a courtesy that had become a custom now between them when the worst was over, transmit, 'Thanks, little friends — that's one more out of the ass.'

Mike told his squadron to land first, and himself did two circuits in a more thoughtful and depressed state of mind than he could remember experiencing. At least he was fighting well three years ago when he had been so suicidal about Eileen and should never have survived the risks he had taken every day. Now he was flying worse than he had ever flown. He was not fit to fly when lives depended on the quality of his flying and shooting. Certainly he was not fit to lead a squadron.

Below, the Cambridgeshire countryside stretched out flat and multi-patterned, summer crops already beginning to lose their green. The main railway line from Cambridge to the north pointed dead straight towards Ely and its Gothic slab of a cathedral, which his pilots found such a useful landmark when they had first flown over this damp and confusing country.

At any other time I would have got that damn 88, and that 109, he told himself angrily. I should have killed four Luftwaffe crews instead of getting my own countrymen killed. Unfit to fly. Unfit to lead.

'Highstrip Leader, are you O.K.? Over.'

'Sure. Coming in now. Out.'

A lurch as the Jug's big undercarriage reached out and locked home. Full fine pitch. Flaps full down. Mike lined up with the centre of the runway, skimmed the fence and put the heavy plane down as if caressing the tarmac with his wheels. But it would take more than a 100 per cent quality landing to put things right for Mike. Much more.

Colonel Harvey said, 'Why don't you take a week's furlough and see how you feel? And let the doc look at you.'

'I guess I'm just damn stale. Nerves are O.K.' And Mike held his arm out straight, palm of his hand pointing down. The smoke from the cigarette arose in a dead straight line, like a bonfire on a still day. He laughed and blew at the smoke. 'That's real nice of you, sir. Maybe a break'll do the trick.'

'I'll look after your boys, Mike.'

'That's swell. Thanks a million.'

There was no one in the bar when he first went in, not even Rex, the Negro bartender. Mike looked about him, at the pin-ups on the sloping walls of the lined nissen, the notice-board at the far end, and above it the double lifesize outstretched brunette with legs unanatomically long and high heels like needles. For the bar to be empty at this time of the day was an almost unknown experience, and for one unbelieving moment Mike's mind beat with the awful answer — 'They're ignoring me, they're keeping away — and Christ after today I can't blame them!'

And then, almost at once, as he was rejecting his crazy, para-noiac thought, Milt came in; tall, dark, serious, steady as a Thunderbolt in calm air. 'Starting early, chief?' He smiled at Mike who glanced at the clock for the second time and saw that it showed 1705 and not 1805. 'An hour early, Milt. I'm not doing much right today.'

'Well, I guess I've got a thirst, too.' Milt swung his long legs over the bar and poured out two big slugs of Bourbon, sliding one to Mike and raising his own. 'Here's hell to the Krauts.' (Down at the dispersal they were painting another big swastika beside the Mickey Mouse on Milt's Thunderbolt.)

'The Colonel'll be looking after things for a week, Milt,' Mike said. 'He'll make you acting C.O. O.K.?'

From the other side of the bar, Milt glanced quizzically at Mike. He had flown with him for five months now, ever since they had converted from Spit Vs, recognized Mike's remarkable record of experience and qualities of leadership as well as his sparkling humour and jaunty style that attracted such strong loyalty among ground crew and pilots alike. He had also heard about Eileen and had made a note of the very deep love he evidently had for her, and had seen possible danger in their closeness too. Now he asked, 'Be seeing that swell girl of yours?'

'Maybe.' Mike looked up sharply from his glass. 'You think a steady's a bad thing?'

'I didn't say that.'

'See here, Milt,' Mike said with no trace of unfriendliness in his voice, but firmly. 'I've loved that girl since long before I shared my first Hun with a buddy nearly four years ago. Two years before the States started fighting. Before you had soloed, for Christ's sake. I'm not pulling rank or experience on you, but I came to terms with flying and women since before the American Ambassador in London started his campaign to keep the States *out* of this goddam affair.'

Milt poured Mike another Bourbon, twice the size of the first. 'O.K. Sorry, chief.'

'No need to be sorry. I'm sorry. Just now, I'm a lousy, useless commanding officer, and I don't know what's wrong. I'm not yellow, that's no problem. And the Doc passed me A1. Milt, I guess I'm just tired — goddam stale. A Fiesler Storch with a rookie pilot could have jumped my ass today and put me down with one Luger bullet. But women — or woman. Eileen just doesn't figure.'

At that moment, the telephone shrilled out at Milt's elbow, and he moved his big right hand slowly towards it, his dark eyes on Mike. He was still looking at his C.O., affectionately and with understanding, as he spoke. 'Yeah. I guess he's around somewhere. Yeah, ma'm, actually he's right here with a bathful of Bourbon in his hand. And he deserves it.'

Milt passed the telephone across the bar, his palm over the ear-piece. 'And this,' he said slowly and with a smile as broad as the Grand Canyon, 'is the doll herself.'

'I've been trying to get you all day.'

'I'm sorry, I was out.' There was a pause and Mike added, 'What is it, darling?'

'We were bombed last night, Mike.'

'Bombed? Where in hell are you?'

'At Rising Hall, or what's left of it.'

The line was very bad and he thought he had mis-heard her. But she repeated it. 'Yes, here. Mike, Mummy was killed. And Stokes. Both the maids were terribly hurt.' He could hear her sobbing and he broke in to say:

'Take it easy, Eileen. Take it slowly.'

'And, oh Mike, so is Daddy. They don't think he'll live. Can you possibly come?'

'Sure will. Right now.'

He got there at 2 a.m. in the Jeep he scrounged from Transport. He had lost his way a dozen times on the unsignposted roads, and was greeted with much suspicion at a police station where he called for guidance. It was a very dark night and the black-out masks on the Jeep's lamps offered only a faint glow on the road ahead. At any other time he would have dropped with weariness on arrival.

He caught the stench of stale smoke and burnt timber before he turned in at the drive, past the lodge where Keith had lived as a young boy before his parents were killed. And now it seemed as if both his adopted parents were dead. Double orphan. Poor Keith! And Mike wondered if he would be here, too.

There were criss-cross lines of fire hoses all over the sweep of gravel in front of the house, like exhausted snakes in the dim light from his lamps. The lovely rose beds of which Constance Barrett had been so proud were churned up by a hundred wheel marks. A single fire appliance sat unmanned in the centre of the drive so that Mike had to drive onto the lawn to get round it. Then there was a small A.R.P. car, a figure standing beside it.

'I've come to see Miss Barrett,' Mike told the man from the seat of the Jeep.

'I'll show you the way. There are several people with her.' The man wore dark A.R.P. uniform with an armband, and carried his tin hat from its strap on his shoulder. Mike realized that this must be the first incident he had had to deal with in this remote rural area.

'Why in hell did they pick this old place?' he asked as he swung out of the seat and walked towards the house with the official.

'Seems there was a raid on the Rolls-Royce works at Derby. Only a small one. But the fighters got in among them and a raider panicked and dropped his incendiaries on one of Sir Richard's hay fields. The hay was lying dried and ready for stacking and went up in a blaze like nobody's business. Another Jerry mistook it for the target. Dropped a stick of bombs clean across and the last one caught the house.'

The man pointed the beam of his torch towards the front door, or where the Inigo Jones Doric portico had been until twenty-four hours ago. Rising Hall, 1650-1943. The whole of the centre of the classic building had gone, the magnificent mullioned windows on two floors, the roof with its fine decorated brick stacks, everything, leaving only the west wing standing, where— 'Thank God!' Mike muttered — Eileen would have been sleeping.

A soft light was showing through an imperfect black-out in that wing, and the A.R.P. official led Mike round by the gravel path to the front of the house, past stacks of rubble, smashed guttering and endless charred beams and boards. He knocked on a double door the glass of which was still intact, and the curtains were drawn aside and the doors opened. Mike stepped inside, feeling his way past the curtains, and blinked, shading his eyes for a moment and then opening them to a scene like a stage set for an old-fashioned candle-lit country house melodrama. They were in the old card room, six people in all, two middle-aged women Mike had never met before, the Barretts' housekeeper Mrs Mousehole (stout, in bedroom slippers and old brown woollen dressing-gown), Eileen, Keith and the woman who had opened the doors.

They had resorted, at two in the morning, to that British panacea for all stresses and strains, and especially bombing, a pot of tea. The women got up when they saw Mike, thus revealing that they were from the village; so did the housekeeper, looking embarrassed as if one more to see her dressed for the night was too many. Keith had his back to the fireplace, a bandage across his forehead making him look the very essence of the blonde gallant warrior, and he smiled and held out a hand towards Mike.

Eileen rose from her chair in front of the table and tea things. She was dressed in a tweed suit and heavy country brogues. Mike's eyes ran over her face, with its fair, sensitive complexion, a hint of freckles, the well-formed chin so like her mother's, and the hair, too, like her mother's, fair, light in texture, a shade of auburn, the small nose — and, of course, those eyes, pure

82

Richard Barrett, deep, piercing green, large and lively, but now reduced by so much crying.

'Don't get up,' Mike said, but she was there, in front of him, arms held wide in unself-conscious greeting. He held her, her hair all over his face, her mouth close to his ears and whispering, 'Tell me I'm not allowed to cry, darling. Order me not to cry. I don't want to cry.'

Mike did as he was instructed, very gently and in a voice so soft that he could not hear it himself. She let him go and introduced the women to him in the assured manner of a woman born to be a hostess, smiling from one to the other.

The women said in turn that they thought they really ought to go now — now that both these young men had arrived, and the A.R.P. official said he would drive them back to the village. Mrs Mousehole said she would like to go to bed, too, and Eileen kissed her on the cheek. Then the three of them were alone, and for a moment Mike felt tongue-tied and awkward and wished the others had not gone. He turned to Keith and asked him when he had arrived and what he had done to his head.

'Loose straps dive bombing,' Keith said. 'How did you get here so quickly?'

Eileen was handing Mike a cup of tea, but withdrew it hastily and laughed briefly and apologetically. 'I'm so sorry. What *am* I doing? Keith, pour him a whisky — at least a tumbler. Poor Mike, you must be dead.' She stood beside him, the same height as he was, and looking into her eyes again Mike knew that she was well, quite well, even if her heart was broken and she was facing months of grief.

'It was really sweet of you to come. I felt awful. I shouldn't have asked you. But when I spoke to you I wasn't sure when Keith could get here and I couldn't face the night alone — or alone in spite of all these kind people. Mrs Cartwright and dear ...' She was talking faster now, and Mike knew what the culmination must be and even placed his whisky on the table in anticipation. 'And of course the Vicar was wonderful. He was here until an hour ago, and the doctor stayed for ages, and it was he who told me about Daddy, and then ...'

Here Eileen collapsed. She fell sobbing into Mike's arms and he just let her drain herself on his shoulder, whispering to her from time to time. She pulled herself away again after a while, quite a long while, searching her pockets for a handkerchief and saying, 'Oh damn, damn, damn, I promised myself I wouldn't, not with you. Stupid, hopeless. Oh, where's that bloody hankie? Not that it's any good. Soaked. Give me yours, Mike, then I'll shut up.'

* * *

They had so much to do the next day that there was little time for reflection or even grief. Eileen could not remain in her rooms in the undamaged wing of the house because the services had been destroyed in the bombing and fire, even if she had wished to stay in such close proximity to the scene of carnage. It was Keith's idea that Eileen should move into the lodge. Mr and Mrs Ewhurst, who had been evacuated from the Eaton Square house in London at the beginning of the war and been given a cottage in the grounds, could look after her. So the four of them, helped by the elderly couple, stripped off dustsheets and cleaned and dusted the little house where Keith had been brought up, and Mrs Ewhurst kept them going with meals and cups of tea.

It was not until nine in the evening, with the sun going down over the oaks and beeches of Rising Hall park, that they felt able to settle down outside on the neglected little lawn beside the lodge. The wood pigeons were cooing and the swallows swooping above making their sweeping whistle sound. The ruins of Rising Hall were out of sight, and it seemed incredible that so recently and in this place of peace and remoteness, 500 kg. bombs had torn up the soil and trees and shrubs and finally the irreplaceable Inigo Jones house, along with its owners.

Mike had ferried up the surviving drink from the house in his Jeep, and now there was a bottle of Haig and a jug of water on the table between them. He had said nothing of his professional problem, which in any case had been pushed clear out of his consciousness since his phone call the previous evening. At one point, when they were getting the old range going in the lodge kitchen, Keith had told him briefly about the change of role of his squadron, and when he asked Mike about his affairs, he replied equally perfunctorily, but adding that fortuitously he had just been given a week's leave, which would allow him the opportunity of looking after Eileen when she really needed him.

And now, inevitably, Eileen's own future came up. As sole

heir to the estate there would be interminable dealings with the family solicitors, Hartley and Hevershed; and family meetings with the numerous members of the Barrett and Huntley families. Eileen, however, seemed to shrug all this aside as of no importance.

She had recovered from the exhaustion of grief of the previous night, and Mike, as he topped up her glass, discerned what he believed to be a new gritty sense of determination in her bearing and expression. This was in strong contrast to the wistful, purposeless Eileen of the long period of her convalescence. And it was different, too, from the first Eileen Barrett he had known, back in that period just before the war, when she was all coltish eagerness for fun and activity. It was closer to the Eileen of the Battle of France in 1940, who had precipitately joined the W.R.N.S., with her personal tragic results that followed.

Keith said, 'I think you ought to go and stay with Aunt Nancy for a while. You can't really stay here long on your own, even with the Ewhursts looking after you. You'll always find yourself thinking about your parents when you're so near.'

'I'll stay with you for a few days after the funeral,' Mike said.

'Thank you, darling. That'll be lovely. But no Aunt Nancy, or Uncle George or any of the cousins. Not for me.' She was talking very firmly. 'I'm going to stay here and sort things out. Then I am going to do something really useful, for the first time in my life.'

Keith broke in to say, 'But Eileen, you're not fit yet. And you'll be lonely. I mean, the Ewhursts will look after you, but they're not quite your sort for company.'

Eileen sat up and swung round on him, her green eyes blazing as they used to blaze when they quarrelled as children. 'Don't you dare talk about the Ewhursts like that! What a piffling, lower middle-class thing to say!'

Keith looked at her in astonishment. He had taken off the bandage on his forehead, revealing a large black-blue bruise with a nasty contusion at the centre. So it was the old class business again. A four-year-old war, more than 700 operational hours in his logbook, crash-landings, bailings-out and a few wounds — well, it still all came back to class. Back to his being lower middle-class, his father a platoon sergeant, and then an agent to a country estate; Eileen's father a commissioned officer and a Baronet. Those resentments he had felt as a boy, brought up above his station by the Barretts. And the sharp, wounding remarks Eileen used sometimes to make. And it was still, 'What a piffling, lower middle-class thing to say.'

'I'm sorry,' Keith said briefly.

Mike, for once clearly embarrassed, resorted to the mock English accent that used to make them all laugh. 'I say, a bit below the belt, what, what?'

They did not laugh. But they smiled, Keith first, and then Eileen. 'Yes, I'm sorry, Keith. You're a big boy now. And I'm a big girl. And we mustn't be silly. There's enough silliness going on in the world.' Mike watched her as she paused, and she seemed to take a grip on herself again, driving out determinedly the picture of her father and mother which would always be there, like portraits in a gallery either on show, or stored unseen in the basement.

Then she went on, repeating what she had said earlier. 'I'm going to do something really useful, I promise.'

'Of course you are,' said Keith. 'And you'll be very good at it.' He whistled up Sheila, who was asleep under Eileen's deck-chair. 'Come on, walkies for you.' He left them alone as the dusk at the end of a perfect summer day began to close slowly about them.

Mike and Eileen did not speak for several minutes. Then Eileen asked a question that took Mike by surprise. 'What's it like to kill someone? I mean, really *like*?'

Mike hated talking about his fighting life to anyone outside the service, and especially to Eileen. He knew it was different for Keith because he and Jenny were in it together and they spoke the same language, even spoke to one another in the furnace heat of conflict.

'Why do you ask?'

She said sharply, 'Because I want to know. Tell me.'

Gee, this really is a different Eileen, Mike was thinking. And then, knowing that he had to answer, he felt uncertain in what terms to do so. He sipped his whisky and water and at length said, 'Well, I guess, like making love and dying or even being born. It's *how* it happens that counts. Making love can be a sad and disappointing business. Dying can be a sublime relief, a joy even — so people say. I've never stabbed someone I've never seen before in the back. I guess that'd be pretty grim.' He was doing better than he had expected, but it did not satisfy Eileen.

'What about your sort of killing, then? Tell me about that. What does it feel like? Are you scared when you do it? Do you lie awake at night after you've killed someone during the day?'

He looked at this pretty girl he loved. This pretty girl who could be so many people. This Eileen he would one day marry, if, if ... O.K., no more messing about. No more procrastinating.

'I'll tell you what it's like. It's (a) something you've got to do so you do it. It's (b) mostly a question of dire necessity or you'll get killed and you don't want that.' (He left out, because it would confuse the issue, the fact that, because of her, there had been a period when he killed most days without minding too much at all whether or not he was killed.) 'It's (c) a damn interesting challenge of technique and skill and experience to bring guns to bear on a target that may be at any one of an infinite number of angles to you, and is travelling at a speed that may be 100 and may be 500 miles an hour. Related to that is (d) the competitive element. Competition against him, or them, and competition against your buddies. You know, the score.'

Eileen interrupted to ask, 'What's your score?' She was listening to him talking about his work, his fighting life, for the first time with complete and fascinated attention.

'It's sixteen confirmed. The Americans have three-class scores, say five — two — seven. Five confirmed, two probable, seven damaged. I don't know what my second two figures are. Don't much care.'

'So you've certainly killed sixteen men?'

'No, darling.' Mike was not enjoying this, and he was feeling frightened by her intensity. But he knew she would not allow him to leave it there. 'No, those are planes destroyed. Sometimes the pilot got out. Sometimes it was a complete bomber's crew. All dead. Or you might strafe a line of army trucks and kill a couple of hundred and that wouldn't figure in your score.'

Mike poured himself another Scotch, feeling he deserved it. The light was going fast and a barn owl shrieked from somewhere over by the stable block.

Eileen said, 'And?'

'And what?'

'You still haven't told me what it feels like.'

'It's a business. You feel nothing,' he lied, recalling the needle-sharp prick of compassion when he had watched a flamer going down, when he had seen a 'chute fail to open. 'It's like shooting grouse. I don't mean you enjoy it. But it's a calculation. And the calculation is that it's better to kill the pilot and crew of a bomber as well as destroy their kite. If they become prisoners of war, they're expensive to keep and may try to escape. If they land on their side, then they'll soon be trying to kill you or your buddies again.'

Her face was a faint pale circle in the last of the twilight and he had to imagine her solemn expression as she said, 'I want to know.' A pause. 'I want to know the truth, Mike.'

There was a sound of breaking twigs and rustling branches from nearby, and then a bark of pleasure from Sheila as she raced for Eileen's chair and jumped onto her lap. She said, 'Was that nice, Keith?'

'Gorgeous. That dotty animal put up more rabbits than there are in Australia, and didn't get near one.' He leant down and kissed Eileen. 'Let's go inside. There's a dew like a deluge.'

* * *

Mike looked at himself in the mirror of his bedroom in the Ritz, undecided whether or not he liked the figure he cut now, or the earlier one in the American uniform. 'I guess it doesn't matter,' he told himself. 'The die is cast, the decision made, no going back.' He smiled at his own clichés, put on his old R.A.F. cap, battered from so many mess scraps, soaked in so much warm, weak English beer, picked up his gloves and gas-mask, and let himself out of his room.

He was off again on his own personal three-act war drama. Act One had been 'Joining the R.A.F.' which had required a good deal of influence-swinging through his father in Washington. Act Two, 'The Transfer' had been easy, even forced upon him though he had not minded taking a commission in the U.S.A.A.F. instead.

Now for Act Three, 'The Return'.

After leaving the ruins of Rising Hall, and Eileen, he had considered his future with his squadron and had decided that his state of mind, his staleness had not changed, and he had telephoned his Colonel to tell him.

'Shit, Mike,' (he talked like that) 'you take a month an' see how you feel. Or d'yer wanna go back to the States?'

'No, sir, I don't want to go back to the States. But all I'm offered here is more lecturing, conversion instruction for newly arrived pilots, radar liaison calibration flying or target towing. I guess I'll take the month's furlough.'

'Take two months. With your record, if you'd been in the U.S.A.A.F. all the time you'd have the Congressional Medal of Honour, dinner at the White House, and every damn Congressman's wife after your prick. Take it easy, boy.'

But Mike's mind had been made up before this generous offer had been made. He did not want two months' furlough any more than he wanted Congressmen's wives. He did not want radar liaison calibration flying or target towing. He wanted Special Duties with the R.A.F. And he was now going to set about getting it. Act Three, 'The Return'.

* * *

At Air Ministry, no one seemed to know, or were they being deliberately evasive? Mike, still trying to adjust himself to the blue uniform and reminding himself to salute in R.A.F. style, wandered about the linoleum corridors all morning, knocking on doors, drinking innumerable cups of tea and exchanging innumerable cigarettes with officers he knew well or slightly. An Air Commodore said, 'Don't know what you're talking about. Never heard of it,' and dropped his eyes to his papers. A grounded bomber pilot, with two D.S.O.s, he had known before the war, said, 'I've heard of something like it. But I don't know where you'd start to find out. Not in this mad-house anyway.'

A tremendously senior W.A.A.F. was more helpful and made some telephone calls on his behalf. She was so nice that Mike invited her to dinner at the Ritz where he was staying.

And so it came about that, shortly before midday, Mike found himself in a very small, very hot office on the ground floor of the Ministry, looking across a desk at the white, mask-like face of Buffer Davies.

'Ol' boy, ol' boy, ol' boy!' he exclaimed as Mike came in and extended a hand. 'What a toppin' show!'

Mike glanced down at the hand and Buffer showed him the other one, palm up. 'Mac didn't do a bad job on the flappers, what? Bit stiff, but they work.' He held up his face, like a woman wanting to be kissed. 'What do you think of the new bark? Not bad, what?'

On 4 July 1940, over a convoy off Rye, Buffer had been shot down in flames by a 109. No one who saw it gave him a chance. But the irrepressible chum of one and all was plucked out of the sea, desperately burnt about the face and hands, and after emergency treatment, had been taken to East Grinstead, where that great surgeon, Archibald MacIndoe, had a burns unit which had saved so many lives. Keith and Mike had visited him there once, and it had been an appalling experience to see the state to which the jaunty, woman-hunting pilot had been reduced by countless plastic surgery operations. Even now, three years later, it seemed inconceivable that any woman would bear to be touched by this young man with his Frankenstein-like face, two small eyes above a white rubber-like nose, and lips like those of a ventriloquist's doll.

Now a bottle of scotch emerged from a drawer, two tumblers from another, and Mike raised his glass to his old buddy. They talked of Keith and the tragedy of his adopted family, of their girls, of ops of all kinds, from night rhubards to long-range escort.

'You ought to be with the Yankee boys, eh Mike? Bags of dough and the popsies like wasps round the ol' jam jar.'

Mike laughed. 'Sometimes I offer my services to Uncle Sam,' he said, holding his empty glass to the proffered bottle. 'Had a Jug squadron for a while. Swell lot of guys, too, But I've gone stale on single-seaters so I thought I'd come back to the Raf.'

Buffer laughed, the old rip-roaring laugh that used to identify him in the most crowded mess parties, when his face was so expressive and his moustache was such a wow with the girls. 'Jolly good show,' he said. 'I like that. Put up a black in one service and you go over to the other till the dust settles.'

He poured another drink for Mike, who said, 'Before we get tight as ticks, Buffer, can you tell me about Special Duties?'

'What sort of Special Duties, ol' boy. That covers a multitude of sins.'

'Special Duties across the Channel.'

'You don't want to be a flippin' spy, ol' boy, do you?'

Mike laughed. 'No, you ignorant sap. Resistance. S.O.E. Dropping guys and guns and all that crap.'

Buffer thought about this for a moment and said, 'It's got a fairly high chop rate. Not so bad for the big boys. But the Lizzies take a hell of a beating.'

'Never mind about that,' said Mike. 'You just extract your goddam digit and tell me where I go. Yeah— O.K., one more for the road,' and he watched the rising level of brown liquid in the glass with eyes that would have laid off a very unsteady deflection shot.

Buffer pulled out a buff folder from the bottom drawer of his desk. 'Somewhere in here.' He was bending over and Mike could see the faint line where skin had been grafted onto his ears; and he felt like crying.

'Here we are.' Buffer held up a sheet of typed foolscap. 'It doesn't say anything about it, but I happen to know, ol' boy, that this asterisk against this ruddy ol' airfield in ruddy ol' Wales is where those poor types do their special training.' He put a pale finger on the line and read, 'Tryngarth. That's the place. I'd just turn up with faked posting papers if I were you.' He drew a block of headed forms from another drawer, and stamped it 'Air Ministry. Official'. 'Get the porter at the club to sign it. I always do. But I still think you're stark, starin', ragin' bonkers, ol' boy.'

Mike took him to luncheon at the Ritz. The restaurant was packed with the very rich, the very fat and a few very senior officers. Buffer cast his little pig's eyes over the scene, no longer shy, Mike noticed, of his curious appearance. 'All dough and brass,' he said, 'didn't know there was so much of it about, ol' boy.'

'Sure makes you feel sick,' Mike said, and signalled to the head waiter. 'My table please, Marcel. And a word with John about a couple of bottles of champagne.' He stood to attention and gave a mock salute. 'Tell him to remember "The Few".'

'Rather decent show, this,' Buffer commented, sitting down while the waiter unfolded and spread his table napkin. 'Not often one gets decently drunk at the Ritz. Midday, I mean. Better midday. Gives you more time to get drunker in the p.m., what?'

'It's a pity we didn't come in Garbo. That would have been the last touch to a good piss up,' said Mike.

'Garbo's up on blocks, poor ol' girl,' said Buffer. He always got maudlin talking of his massive Bentley Special which he used to race officially at Brooklands and unofficially, and highly dangerously, on the roads. Long, long ago, when Mike still had no wings and Buffer still had his original, handsome face that made the girls swoon, Buffer had driven Mike out in Garbo to cheer him up in a pub in Lincoln. Mike was, Buffer suspected, about to be flunked from the course, and he had figured that a night on the booze might give him Dutch courage the next day. By any sound reasoning, it should have had the reverse effect, but it had worked.

Over the butterless cheese and biscuits, Mike noticed two middle-aged women staring at Buffer, returning to their food, talking quietly and then renewing their staring. Outraged, and by this time quite drunk, Mike got up and walked not all that steadily over to their table.

'Do you find something unusual about my friend, ma'am?' he asked one of the women, who stared back at him with cold, grey eyes. She wore spectacles and bore the evidence — hair, hat, clothes — of commonness as well as wealth.

'I don't think we have been introduced, young man,' she said in an icy voice.

'You have not yet earned that privilege,' said Mike. 'Nor have you earned that luncheon. My friend, however, has earned your gratitude, not your goddam rude stares for helping to save this country so that you can stuff yourself sick at the Ritz after a morning's shopping at Harrods and Fortnums.'

With that, Mike put his arms under the table and raised it with one sweeping movement and carried it high above his head like a veteran waiter towards the kitchen, leaving the women with nothing between them. On the way, Mike met the head waiter. 'Marcel, those women there have changed their minds. They are not taking luncheon here after all. They say your food stinks. Bar the doors to them in future.'

Buffer's laughter was still echoing about the dining-room when Mike returned. 'Bang on, ol' boy. Quite like old times at The Spider's Web on Saturday nights. Those two belted off like a couple of Dorniers with a squadron of Spits on their tails. That's two more down in flames for your log book.'

Mike was dimly aware that he was not behaving like an officer and a gentleman, and that it was time to leave. Buffer agreed but thought they ought to celebrate their victory. So he grabbed Mike, lifted him without trouble onto a waiter's trolley, gave him the two empty bottles of Krug to hold and placed the ice bucket on his head. They sang 'Bless 'em All' all the way to the lifts, where Buffer tried to do a slow roll, which set them both sprawling. Then they went up to Mike's room to sleep the afternoon away.

5

Randall's Night

The bombs and their racks were received by 727 Squadron with outrage. They were fighter pilots, weren't they? The élite: top button of tunic undone, silk scarf instead of collar and tie, flying boots in the mess, a swashbuckling air of self-confidence in all that they did. Bombs were for bombers, for those poor sods who sweated it out in the dark over the Ruhr amongst the flak, the searchlights and the German night fighters, with one chance in three of finishing a tour.

Not that 727 pilots were scared of those squat, ugly steel objects with fuse and fancy tail that had been unloaded down at the dispersal and placed in the extemporized bomb store at Southdean. Not scared, affronted. They had trained for fighting the enemy in the sky, freely, independently, man against man in their nippy single-seaters. Now they were to be loaded down with these burdens and told to blow things up with them.

Keith got his two flights together after lunch. It was a cold, wet day in late November 1943, and during the previous three days, when he had been away at Aston Down on a bombing course, there had been no flying. He had noted a certain measure of torpor and boredom amongst them recently. Thanks to their own efforts, and those of other Typhoon and Mustang squadrons, the tip-and-run menace had been mastered. Keith had organized some rhubarbs, there had been a few patrols, half a dozen shipping strike escorts, and on one more lively September afternoon, they had escorted some American Marauders to St Omer.

But it had been an uneventful time on the whole, the weather had been mainly awful, the war seemed to have lasted forever, and still there was no sign of the Second Front that might signal the beginning of the end, one way or another.

Keith ran his eyes round his pilots, wondering momentarily how many would last out the war, and what they would be doing with the rest of their lives if they did. Polo Satterthwaite, as usual smoking his foul pipe, stalwart, straight-talking, unflappable; and Range Powell, equally hard but quarried from a different seam of granite — these two, who had served with Keith for so long, seemed indestructible. Both, like Keith, with a bar to their D.F.C.s. Pricelessly valuable Flight Commanders.

Then that other tough veteran, Bill Watson, now a Flying Officer, but with five years as a non-commissioned pilot before that. The ex-Halton boy who had fought for so long to get into aircrew, had more service than any of them except for the middle-aged Chiefy, who knew more about the vagaries of Rolls-Royce or Napier aero engines, Hawk or Avro airframes, R.A.F. officers, non-commissioned officers, and other ranks than all of them put together.

The rest of the pilots were all V.R.s, some who had had their wings for little more than a year, like Ron Easton; others much longer like Titch Brambell and the tall, grave South African, Inch Samuel. Some he knew well, some of the newer Sergeant Pilots he had talked to only a few times, and he knew their flying characteristics better than their personalities. A mixed bunch, mainly English and middle class, a few welcome New Zealanders, two Canadians. But all skilled in their difficult, complex and dangerous trade; all, he considered, reliable in a tricky corner.

'Well, chaps, I hear you're binding about bombs. So let me tell you something. It's good news, not bad. It means we're really going over to the offensive. Believe it or not, the Second Front's going to happen — and bloody soon now.'

Range handed him a lit Players cigarette according to custom at briefings, and Keith drew on it. 'The Luftwaffe is about played out in the West. Almost all the fighters have gone to the Russian front, where they're taking a hell of a beating.'

There was a thin cheer from his men, and Keith went on to

explain that the new rôle of the fighter was ground attack. Strafing, bombs and rockets. 'Targets: communications, supplies, tank concentrations. We're going to prang anything useful to the enemy after the invasion. The dizzy days of dicing with death in the clouds are over. We're fighter-bombers again now, flying Bomphoons or Tiffybombers — whatever you like to call the kites.'

Finally, he told them of a white circle target set up in a field near Lancing. They would start practising dive bombing the next day with small smoke bombs. 'Those of you who never did it with the old Hurricane, you'll soon get the hang of it. Polo, your kites are all fixed with racks now. So it'll be A Flight at 0800 hours.'

* * *

After the first session, Polo Satterthwaite said at the bar, 'It's a reet bastard getting low enough to hit anything and high enough to pull out of your dive without pranging. I'm still bloody blacked-out from my last dive.' And he mimicked a blind man groping about the bar, spilling his beer.

Later, Range Powell said, 'Stone the crows, I brought back half a bloody forest in my air intake.'

727's first efforts were wildly inaccurate. You dropped twice as fast as the Hurricane, and there was still no special sight. You simply turned over onto your back, went down as steeply as you dared, estimated by eye your lowest safe pull-out point, took the centre dot of the gunsight through the target allowing for the angle you were off the vertical, and pressed the red button on the tip of the throttle handle.

Keith took a mobile R/T set in a van out to the target. 'Steeper, Red Two,' he would call out, sharply but without fuss. 'You're only about 50 degrees. Pull out and try again ... Yellow One, you come down. That's better. You're nearer 75.'

The heavy fighter, put on its back at 8,000 feet, would at first appear to be hardly moving. Then it would gain momentum fast, the small dot would assume the strong-jawed heavy shape of a Typhoon racing towards the earth, and Keith would call out from the driving seat of his van: 'Hold it, hold it a shade longer, steady — now!' And the two small practice bombs would detach themselves from under the wings, and at the same moment the plane would be dragged out of its dive low to the ground with an ear-splitting shriek from its Sabre and climb away again.

What Keith feared, happened on the third day. The youngest sergeant-pilot on the squadron with the least experience, and too conscious of it and too determined to impress with a bull's-eye, came down very steeply. Keith knew he would need more than a thousand feet to get out safely, and called out to him when he estimated he was at 2,000 and doing at least 400 m.p.h. 'Leave it at that,' Keith told him. 'Let 'em go — pull out now.' The Typhoon continued its dizzy descent. 'Now, Green Two—*now*!'

The pilot did not even drop his bombs. Suddenly panic-stricken, he started to drag his machine out of its headlong dive. Keith could imagine the boy pulling back on the stick with all his strength, knowing — as Keith could calculate by eye — that he was not going to make it.

The Typhoon struck the ground at a shallow angle three fields away. Keith saw the fuselage in the air again, shedding tail unit, wings and panels at the same second that the sound of its first impact reached him. It appeared to be held in mid-air momentarily before falling back. Debris and smoke arose into the sky, and just when it seemed to be all over and a merciful mourning silence had fallen upon the scene, a great blast of smoke went up, black and oily, and the dull sound of an explosion reached Keith's ears.

What was the point in running? What the hell was the point in running? But Keith continued to run, veteran witness to catastrophe though he had become. He scratched himself bursting through a hedge, almost fell in the mud by a gate, and suddenly found the ruin of alloy and steel in front of him, smelling of hot death. One wing, complete with projecting cannon and a hundred yards away, appeared intact, a freak survivor of the holocaust. The rest was lifeless anarchy, smoking shreds of air-craft, pieces as small as a thumbnail, half the size of a bed, at all angles, in all shapes. The engine had buried itself in the soft soil. One of the boy's forearms, blackened and without thumb, lay like a rebuke at Keith's feet. He turned away, ready to be sick, but awakened to his situation and rank by the sound of a low-flying plane. It was Watson's T-Tommy, circling, his window wound down, his goggles raised. No evidence of squeamishness in front of Watson of all people, thank you.

Keith walked slowly back to his van. 'I very much regret to

inform you ... a most promising and likeable young man ... the events surrounding his death will have to remain secret for the present, but believe me ...' Or don't believe me. What did it matter? There was no one, absolutely no one, he could talk to about it except Jenny. And she was sixty miles away in her new T16 at Swingham.

There was an urgent message from Ops for him when he got back to his office. The squadron was to fly to Rampton that afternoon. Temporary detachment, overnight kit only. There was to be a maximum wing strength show at dawn. What in heaven's name was suddenly on?

727 had a new I.O., a pleasant, schoolmasterly officer, very calm, very conscientious. Ex-Army, Desert Rat, M.C., tin right leg, Flying Officer Jerry Owen. 'What's the flap, Spy?' Keith asked him.

'Search me, sir. They never tell I.O.s anything. But sometimes we find out in spite of all Group's efforts.'

'And what *have* you found out?' For Keith the image of that burned arm kept re-projecting itself in spite of the distraction of activity and speculation.

'Something rum going on in the Pas de Calais.'

'Secret weapons, I suppose,' said Keith. Hitler's secret weapons had been a German propaganda threat for so long that few people believed in them any more, and in many quarters they had become a sour joke.

'Could be.' The Spy raised an eyebrow enigmatically, put on his forage cap, saluted, and limped metallically from the office.

It was not the first time that Flying Officer Owen's suspicions proved to have substance.

At Rampton, nearest airfield to the French coast, there was more activity than at any time since the Battle of Britain, when it had been bombed into unusability and dozens of aircraft had been smashed on the ground. Keith recalled it at the time of the Fall of France when Hurricanes had used it, in the fever of the evacuation from Dunkirk. Now it was again overcrowded for some new crisis, with Spitfire IXs, Mustangs and two more Typhoon squadrons competing for space about the dispersals, the blast pens long since filled.

It was just as crowded about the officers' mess bar, where there was much drinking by pilots of three generations of this long war

— a handful of Auxiliaries and pre-war regulars like himself, more who had joined as V.R.s at the outset of hostilities, and by far the most numerous, the junior officers with a single narrow or broad ring on their sleeves, products of the huge expansion of '41 and '42, very respectful of Keith's generation, quick to glance at decoration ribbons, quick to emulate their style and language.

Keith expected to see Maitland here as Wingco Flying and found him in a corner talking to the Station Commander. Maitland — solemn, austere, with his statutory one pint of beer — greeted Keith with a smile, introduced him to the Group Captain, and then apologized for the crush.

'What in hell *is* going on?' Keith asked. 'All I get is dark hints from my Spy at Southdean.'

'Let's get out of here and I'll tell you. As much as I know.' He turned to the Station Commander. 'Is that O.K., sir?'

'Yes, that's all right. All the Squadron Commanders will be informed. But no one lower.'

It was only ten minutes' walk to the cliff edge. Dusk was falling but it was still possible to see the undulating white line of the French cliffs twenty-five miles distant, a replica reflection of the chalk cliffs beneath them. In front of them there was a double row of barbed wire, rusting now after $3\frac{1}{2}$ years of invasion threat that had now receded to nothing. But it was the only reminder of war. There was a strong, invigorating smell of the sea, the gulls were wheeling and crying before settling down for the night. Maitland's news, spoken in his soft Canadian accent, sounded grotesque, almost surrealist, on this quiet and peaceful evening.

'These German V weapons are no joke, Keith,' he said. 'They're being taken very seriously. We've got some P.R. photos now. I've seen them. There are long-range rockets. And something else — another of the *Vergeltung* weapons. I guess they're pilotless bombers — just one big bomb, a pair of stubby wings, and an engine.' He pointed out across the grey waters of the Channel. 'Just inland from there, we've found signs of great activity. Deep gashed suddenly appearing in the fields. Camouflaged buildings springing up overnight. Shapes like damn great skis on their side. And a lot of the way along the coast, to the Cherbourg peninsula. Most of these slits point towards London. Others towards Portsmouth and Bristol and Plymouth. Those Krauts ain't shamming, Keith. It all figures.'

Was the sky going to be filled with pilotless bombers designed to lay London and other big cities flat? A thousand a day killing tens of thousands, forcing the Allies to sue for peace before the invasion was launched?

The smoke from Maitland's pipe and from Keith's cigarette rose straight up into the still dusk air. There was a party going on in the Sergeants' Mess and a band was playing 'I Don't Want to Set the World on Fire'. It occurred to Keith that this popular melody could hardly be more appropriate, but he said nothing. The music was, in any case, soon drowned by the grumble of distant bombers climbing laboriously with their heavy loads and heading south from their Midlands and Eastern bases for their French target. In an hour or two some great factory, some marshalling yard, would be torn asunder, and maybe thirty or forty of the great dark Lancasters and Halifaxes would be shot down. But if the Germans had really designed, and built in great numbers, cheap pilotless machines, R.A.F. Bomber Command would be an insignificant weapon by comparison.

Keith turned to Maitland, who was knocking his pipe out on a rusty steel barbed wire stanchion. 'Does Intelligence know how many of these things they've got?'

'Not a clue. But if these are launching sites, there're a helluva lot of them. A hundred or more maybe. You'll see tomorrow.' The head of the bomber stream was directly above them and Maitland had to raise his voice. The earth seemed to tremble beneath their feet. Maitland looked up, but there was nothing to be seen. There never was, until the enemy searchlights began to finger the sky, and the multi-coloured flak overwhelmed the light of the moon just as the sound of the bombers now drowned their voices.

Back in his office, Maitland produced a large glossy print from the safe. 'This is what P.R.U. found. At Peenemunde, an island in the Baltic. We'd got wind that something kind of special was going on there. Everyone looked at it all ways — couldn't see a damn thing. Then some bright W.A.A.F. with a keen eye picked this up. On the original it was invisible, near as damn it. But blown up ...'

The Canadian indicated with the point of his pencil a very faint light grey cross against the darker grey of the background. 'That was the first clue. We know a bit more now, mostly from our agents. There've been launchings from this ramp — not all successful. Then Bomber Command gave the place the once over — take a look at that.'

Maitland placed another photograph over the first. It showed a scene of utter devastation, the whole site pockmarked with craters, scarcely a building left standing. 'O.K. — but those Krauts are tough guys. That was just a temporary setback. And unless we can do something about it, there's going to be a helluva lot of killing right soon.'

* * *

First time. First time with live bombs. First time with 500-pounders. First Tiffy bombing op. For Pilot Officer Crawley, first op. Over the past two weeks, they had gained proficiency at dive bombing, finding an angle that was not so steep that you had to start pulling out at 1700 feet, or so shallow that accurate aiming was a too speculative business. They had all got hits into the 100-yard circle, most had been successful with the 50-yard chalk mark. They had taken off singly with 250-pounders and dropped them into the range at low tide along the coast.

Now, with twice the weight hung beneath their Typhoons' wings, they were taking off in four-formation, on their first raid. About a month, Keith reckoned, before they were ready for it. But he had few anxieties for 727. The challenge was good for them. If Crawley got back O.K. he'd be twice the boy....

With four squadrons of Typhoons, all at maximum strength, to get off the ground, formation take-offs were essential. 727 was the second to go. Keith had them close bunched on the perimeter track, big props turning, shuddering with eagerness to get off— a serious need it was, too, because the Sabre quickly overheated if kept ticking over for too long. The last section of four of the previous squadron blasted off down the runway, their clean configuration broken by the big bomb suspended beneath each wing.

Before their tails were up, Keith taxied his section fast onto the runway, swung them through 90 degrees. Quick mag. check, then throttle open to 1500 revs on the brakes. Keith glanced to right — young Crawley — and to left — Bill Watson and Titch Brambell. They all had their eyes on him. He nodded once and raised his right hand, dropped it to release the brake, and they

were away. Hard on left rudder as the torque bit. The accelera-
tion was slower with the extra 1000 pounds and Crawley was
losing ground, a common weakness of a novice who is anxious
not to overshoot his leader. The other two were all right. For
Watson, with entries for Furies and Audaxes, Harts and
Gladiators, in his oil-stained old log book, this was like walking
to the bus stop in the morning, and his wingtip was never more
than six feet nor less than one foot behind Keith's own port
wingtip.

'Close up, Blue Two,' Keith told Crawley as soon as they were
airborne, wheels and flaps up; and he delayed his port turn a few
seconds to allow his number two — throttle wide open and no
doubt sweating heavily with the concentrated effort not to overshoot— to come alongside. On the way out to their planes, Keith
had said, 'Just follow me as if you're my shadow. Nothing to it,
kid. Don't pull out below 1500. And then start kicking like hell—
they'll be expecting us.'

The four squadrons made fifty Typhoons altogether. An
improvement on Dieppe, in machines and bomb weight. Keith
counted them quickly while they circled and climbed slowly to
8,000 feet, waiting for the last two squadrons to catch up. Maitland was leading the show— that made forty-nine. Then another
kite had hitched itself onto 727, flying as a sort of tail-end Charlie
to Polo's section — a Typhoon without identification letters.

'Sideline Green One, you have a stranger,' Keith transmitted.
But Polo said he knew nothing about him, and as the pilot did not
answer Keith's call to identify himself, he gave his attention to
forming up his own three sections to the starboard of Maitland.

There was scattered cloud at 6,000 which thinned over the
narrow strip of Channel, glinting in the late October sun. The
countryside of south-east England and the north-east countryside of France, and the two undulating lengths of white cliffs,
appeared so similar it was as if some recent geological slip had
split them apart. That the other side was all hostile, and this side
all friendly, seemed ridiculous. But not for long. It took only four
minutes for the massed formation of Typhoon bombers to cross
the sea, instruments showing 240 m.p.h. A.S.I., $3\frac{1}{2}$ boost, and
2,900 on the rev. counter. Before they were over the other side
the heavy flak started coming up.

'Fishguard here,' the Wing Commander identified himself.

'Spread out. Target eleven o'clock, ten miles.'

Keith glanced down and recognized, through the cloud breaks over the Pas de Calais, the big rectangular wood which had been so promiment on the P.R.U. photograph at briefing. It conformed, too, to the map strapped to his right knee.

'Fishguard — fuse bombs.'

There were Spitfires high above them, wings glinting in the sun, two squadrons of Mark IXs as top cover in the unlikely event of Luftwaffe opposition. But flak was to be their enemy, not 190s or 109s, and the importance the Germans were attaching to these mystery sites was matched by the intensity of the heavy shellfire coming up at them. At 8,000 feet, every one of them jinking and ruddering hard, they made difficult targets. But the German gunners were unsurpassed for efficiency and accuracy, and the ugly grey puffs seemed to follow each one of them individually, anticipating every evolution.

Far away to port a sharp light, a glow and trailing black smoke, marked the end of one Typhoon, and a voice called out at the same time, 'Dud engine, returning to base'. Someone else was in trouble in his squadron, too. No voice spoke, but there was glycol streaming from Range's number two, and as Keith watched, the bombs and canopy were jettisoned, there was a brief pause while the pilot — it was Flight-Sergeant Mackie, married only three weeks — tussled with his straps. Then he threw himself out over his starboard wing and — 'Oh the fool, the poor sod!' — was hurled by the slipstream from his dying engine against the tailplane. For a second his body stuck there like a torrent-swept log against a rock, and then fell away.

There was nothing more to see — nothing that Keith had not seen again and again before: the slow turning over and over, head down one minute, legs spread, arms together, arms apart, a limp puppet thrown about by the vagaries of wind and gravity. Then, if the ground were soft enough, he would make his own shallow grave in about twenty seconds' time.

Bostons of 2nd T.A.F. had been here yesterday, plastering the target, pockmarking the fields all around. Poor bombing, too, caused no doubt by this ferocious flak. But it confirmed the position of the construction sites set among the woods. The Germans, past masters at camouflage, had concealed everything else, but they could not alter the chalk of the soil, nor hide the

103

whiteness as they dug their long, narrow trenches. And these were what they were to hit, these slits in the soil of France, no doubt dug by French slave labour, and the giants' skis alongside. As Jem Maitland had pointed out, every one aimed towards the heart of London.

Maitland himself was calling up, 'Fishguard going down. Make it snappy.'

Keith saw him throw his Typhoon onto its back, revealing its two big bombs. The flak followed him down, followed his number two down, and all the squadron, 3.7 cm. tracer joining in the tumult; and soon it would be 20 mm. from the Flakvierling 38s. Every foot of the way the high-explosive and splinters would be following them.

727's target was a mile to the west, two almost invisible white slits in fields, a third in a wood. 'Sideline going down!'

He glanced across at Crawley and threw over the stick to port, pulling back the nose to the vertical, then pulling it back to 70 degrees. A touch of aileron, a glance at the A.S.I., the altimeter needle spinning round the dial.

It was like running fast through falling leaves in a thunder-storm, the tracer lines forked lightning. The flak bursts brushed past on both sides, and sometimes you hit them, and the heavy, swift-diving Typhoon lurched; and there was the rattle of shrapnel like gravel on a steel barrel. You just kept on. There was nothing else you could do. For a few seconds there was no possible escape, so you might as well concentrate on keeping that little dot in the centre of your gunsight on that ridiculous little trench. Bombing a trench! What bloody next? as Range would ask.

The merciful thing was that it was only for a few seconds. Not like the high-level boys who might have this for half an hour at a time. And, like a cavalry charge, it was breathtakingly stirring.

There were camouflaged huts in the wood. And as Keith fell closer, he saw for a fraction of a second paths between the huts, vehicles and earth-moving equipment beneath artificial branches that should have no leaves by this time of the year. He knew now, without looking at the altimeter, which in any case was subject to lag at this rate of descent, that it was time to pull out.

Left thumb on button. Right thumb on gun button. A short burst to keep their heads down. Now pull through the dot, not too far. There! Squeeze. A momentary lift of release from his plane. Then hard, hard back with the stick. The black blind across his eyes. Kick hard right rudder. The machine-guns would be joining the party now. Many of them concentrating on his belly at this most vulnerable of all moments.

He climbed away at full boost, aileroning and ruddering all the way. Crawley was close alongside him. Good boy. A glance back showed the three-second delay bombs exploding on and about the sites like a sudden rain squall against a window. Ninety or more H.E.s all in ten seconds, shock waves spreading out from each, white chalk columns rising high. And still the flak came as if the gunners were invulnerable automata, following the Typhoons that spread out and up from the target area like great splinters from the holocaust they had created.

All except one. Some suicidal fool was going back in again. Keith saw the tiny shape far below, racing across the target area. He could only be doing one thing: beating up the flak guns, the shortest known route to a quick death. Some people never learn.

Keith lost him in the haze, and two minutes later was calling up, 'Sideline Leader. Over Calais angels twelve.' Several of his squadron were already there, and Keith did not hang around waiting. They had had enough for the morning, and he took them back to Rampton, circling and waiting for the O.K. to land.

'Yellow One,' he called Range. 'All O.K.?'

'Bloody right, cobber.'

So it was only Mackie. Poor young Mackie. A seventy-two-hour honeymoon at the Strand Palace. And that was that.

Keith walked into the dispersal with Crawley as he had walked out with him. No fuss now, he told himself. Then he glanced across at the twenty-year-old boy, fair hair like his own. Freckles like a prep school kid. 'O.K.?'

'Yes, sir. Quite a bit of flak.' His voice was tentative, but not as uncertain as before.

'Yes.' Keith offered him a cigarette and then paused to light up before going on. 'You hung on very well. You'd better stay as my number two.'

* * *

They may have had enough for the morning, but there was more to come. By 11 o'clock they were rearmed, refuelled and bombed up again. Back in the cockpit, Keith selected the first Coffman cartridge and pulled to detonate it. The Sabre did its usual spitting and gasping, trembled on the brink of expiring, recovered, blew out smoke and banged into rackety life.

So it was back to the Noball targets, as they had been code-named. Little white slits of no apparent significance to the course of the war. The mixture as before, as the family doctor used to prescribe....

This time they all came back. All peppered, more or less, with flak splinters (Titch Brambell actually got one through his gauntlet — 'Bloody presumptuous!') but no one shot down.

It was like the Battle of Britain in reverse. At lunchtime the officers' mess bar was packed and heavy with tobacco smoke, and there was talk of a third op in the afternoon. Keith bought Crawley a pint and fought his way to a quieter corner. There was only one person there, brooding over the scene with an expression of world-weary wisdom. He winked, his forehead scar twitching in conformity, when he recognized Keith. It was Flight Lieutenant Randall, looking more battered than ever, collar undone, his oil-streaked hat on the table beside his mug of bitter.

Keith introduced him to Crawley, who could not entirely conceal his surprise at the sight of this middle-aged regular pilot with his Great War decoration and modest rank.

'I taught this bugger to fly,' Randall informed Crawley, indicating Keith with a thrust of his grizzled head. 'You'd have been at bloody prep school then. Christ, even Boom Trenchard's beginning to look a kid.'

Keith suddenly realized who his mystery thirteenth man had been on the first op, and said, 'Don't give me that "old man" stuff, Randall. You were dropping 500-pounders on those Noball targets this morning.'

'Never.' Then Randall began singing off-key:

> 'Hitler's only got one ball,
> Goering's are really very small,
> Himmler is somewhat similar,
> As for Goebbels —
> He's got no balls at all
> No balls at all ...'

'And I'll bet it was you beating up the flak, you bloody fool. You're expendable, but we need that kite.'

Randall was rolling himself a cigarette with fingers that might have been washed a week ago but not more recently. 'You had a bloke go for a Burton. Saw him prang. Tough tit. So I thought I'd tag along again this afternoon. Gen is there'll be another op. Bloody good sport, this dive-bombing. I've got a century's service in, but never done it before.' He stuck the thin and untidy cigarette into his mouth and demanded a light. 'Of course, we used to drop twenty-five pounders from Camels into the Hun trenches. That was all right. But not as good as this,' he said with relish.

'You'll get me shot,' said Keith.

Randall's talent for keeping his ear to the ground and for getting himself onto what he called 'the better class of show' had increased rather than diminished as the war continued. 'I picked up the gen about this secret weapon balls-up at the Priory,' he told Keith later, 'stooging around the offices of some chums of mine. So I said to myself, "Time to get weavin', Randy boy," and got myself a delivery job. I thought it'd be Rampton, being closest 'drome to Frogland and all that.'

The afternoon op had been casualty-free, too, though one of 727's sergeant-pilots had had to bail out over the Channel, and had been picked up by Air/Sea Rescue. 2nd T.A.F. medium bombers had been out to the Pas de Calais again and there was talk of American 8th Air Force heavies being diverted to the sites from the irregular operations against aircraft plants in Germany.

Keith was in Maitland's office in the early evening, discussing the next day's ops over a whisky, when Randall walked in. He apologized perfunctorily for failing to knock and gave a sloppy salute. 'Well, what's the griff, Wingco?' he asked. And Keith wondered for the hundredth time how this veteran Flight Lieutenant had survived the wrath of superior officers for decades. The answer, he supposed, was that he was a character — an indestructible character. The R.A.F. could tolerate one or two insubordinate eccentrics and Randall was one of them.

'Would you care for a drink, Randall?' Maitland asked in his Canadian drawl.

'Sure thing, boss.' The voice was a terrible mockery of an American accent.

Maitland had big P.R.U. prints of photos taken in the early afternoon, and still damp from processing. The ski sites and the whole area about them was pockmarked like the face of the moon.

'That's a bloody wasteful way of knocking 'em out,' said Randall, leaning over the desk. He picked up Maitland's magnifying glass and held it over one area which Keith recognized as their first target of the morning. Randall was counting aloud. '...thirty-eight, thirty-nine, forty. There must be nearer 100 craters around this site alone. Some of 'em are 1,000-pounders from Bostons, some 500s. Say 70,000 pounds, nearly fifty tons. All bloody waste, Wingco.'

'What do you suggest?' Maitland asked.

'Cut off their sodding supplies.'

'They'll be bringing them up at night.'

'Cut 'em off at sodding night, then. It's nearly full moon. What about a night rhubarb? Might find a few lorries, or a train or two. The least you can do is cut the railway lines. Interdiction.' He pointed a finger with a black nail at the large-scale map beside the photograph. 'Here, here, and here. Best of all *there*, at the intersection.'

Keith said, 'There might be something in that, Jem.'

'Do you want to have a go?' Maitland asked. 'I'll have to get on the blower to Group, but there shouldn't be any problem. So long as you don't prang yourself.'

Keith had done night rhubarbs in Spitfire Vs, and earlier in the year on Typhoons. They had always been free-ranging affairs, searching for targets of opportunity. There were certain exclusions in the occupied countries where needless loss of civilian lives had to be avoided, but all non-passenger trains, sidings, canal locks, and of course obvious military targets like airfields, were permitted.

The next day, there were two more shows against the Noball targets and Keith ordered Polo to lead one and Range the second, while he kept himself fresh for the night and prepared his route with great care. Randall was still hanging around Rampton, hands in pockets, chatting to Chiefy and the troops down at the dispersals one minute, air testing a Typhoon the next, or wandering restlessly in and out of the I.O.s' offices and flirting with the station's W.A.A.F. officers. He took a particular interest in Keith's self-briefing and watched him lay off his route to Doullens, which he was using as a hub for low-flying sorties up and down the railway lines that ran out from the town.

'Last time I was there, there were more whores than smashed houses, and that's saying something,' Randall reminisced; and made Keith laugh at his stories of wild nights of champagne drinking in bed with two at a time in the final triumphant days of 1918 when they were at last rolling the Kaiser's armies back to their fatherland.

'I'd like to see the old place again. I suppose all those poor bitches are grandmothers now.' Randall sighed. 'Won't be able to tell from 100 feet.'

Keith said, 'Why don't you stop gassing and let me get on with my work? Anyway, I stick to 200 feet. Keeps you clear of the high tension cables.'

'I meant me, you bloody fool.'

Keith looked at him sharply. 'You're not coming.'

Randall sighed again, rolled himself a limp cigarette and slouched off in search of fresh company.

Keith drove down to the dispersal after dinner. The moon did not rise until 10 p.m. but he wanted to check again on the state of his plane, talk to Jerry Owen and have a last word with Group. It was a cold, star-lit night and his rigger and fitter were stamping their feet and rubbing their hands when he walked out to his Typhoon.

'Everything O.K., Bertie?' he asked his rigger.

'We got those last holes patched up about two hours ago. The kite's beginning to look like a colander, sir.'

Keith walked slowly round the big, lowering machine. She looked even more menacing in this faint light, her two 500-pounder delayed action bombs scarcely visible.

'They've had a spot of trouble with F-Freddy, sir. Bomb release mechanism. But I think she's serviceable now.'

Keith turned to the airman. He was wearing a knitted bala-clava, a wool-lined waistcoat and gumboots with the tops turned down. 'What do you mean?'

But Keith knew the answer to his own question. He knew the answer before he had turned and identified a second Typhoon thirty yards away, the two big underslung bombs just visible in the faint light of the crew's torches. He walked over to it and recognized Randall's stooping figure talking to Chiefy Norton. Keith said to him sharply, 'Can you spare a minute?'

They walked down the perimeter track out of earshot of the crews. 'What the hell is this ? I told you you couldn't come, Randall.'

'I thought you'd like a bit of company. Two's company, one's none.' Randall stamped his cigarette butt out with the toe of his flying boot, and Keith saw that he was looking at him, no doubt with that crafty grin he put on when he was flouting authority.

'I can't have you ordering my troops around like this,' Keith protested. 'It's lousy for discipline. And there'll be all hell to pay if you get into any trouble. There'll be all hell to pay anyway when Group finds out you've gone off on an op without authority.'

'They're used to me at Group. Come on, boss, it'd be a bad show if you scrubbed me now — after all the trouble Chiefy's taken to get my kite ready.'

Keith knew that he was going to yield, just as countless officers in authority had yielded to this ageing, brilliant pilot and had covered up for his crimes, or forgiven him. Randall's marriage to flying had been consummated before Keith had been born, and there had been no other love in his life ever since. No wife or children, no home except R.A.F. messes, no other interest except planes and flying and fighting — if you except occasional fornicating, steady heavy drinking, and smoking endless cigarettes.

Keith said briefly, 'It's time we signed the form and emptied our pockets,' and began walking swiftly back to the dispersal. He glanced at the luminous dial of his watch. 'Take off in twelve minutes.'

The moon was rising, blood red, beyond the cliffs. There was already a sharp frost. Visibility would be almost like daylight. A good night for a rhubarb.

They climbed above the shimmering Channel to 8,000 feet in loose formation half a dozen wing-spans apart, keeping radio silence. Keith had never flown a night rhubarb as a pair, and found himself glad of the company. There was not a sound on the earphones except a faint crackle of static above the roar of the Sabre, and the world below might have been dead. There was not a ship on the sea, not a glimmer of light on the land. Only moonlight, which etched out clearly the coast of Sussex and Kent and the familiar configuration of the northern French coast.

They crossed in midway between Fécamp and Boulogne in a fast shallow dive. Long experience had taught Keith that there was a narrow air passage, just north of a village on a small estuary, where the flak had some difficulty reaching you, as if the guns had been poorly sited. You did not get away Scot free, but at least the density was much reduced if you went in fast at about 6,000.

This was the line he took now, with 400 on the A.S.I. and Randall formating to port and a short distance behind. He waited for the inevitable searchlights and the arching 3.7 cm. tracer, ready to break into evasive action. But nothing at all came up, not until they were down to 3,000 feet, when the coastal searchlight came on behind them and swung down low, groping about belatedly and unsuccessfully.

The first time he had ever crossed this coast without trouble. Good omen? Far to the south, like a distant fireworks display, the sky was patterned with the sparkles of heavy flak and criss-crossed with multi-coloured tracer, where some intruder was experiencing a rough reception.

There was the landmark he was looking for, a sharp loop in the river, a railway line beyond going north-south. Now, a true compass course of 095 degrees for six minutes at 290 A.S.I. Keith dropped thankfully down to the safer altitude of 200 feet, with the fields flicking past the trailing edge of his wings — square fields, triangular fields, fields dark from winter sowing, pasture land with stock. A herd of cows in the first stages of panic, only half on their legs as the two Typhoons shot past above them. (How Keith, country bred, hated scaring farm animals!) The moonlight was so bright that he could even identify a man on a bicycle, no doubt full of wine from the bistro, halted at the road verge, wondering if his bleary eyes were deceiving him with visions of the devil incarnate and airborne.

Then a village on a dead straight road. Keith remembered it from daylight rhubarbs and broke radio silence to warn Randall of the church spire, which they passed three seconds later, Keith to the right, Randall to the left, shying away from it. They were dead on course. Keith did not have to consult his map to satisfy himself of that. This was the fruit of two hours with the maps in

111

the afternoon, and of the sum of knowledge he had collected of the Pas de Calais's geography and topography over the years. St Omer was just eighteen miles due north, a vast and powerfully defended airfield to be avoided at any time. But they were unlikely to scramble any fighters. Even on this brilliant moonlit night, fast-moving low-flying Typhoons would be almost impossible to pursue.

There were sidings half a minute ahead, a shade to the right. Randall had heard him musing that they might be worth deviating towards, and now he transmitted, 'Target one coming up two o'clock. If there's any joy, follow me in, but there could be a flak wagon. Over.'

'O.K.'

Keith fused his bombs. He would be glad to get rid of them, but only on a worthy target. Now they were over the double track leading to the sidings, rails glinting in the light of the moon dead ahead. And here were the sidings, fanning out, sheds beyond, the town beyond them, twin chimneys of a small factory. But the scene was not as Keith remembered it. The bombers had come, probably 2nd T.A.F. Bostons, spattering the sidings with craters, tearing up the rails, throwing wagons and locomotives crushed onto their sides. And the sheds were roofless skeletons.

'No joy there,' Keith said laconically. 'Someone's been here before us. Chimneys ahead.'

'I've got 'em.'

They found the train five minutes later, beyond the intersection they were going to bomb if no better target showed up. They saw it simultaneously, and Keith at once ordered, 'Break port'; and himself broke starboard. Like a predator, he wanted to study and sniff his victim before attacking.

It was a long train, forty or more wagons long, double-headed, and moving very slowly, as if the weight was almost beyond the capacity of the two locomotives. When he had completed his 360 degree turn, he was able to identify the faint red glow from the cabs and could see the smoke, white in the moonlight, streaming away on the gentle westerly wind.

'You take it first,' he told Randall. 'There'll be a flak wagon somewhere but I can't see it yet.'

He was flying very low, parallel with the line and about half a mile from it. It looked the fattest railway target he had ever seen, some of the wagons open with bulky loads shrouded by tar-paulins, others closed, long flatcars loaded high. And then in the middle — yes, the flak wagon, there it was, gunners no doubt poised behind their quadruple-mounted Oerlikons.

The locomotives had halted by the time Randall came in. Keith had lost sight of him, but picked him up again by the muzzle flashes from his Hispanos. His Typhoon was very low and coming in from three o'clock. Keith was banking, heading for the wagons immediately behind the locomotives, timing his run to avoid Randall's three-second delays.

The ex-R.F.C. pilot was firing with sublime accuracy, just as if he were a boy of nineteen in his Sopwith Pup. Keith could see the pattern of hits all over the boiler of the first locomotive. Already there was rising steam. Then the fleeting shape, like a shadow, as the Typhoon lifted up over the big, black, multi-wheeled engines. One, two, three — and the searing, shocking, flash of the two 500-pounders exploding, the glare spreading like an instant pool of light over the countryside, illuminating trees and hedges, a single-story cottage, a length of road flanked by telephone poles.

The bombs appeared to have landed and exploded dead bet-ween the locomotives, but Keith was now too concerned with his own run in, and with the flak which — again belatedly — was spitting out from the wagon half-way along the train. He raised the nose of his machine fractionally, saw the first hits, and was at once picked up by the yellow beam of a searchlight from the flak wagon. He kicked left, right, like an evading hare, failed to throw off the beam, and with shielding hand half over his eyes, saw the tracer whistling past his port wing.

Jerk the stick forward, praying that he had height, up again, left, right, right, and right rudder again, into a full sliding, climb-ing turn. Then he was free, and he could see the beam, foiled of its prey, fingering the sky, could see the fire he had started in the foremost wagons, could see Randall suddenly caught in the beam as he came in on his second run.

'Duck out!' Keith shouted.

But the Typhoon continued on its shallow dive, straight down the line of the beam, fighting it out with the flak. Keith aileroned down, in a 40 degree dive, finger on gun button although a long way out of range, closing fast, another long burst. He could see the figures at the guns — two *Flakvierling* 38s — firing for their lives, and his own shells slamming home. Three seconds. Now pull out hard. He saw the searchlight beam had been doused — blown up? — just before he blacked out at the bottom of his dive. Then through 180 degrees, back again.

Randall was calling out, 'That's a wizard prang. Now watch this!' Keith did so, and saw Randall's Typhoon outlined against the glare of the fire, his shells racing like a fuse along the length of the train, from the rear forward to the flak wagon. Every shell was on target, every damn one. Keith swore it, and had never seen shooting like it. And fires were breaking out behind him, one, then another, bigger, a flash of blue flame, another sulphurous yellow. My God, there was going to be nothing left. A clean wipe-out.

Keith, behind Randall, dropped his bombs, felt the lift, pushed forward his stick and used up the rest of his ammunition in a long burst. It was good shooting. Nothing up to Randall's standard, but good for him.

Then the flak started again. The gunners must have cleared the steel wagon of dead bodies and mangled equipment, and some-one had got one of the *Flakvierlings* going again. Was it aiming blindly? Keith asked himself. He could see Randall above him, and the shellfire was not in his direction.

Then it was. It was as if the gunner had seen his error and simultaneously spotted the Typhoon at 500 feet coming in again in a shallow dive. Keith saw Randall being hit, saw the strikes on wings and fuselage. Heard Randall, in his coarse-edged voice, say, 'I've had my fuckin' engine,' saw him opening fire again, not at the flak wagon, at the wagon immediately in front of it, saw the Typhoon following the line of its shells as if hell-bent on adding its own six tons to the holocaust of destruction.

Keith saw it go in, the whole process of destruction, and it was not even very fast. An almost leisurely nemesis, or so it seemed. The ammunition exhausted, or Randall already dead, the dark, punchy body of the Typhoon, a speeding coffin carrying the veteran killer of a pilot. The impact against the wagon, still a slow event. Then the result, tearingly fast. A jet of flame, like a cigarette lighter's. A rush of flame. A mountain of flame, and it was no longer moonlight, it was glaring daylight, bright enough to hurt the eyes. Keith flinched back in his seat, covered his face with one hand, threw the stick to the left as the shock wave struck him.

him. He felt the heat, and knew then that it was the end for him, too, engulfed in Randall's explosion — Randall's volcano, Randall's earthquake, Randall's holocaust, France's biggest ever explosion. For several seconds Keith had no control of his machine. His Typhoon was no more than a fragment of litter on a windy day, tossed about, the controls out of his hands and feet. There was nothing for him to do except await the disintegration of his machine, or its impact with the earth.

Then the weight on his shoulders told him he was upside down, and he at once pushed forward the stick and put it over to the right. Astonishingly, his Typhoon responded, and as his night vision returned (although the glare still beat at the centre of his retina) he saw that he was at some two hundred feet, tearing above the French countryside. The flat fields, the trees and their shadows, a long straight road, swept past under his wings as if nothing had happened and he was still searching for targets of opportunity.

He could not be far away. Surely he could find some evidence that this had not been some fantasy explosion. And then he heard a voice, distantly on the R/T. It was a gasp over the ether. Simply, 'Christ! Did you see that, Charlie?' Then another voice, 'Wow! That's north-east France gone for a Burton.'

So it had happened, and a couple of Intruders had witnessed it, too. And Keith's machine was O.K. Everything felt all right. A wing might fall off at any moment, the engine expire from delayed shock. But his sturdy old Typhoon was still flying, and when he pulled back the stick, up she gamely went. He turned through 180 degrees, tipping port then starboard wing. It was some moments before he recognized the scene, a mile or two to the east, his eye caught by a pall of smoke and numerous scattered fires. There was still enough heat to throw him about when he flew above the massive crater and the fragments of train spread wide. The cottage had disappeared, seemingly wiped off the map. And a length of road running beside the twin-track line, as well as the line itself, had disappeared, as if the civil engineer who had laid it had decided, 'We'll dig a pit here instead — a big one.'

Keith wondered if they would ever find anything of Randall and his machine, the perpetrators of this fearful wreckage. Perhaps a tattered piece of flesh, perhaps an intact piston, one of the Sabre's twenty-four. Not much more than that, Keith guessed.

No forced landings for Randall. No regaining height and bailing out, and then the evasion and capture, and sodding Stalagluft something-or-bloody-other all in Roman numerals. Randall had always believed in finishing off a job. No half-way stuff. That train, he had known, was full of supplies for Hitler's V-weapons. Maybe the weapons themselves, perhaps rockets or these missiles, these flying bombs. A target of opportunity all right, and there was no other way Randall would consider going, 'In my sodding cockpit,' as he would say in his harsh voice, rough from decades of smoking his rolled cigarettes, 'hitting something hard, a real bloody wizard prang'.

Back in the UK, in messes from the Shetlands to Cornwall, they would soon be saying, 'The Raf'll never be the same,' 'The end of a bloody era, old boy,' and 'He had an innings all right—a really wizard innings, never stopped. I can remember back in ...'

And Keith, as he flew home, uncaring of flak or fighters, not even much caring about his compass, felt a stab of grief that pierced even his hardened steel armour plate. The ultimate survivor had succumbed. It was no relief to condition it with clichés like 'It was the way he would have wanted to go,' or considerations like, 'This is where he liked to fly best, in a Camel strafing the Hun trenches in '18.'

And for all time in the Service, Keith would be known as the pilot who had been with Randall when he had bought it. When Keith was one day grounded and a snappy-tempered old Station Commander, newcomers would be told. 'Yes, the old man was number one to Randall when he got the chop.' Notoriety, of a kind. But all that was in the future, if he was, after all, to have one. For the present, there would be a Court of Enquiry, perhaps a Court Martial, for authorizing a non-operational junior officer to fly on a night show. He would get by, under the circumstances. Perhaps a reprimand and a note on his records.

The moon appeared to have scarcely changed its position in the night sky when Keith went out somewhere south of Calais, its angle almost the same relative to the Channel waves upon which its light glittered softly and peacefully by contrast with the blinding violence Randall had created minutes before. The flak gave him a desultory once-over and Keith did not even bother to jink.

116

He was giving his mind to little things, of no consequence. To the usual streak of oil on his screen, to the shape of the English coast ahead, to the faint glow of his instruments — A.S.I. 220, R.P.M. 2,700, Boost 3.5, time: ten to twelve. Just figures. And when he touched down, it would be another December day.

Keith flashed the letter of the day and transmitted, 'Hello Matchmaker, Sideline Leader calling. Five miles south of Dungeness, angels five.'

Then Keith was in the Rampton circuit, wheels and flaps down, green light showing on the panel, everything working like a dream. Control gave him the Drems for the last of the final approach and touch-down, and were off again before he taxied off along the perimeter, following the guide van to the dispersal.

'Any joy, sir?' Bertie Silver asked, as always, as he took Keith's helmet.

Keith thought, No, no joy. No joy at all. And what a bloody silly R.A.F. expression that is. He said aloud, 'Yes, we pranged a train, Bertie. But I'm afraid Flight Lieutenant Randall went for a Burton.'

'Sorry to hear that, sir. Still, he had a fair enough innings.'

* * *

It was not until he got into bed that night that Keith realized how badly he needed to see Jenny again. It was always the same in times of stress or distress. He rebuked himself for having this need as a reflection on his strength and masculinity, but it never seemed to make any difference. He calculated that he could go on for ever — or at least as long as Randall, if Jenny was there when he got back, and beside him in this bed. Without her, it was hard. 'Tough tit,' as Randall would growl in another context.

* * *

It was Christmas Eve before he saw her again. He had given himself a week's leave, and she had promised him forty-eight hours. They met at a hotel at Eastbourne, a vast and ostentatious place on the sea-front, with pre-war potted palms, the gilt and paintwork tatty from neglect, the porters and waiters ancient and unsteady on their feet.

Everyone else was over seventy-five, permanent residents long since returned with the end of the invasion scare, each with their jealously guarded citadel of sauces and cordials and minute butter and cheese rations at the centre of the table.

Watery eyes behind spectacles followed them suspiciously. Jenny said, 'Cripes!' and giggled.

Keith withdrew from his pocket the two £1 notes he had taken from his wallet earlier and pressed them into the hand of the head waiter. 'This is a special occasion,' he said into his ear. 'See if you can dig out a bottle of wine — champagne if possible.'

It was not champagne, but it was a very good Pommard, and they looked at one another over the glasses and drank.

'What's so special about it?' Jenny asked.

'That's a very silly question. If you don't know, you don't deserve to be told.' Then he looked at her with loving concern. 'You look gorgeous. But tired. Why don't you ever let up?'

'I've been on nights. I find it difficult to sleep during the day.'

Keith asked, 'Were you on night duty last Tuesday?'

'Yes, and I heard you calling up. I thought you had a number two. What happened?'

He told her about Randall and she held his hand across the table. 'Oh Lord, I'm sorry about that. Was he a great chum?'

'I don't think he had any friends— not what most people think of as friends. Drinking cronies. But no enemies. He used to exasperate senior officers, and the more he became a legend, the more legendary he grew. He got into the habit of being a character in about 1923, I'd guess. And he could no more stop than he could stop flying. And my God Jenny, he could fly all right!'

'Did he kill himself?'

The question surprised him and he did not reply at once. 'Yes,' he said at last. 'No one will ever know for sure, I suppose. And no one will know how many lives he saved. Whatever it was that went up, it was due to come here. With intent to kill.' He lowered his voice. 'It was V-weapon stuff, almost certainly.'

Soon, the aged guests rose to their feet and shuffled silently out, the men with their *Daily Telegraphs,* the women with their knitting and Boots Library books. Keith and Jenny were the last in the huge dining-room, watched resentfully by their waiter. Their mood had changed with the wine and they talked about the Christmas dinner they had planned with Mike and Tom and Moira the next evening in London.

'The time has come,' said Keith, 'when we should go upstairs to that impossible, freezing bedroom and get undressed rather quickly and between those welcoming sheets.'

'And?' Jenny's eyelids were heavy with the need for sleep, but she was smiling quizzically.

'I am going to wrap you up in my arms like a Christmas present for tomorrow, and I shall kiss your breasts freely and frequently and touch you elsewhere that has pleased you in the past. A thousand or a million years ago? And we shall slip together as easily as can be. Your face will be even lovelier than it is now, and if I have *my* way it may even crumple a little with pleasure. And then we'll lie still for a moment and ...'

Jenny's eyes had left his and were glancing above and to his right. Keith turned at the sound of the slight cough. Their waiter could bear it no longer and was proffering the bill. Reddening slightly, Keith initialled it and gave the stooping man a pound note.

'Do you think he heard me?' Keith asked quietly on the way out.

'Yes, and I think he wanted you to go on, like the next column in the *News of the World*.' She laughed and held his hand. 'I don't mind you going on either.'

It was even colder than they had guessed it would be in the massive bedroom and the water was only tepid so they leapt into bed just as Keith had predicted. Everything else went according to plan, too, and they made love three times before Jenny dropped off into a deep sleep in the middle of saying she loved him.

Keith remained awake for a long time, his arms still wrapped lightly about her, resisting the urge to caress her again. Yes, it had been as he had predicted, and as he had prayed that it would be. The tenderness and understanding were, as always, the one healing balm. And, now that he had told her about Randall, he could bear to think about him without guilt.

* * *

As the train was passing through East Croydon on Christmas morning, Keith said, 'I think we ought to get married now.'

She did not hesitate or ask for time. She looked at him with her clear brown eyes, smiling her slightly uneven smile (no irony, no false sentiment, just uncompromising and decisive pleasure), and nodded. 'I think that's a very good idea if you would like it.'

Later they agreed to tell no one, that she would wear a ring but would not change her name. On the sacred records of the Women's Auxiliary Air Force, she would remain Squadron Officer Jennifer Simpson O.B.E.

6

L for Landing

They were confined like pariahs to the extreme north-west corner of the airfield at Tryngarth, out of bounds to the other personnel, whom they saw distantly going about their duties. It was an O.T.U. for Mosquitoes, and all day and half the night the fast, twin-engined machines were taking off and landing, doing circuits and bumps, low flying practice over remote Welsh forests and firing and bombing practice on the range up the coast.

For the Special Duties Training Unit, with its Hudsons and Lysanders, there were none of the entertainments enjoyed by the O.T.U. people; no cinema, no E.N.S.A. visits, no leave, and they were confined to their area for the entire six weeks of the course. It was cold, the weather mainly awful, the training gruelling; and Mike revelled in every minute of it.

After the first full day's work, and drinking with the five others on the Lysander course, Mike said, 'This is going to be like a goddam kid's dream come true. Blowing up, shooting with everything from Brownings to Brens, how to make a stickbomb and a Molotov cocktail to blow up a car.' He turned to the senior lecturer, a small, cunning Squadron Leader named Jennings. 'Are we going to be taught how to deal with Kraut sentries? Knee in the small of the back? A quick pull with the wire? Or the swift insertion of a knife?'

To all these questions Jennings nodded; and Mike said, 'To think I was wondering what to do with myself after the war. I'm sure going to be the neatest, most ruthless Chicago mobster of all time. Al Capone will be like a lamb compared with Mike Browning.'

The range was a mile into the pine forest behind their quarters. Every other day they went down in a Jeep, loaded with various weapons, and banged away at towed dummy cars, dummy running figures, dummy figures at the windows of dummy houses. The standard was very high and Mike had difficulty in keeping abreast.

They stripped and assembled all their weapons blindfold, learned to accept the odd temperaments of the P.I.A.T. and Sten. They were made fit on assault courses, learned unarmed combat, slept out in the rough in thick sleeping bags. They listened to lectures from S.O.E. and S.A.S. officers who had been in the field, warned of the political divisions in France between different branches of the Resistance.

All this was provided to give them the background to the work of the agents they were later to drop or land, and contingency preparation in case they were trapped and unable to get back. Their primary task was to learn the technique of flying agents to their destinations, dropping them and bringing back safely anyone whose time was up.

Mike's instructor was Flight Lieutenant Jock Wallace, a tough Scot who had done twenty successful lifts and could, he claimed, put a Lizzie down in Sauchiehall Street, 'and I mean crossways'. His formula for success was simple, like most good recipes. 'Preparation,' he told them at their first lecture, 'patience, and don't flap. Indulge yourselves instead. Sit in the warmth and light in a comfortable arm-chair for two two-hour sessions with your half-million, quarter-million and 50,000 maps, pre-reading your course until you know every kink in the rivers, every railway cutting and curve, every lake and village on your route. That's better than circling with the sweat pouring out of your helmet wondering why flak is coming up from *there*.'

He warned them that reception parties could be late, and for very good reasons. 'So in your fuel calculations allow for an extra hour over the target area. Your passengers will be less worried if they know you're not.' Then he showed them a P.R.U. photograph of a real target area, with a 50,000 map on the reverse side, and the field marked in red shading. 'Wood here, see. Triangular, easily recognized, but trees up to maybe seventy-five feet so turn after take-off, and always use full emergency boost for the first half minute anyway. If you see lights from this field,' he continued, putting his finger on another part of the map, 'similar shape, not far away, don't imagine the reception committee have made a mistake. It means the Germans have got the screws on them and are going to get you, too, if you don't beat it fast.'

The tips from this veteran came in a seemingly inexhaustible torrent. He had an engine-less Lysander fuselage in the nissen hut which served as a lecture hall, and he sat in the passenger compartment, his cap on the back of his head, and called out to them below. 'Heaviest luggage under the seat, near the centre of gravity. Money sacks on this shelf so you won't forget them. Amazing how people in a hurry can leave behind a million francs. *Don't* put it down here on the floor. It can slide all the way to the tail. Don't wear flying boots. Comfortable shoes. I had to walk clear over the Pyrenees once. Couldn't have done it in boots. Take a couple of small photographs of yourself and *not* in uniform. They may come in handy for identity papers ...'

Then it was Mike's first practical experience with the remarkable Lysander— that 'miracle of flappery and slottery' as she was called, a high-winged, single-engined machine originally designed for Army co-operation, and for this reason possessing remarkably short take-off and landing runs.

She looked, he decided, like some distorted breed of extinct gull coming in to land. The undercarriage was fixed and massive, with not only wheel spats but light bomb racks secured by little stub wings. Behind the cockpit was the compartment, originally intended for the observer and gunner, now converted to passenger space for three (at a pinch) or four (very uncomfortable) agents.

Mike climbed up into the high cockpit behind the radial engine and cast a practised eye about him. He felt as if he were in a world of his own, with clear visibility above, and visibility below obstructed only by the wing struts. The wing itself was higher still, and behind him, a crank-shaped affair with the slots, that lowered the landing speed, in the leading edge, and big flaps at the trailing edge. He moved the stick right and left, watching the ailerons respond, then forwards and backwards, looking back over his shoulders right and left at the elevators. He looked down at Jock Wallace standing beneath the wing, whose head did not reach near to the cockpit.

'This,' said Mike, 'is the goddarnest aviation joke in history. I guess you'll tell me someone sat down at a drawing board and *drew* it, declaring, "It's gotta fly, it's sure gotta". And of course it doesn't.'

Flight Lieutenant Wallace grinned back. 'She'll peck you if you talk like that to her. Now prove you're wrong.'

Mike started up the Bristol engine and taxied out to the runway, did his cockpit drill with special care, got the green light from the watch office, and opened up. For a moment he did not believe it. But it was true. He *was* airborne, and in less than 50 yards. Goddarn it, the contraption *was* flying! Before he did anything, before he had time to do anything, he was off the ground, and floating (that was it, floating) up into the grey winter Welsh sky.

Mike tested out the controls gingerly, and they responded nicely and quickly. 'Well, you hide your light under a bushel all right,' he said to the Lizzie. 'My apologies.' Yes, he could get quite fond of this contraption, he decided, after a couple of loops and a roll.

The Special Duties Flight had the exclusive use of a length of perimeter track on which transverse white lines had been painted, the first indicating touch-down point, the others at ten yards intervals to measure the pilot's landing run. After three attempts, Mike got the distance from touchdown to a standstill to 150 yards, with very little wind blowing, and taxied in, feeling confident and highly satisfied.

Night flying, landings in clearings in the Welsh forests by day, and then by night; by a string of powerful lights, and then by the light of hand-held torches shaped in an 'L' and with a full load. There were long cross-country flights to 'targets' as far distant as Norfolk and Dumfriesshire, and Mike who had the traditional fighter pilot's distaste for dead reckoning navigation ('follow the railway line and turn left') found himself becoming fascinated by the intricate processes of holding a strict compass course and relating it to his visual observations along the route.

All six of them passed out of the course successfully in mid-December, and were posted to Southdean with effect from 28 December, with leave until then. The informal words from Jock

Wallace at breakfast that they were all qualified for Special Duties, was followed by the arrival of a letter from Eileen. Yes, she wrote, she had heard from Keith and she would love to come to the Christmas party he and Jenny were arranging.

Dearest Mike,
   It will be so lovely to see you again after all this time. How I have missed you!

Mike read the letter three times, studying the rounded hand-writing — a strong, firm hand, he decided, developed from the standard English girls' public school script. Swell writing. Swell words. Swell girl. The other Squadron Leader on the course eyed him across the table quizzically. 'Good news?'

'Yeah, sure.' Mike rapidly folded the sheets and slipped the letter back into the envelope. 'About Christmas. Christmas arrangements, you know ...'

The Squadron Leader winked and got up. 'Well, have a happy one, Yank.'

* * *

Christmas morning 1943, a damp, chill, foggy day. Mike had arrived early at the flat in Half Moon Street, and had to wait, stamping his feet to keep out the cold. He did not care. It could be raining a deluge, London could be looking even tattier than it was — nothing mattered except that he was going to see Eileen again. And Keith and Jenny, too. And perhaps some others. And he had two more clear days before he had to set off for Southdean again.

He saw Keith and Jenny coming down the street from Piccadilly, both wearing long R.A.F. officers' greatcoats, looking just right. Keith, three inches taller, in jaunty cap, Jenny in W.A.A.F. officer's hat; she dark, and Keith with his usual too-long, corn-coloured hair sticking up around his cap; she, holding his arm (against custom in public, of course, but who would care with such a well-matched couple and on Christmas Day at that?) and looking up and laughing.

Neither had seen him, so Mike slipped back into the porch, listening to their approaching footsteps on the pavement. They still did not see him when they reached the front door and Keith began to open it. Mike put his hands over Jenny's eyes from behind and said, 'Happy Christmas, you two.'

Jenny kissed him in turn on both cheeks, and Keith, laughing, pumped his hand. He was looking him up and down. 'So, you've rejoined the Raf. And I was looking forward to calling you "Major Browning".'

They crammed into the little lift. It was Mike's first visit, and he said, 'So this is where you two came on that first night. Does it seem a long time ago?'

'A million years,' said Jenny, opening the gates and searching in her pocket for the key.

It had, in fact, been more than five years ago, Munich Crisis time, and everyone thought London would be bombed to pieces at any time. Instead, Czechoslovakia had been sold down the river, and the bombing had come later instead, France had fallen just the same, and the R.A.F. had been fought almost to a standstill (but not quite, as Keith and Mike could testify better than most) and then Russia had been invaded and America had been forced into the battle at last, too. Now here they were, on the eve of the Second Front, the invasion of Germany's so-called invulnerable fortress of Europe...

'But we're not going to get maudlin about this war. This beastly, boring war.' Jenny let them into the flat and began ripping the dust covers off the furniture before she had even taken off her coat. 'We're going to eat a lot and get rather drunk and play paper games.' She threw one dust sheet at Mike and a second at Keith. 'Happy Christmas everybody.'

Fortnums delivered an enormous hamper half an hour later, and Mike gave the two pre-military-age boys a pound note each. Jenny opened it in the kitchen and all three looked in wonder at the contents: aspic in jelly, a jar of peaches, a substantial jar of caviare, a whole Stilton cheese, Bath Oliver biscuits, luxuries of every kind, even one thermos of ice and one of coffee, all settled neatly in straw around two magnums of Krug and an enormous cold turkey with a label attached. Under the printed holly leaves and Christmas Greetings, was a hand-written message: 'I thought you would prefer not to have to cook, Madame. I trust everything else will be in order for your heroes. Bon appetit — Gaston.'

'Darling Gaston,' exclaimed Jenny, kissing the label. 'I wrote to him from Swingham, reminding him of old times.'

'You must have spent a fortune with him in the old times,' Mike said. 'Gee, I guess the country's not starving after all. I hope it's a big party.'

Keith had put on all the electric fires and drawn back the curtains. Soon they were able to take off their coats, and Jenny got out her old cocktail shaker and Mike showed her how to make a sidecar.

'I guess there's never been a war. Let's kid ourselves it was all a nightmare. The Krauts and Japs never had to surrender because it sure never began.' He raised the shaker above his head in true American bartender style, rattling the ice. 'It's Christmas Day and there'll be no war.'

But the living evidence that there had indeed been a war, more than four years of war, longer than the Great War, arrived before they had put down their first drink. It had been Mike's idea and Keith had agreed vehemently that Buffer Davies must be invited to their party. His step was as jaunty as ever as he came through the door Mike held open for him, his face the crudely sculptured white visage Mike and Keith had seen before, a pathetic stuck-together face, all that could be salvaged from those terrible burns of 4 July 1940.

Without a flicker of consternation, with a welcoming smile on her face, Jenny got up, stepped towards Buffer, and put her cheek against his, first right and then left. 'How lovely to see you again!' she exclaimed. 'You won't remember me. But I was at Elgin briefly, back in '39, and I remember you ...'

* * *

Tom and Moira arrived in the middle of the afternoon while they lay torpid about the flat recovering from their feast of a lunch and preparing themselves for the bigger feast of the evening. Moira stood in the doorway looking about her in wonder at the evidence of undreamed-of-riches, including two empty bottles of claret Jenny had dug out from the back of a cupboard.

Tom said, 'When can we join the orgy? I'll be prescribing some settling drugs by the end of the day, I can see that.' He looked very new and austere in his uniform of R.A.F. officer in the Medical Branch: just one thin ring on his sleeve and the snake and staff on his lapel, by contrast with Keith and Mike with their two-and-a-half rings, and their D.F.C.s and '39-'43 ribbon with the gilt rose of the Battle of Britain star. But, as always, there was a taut resolve in Tom's demeanour, and, as became evident later, a new element of self-discipline in the highly strung doctor who had come so near to breaking point during the '40 Blitz.

Moira, beside him and holding his hand, looked fresher and plumper than ever. 'You don't know how hungry I am!' she exclaimed characteristically.

Keith and Mike kissed her in turn. Keith said, 'I've never known you not, darling Moira,' and held out a huge peach dripping with brandy on the end of a fork.

The plump, always cheerful girl took it in one mouthful and held up her left hand. There was a narrow ring on the third finger. 'Two little mouths to feed now,' she mumbled through the fruit, and began to giggle.

Tom was introduced to Jenny and Buffer, glancing flickeringly a second time at Buffer's mask of a face, Mike noticed, and, as a professional now, who could blame him for that?

'I must apologize for my wife,' Tom said, but smiling at her as she extracted the stone with satisfaction. 'She's about as new to marriage as to peaches in brandy.'

'Both nice,' said Moira, patting her tummy, which was more ample than Mike remembered it. 'And both necessary. You'd think Tom would know, wouldn't you?'

They drank many cups of strong tea, all talking easily together; a sixsome the war had treated in various ways and with varying severity, from permanent disfigurement to serious or light injuries, and temporary homelessness for Keith and the two newly-weds. Then they went for a walk in the dusk through Green Park and St James's Park to work up an appetite for Christmas dinner.

As they were passing the ugly new fortress built onto the Admiralty, Mike took Keith aside and said, 'What time did Eileen say she would arrive?'

'Anytime. Don't worry, she'll be here soon. Jenny left the flat open and she'll probably be there when we get back.' But Keith was not telling the whole truth. Eileen had clearly indicated on the telephone that she would arrive for luncheon. Nor was she there when they got back. There was no telegram or note from her either, as Mike quickly noticed when he had pulled the black-out curtains and switched on the lights.

Mike's own day was beginning to darken with the twilight, and the contrast with the joy of expectation he had experienced in the morning was hard to conceal. Jenny said, 'Don't worry, Mike darling. Trains are hell at Christmas.' But, when they talked about telephoning the station, none of them seemed to know the line on which she was travelling, or even where she was leaving from.

In the end, as Keith opened the first magnum of champagne, Mike telephoned the Ewhursts at the Rising Hall lodge. He wished them a happy Christmas from Keith and himself, and asked them if they knew anything of Eileen. 'No, sir,' came back the distant crackling voice. 'We've heard nothing from Miss Eileen for such a long time. Not like her, sir.'

They played consequences, sitting on the floor and passing round the champagne with the paper, and Jenny dug out some ancient dice games from the top of a cupboard. 'Signs of an ill-spent youth,' she said brightly. They were all trying to be bright, but when six o'clock, then seven o'clock, chimed on Jenny's little French travelling clock, it became even more difficult to keep off the subject of Eileen's failure to arrive, and to keep Mike's hopes alive. Soon after seven, Mike threw down the cards in a game of rummy, and apologized.

'Just can't keep my goddam mind on it,' he said, with the shadow of a bitter smile on his face. 'Can't help remembering last time.'

'Oh no, she'd never ...' Keith began. But Mike was at the door, not listening. 'I guess I'll take a little air.'

When he stepped out of the lift, Buffer was already at the front door to the flats, having run down the stairs fast. 'Don't want you to brood on your jolly ol' own, ol' boy. Any help if I stroll along too?'

Mike looked at the white mask in the dim light of the hall. There was a tentative smile on his grafted lips, and Mike remembered again that other distant evening of crisis they had shared. 'I'm not getting sloshed, Buffer, not like Lincoln in '38,' he said with a short laugh. 'Boy, that was some piss-up!'

'Don't want to get pissed over a bird, ol' boy,' Buffer said as if uttering the wisdom of a young bachelor about town. 'Wouldn't do at all. I mean, not if she's a real bird. And if she's just a fancy piece, then she's not worth the cost of the booze anyway.'

They strolled down Curzon Street towards Berkeley Square. 'Oh, she's a real bird, O.K.,' Mike said.

'Want to spill the jolly ol' beans?'

'Sure. I met her in Germany. She was on a walking tour with Keith, Tom and Moira. Keith was a bit proprietorial — no, protective, I guess you'd call it — about her at first. They aren't related but they grew up together. Her parents adopted him when his were killed. She's really a swell girl. Then she joined the W.R.N.S. and she was spoilt and something snapped and some heel of an officer seduced her.'

'Pupped, did she?'

Mike paused momentarily, then succeeded in interpreting Buffer's English slang. He laughed. 'Yeah, I guess you could call it that. But she went to some quack dive to get rid of it, was sick as all hell for weeks, months. Had a breakdown. Then her parents were killed. She's sure had some war, that girl. But she seemed O.K. again last time I saw her. Gee, Buffer, I'm frightened of what might have happened to her. She's still only a kid.'

They stood in the middle of Berkeley Square. There was almost no traffic on this Christmas evening. The fog, which had cleared earlier, had now returned. And, Mike reflected, there wasn't a nightingale to be heard.

'You know what I think?' said Buffer.

'Spill it.'

'If she's a real bird, she's O.K. You listen to Uncle Buffer, Mike ol' boy. He's knocked about with the ladies in his time. Used to come flockin' down at the Spider's Web and the Ace of Spades. I know birds, and real birds might slip once. But not twice.'

Mike laughed and kicked at the last of the plane tree leaves on the gravel path. In an odd sort of way, Buffer was giving him the comfort and reassurance he needed in the way he wanted it.

'And, talkin' of birds, we mustn't let the ladies down.' He laughed his old deep chortle Mike had heard so often in mess bars and down at the dispersal, and in the dark of Berkeley Square, Buffer might have been the cheerful old womanizing extrovert of 1939 with his own face and the pencil-thin moustache.

'And there's a big fat bird for consumption, too, at the flat,' Mike said.

'You won't mind if I get a bit pissed, ol' boy?' Buffer asked as they walked back up Half Moon Street.

'I'll be goddam offended if you don't, Buffer.'

'I mean to say, Christmas an' all that. A chap's allowed to get a bit pissed, what?'

They all got pleasantly drunk on the second magnum of champagne and a few brandies to follow. They ended up with the caviare on Bath Oliver biscuits, and Moira fell sound asleep on the floor with her head in Tom's lap. At midnight Mike announced that it was Boxing Day and time they went their ways.

Moira said sleepily, 'I suppose we must leave these two in their love nest.' She yawned. 'Love well.'

Tom rebuked her. 'You have a one-track mind. No, correction. Two track. Sex and food.' He lifted her firmly and gently to her feet. They had a hotel room near Euston Station and Moira would be returning to Market Rising the next day where she was living with her parents until the war was over.

Jenny said to Mike and Buffer, 'Why don't you two stay here? Sleep on the sofas.' She had changed into a long white dressing-gown and let her dark hair down. Mike thought how nice it was for Keith to be going to bed with her, and tried again without success to put anxious thoughts of Eileen out of his head.

'Thank you very much but we've got rooms at the Flying Club,' Buffer said. 'Strictly jolly well celibate. Mike by design, yours truly by necessity.' He laughed unselfconsciously. 'Ever since I had my bark knocked off.'

'Oh Buffer,' said Moira laughing, 'I would go to bed with you like a shot. You're lovely.' And she put her arms round his neck and kissed his cheek.

'See what I mean,' said Tom. 'No morals.'

Mike and Buffer got them a taxi by standing in the middle of Piccadilly with arms spread wide. There were already two people in it, but they were really drunk, not happily non-sober like them, and the driver agreed to the diversion without demur.

* * *

At Southdean there were Mustang and Typhoon squadrons, and, like Tryngarth, the Special Duties Flight was segregated in the most distant corner of the airfield with twenty-four-hour guards. There were six pilots, a veteran Warrant Officer, a Flight-Sergeant with a D.F.M. and a Battle of Britain star, the Squadron Leader who had been on the Tryngarth course, and two Flight Lieutenants who had been in Training Command for too long and were pining for some action. They messed with the rest of the station personnel but were forbidden on dire penalty from mentioning the nature of their work.

Once or twice a week during the moon period one or two of the all-black Lysanders would take off after dark, labouring under its full load, head south, and return two or three hours later. Once or twice a week a large black American car would turn in through the special gate to the Special Duties Flight, and after a long security check, would proceed to a building behind the dispersal.

Mike did two trips in the first moon period, one to a target west of Argentan in Normandy, and the second more distantly to a target north of Châlons-sur-Marne, where he had collected not only two tired agents but bottles of champagne for all six pilots in the Flight. Everything had gone smoothly on both ops. The navigation worked out well and the reception committees had been prepared with the correct code and lighting. On the first he was on the ground for less than three minutes and was not flakked once on the way in or out.

But Mike knew that it was not always going to be a piece of cake. He was too old and experienced a pilot to believe in that sort of nonsense.

8 April was a full moon and, two nights later, met. said that there would be only scattered cloud over Northern France. Something big had been blowing up for days, and early in the morning Mike was told he was to do an urgent op that night — 'two passengers and a longish trip', the I.O. told him. By 10 o'clock he had been given his target, and he settled down in his room, where he had worked out a routine self-briefing which had worked well so far. Take-off would be 9.30 p.m., and he would cross the coast nine miles west of Le Touquet. It was left to individual pilots to select their own height for the Channel. Some preferred to keep right down on the deck, under the enemy radar but at risk from light flak from friendly as well as enemy shipping, and from the coastal batteries. And a heavily loaded Lizzie was slow to climb if you did get into trouble. Mike liked to go in as

high as the weather conditions allowed, though not above 8,000 feet where the heavy flak was at its best — or worst for you. He had found on his last trip that he had had to drop down lower to recognize his coastal pinpoints.

He propped himself up on his bed, the maps on one side and a pad of paper on the other, switched on the little Pye portable wireless, tuned in to a concert, and gave himself up to studying his route in and out, making detailed notes of landmarks. At luncheon he had one glass of beer and bacon and eggs, went to sleep at 2 o'clock and was woken up by his batwoman at four with a cup of tea.

An hour later, the agents arrived with their controls, four commonplace men in rather shabby civilian clothes, the agents' suits crumpled and characteristically French in cut and material. One of the agents was code-named Drumbeat, a Pole from Warsaw, a cavalry officer who had actually survived a lance charge against a Panzer division, and then escaped by way of the Baltic, Denmark and Norway. His French was perfect; his English appalling. He had a puckish sense of humour, and Mike took to him at once. 'You fall us smack bang on ze target?'

'Sure thing, smack wallop, right there,' and Mike put a finger on the north-east corner of a field three kilometres north of a tiny village called Poissy-sur-Oise, Department Marne.

His companion, Mailorder, was an Irishman, judging from his accent, a pale-faced, stooping man with craggy eyebrows and an unexpectedly child-like, freckled face. He broke frequently into French and German when speaking to his control, and switched quickly into heavy brogue Irish to talk to Mike.

It was a first trip for both agents, and Mike began the briefing with instructions on landing, Drumbeat to remain in the plane, and Mailorder to jump down the moment they came to a standstill to receive the luggage. 'You then take on board the luggage of the agent I am bringing back.' He spoke clearly and slowly. 'Understand?'

The Pole nodded, and they all glanced at the stack of luggage piled up in the corner of the room: Stens, rifles and a single Bren amongst the weapons; guncotton, Bickfords detonators and gelignite; all wrapped and tied in tarpaulins. Three boxes of ammunition, a million francs in well-used French bank-notes, a kitbag packed with doubled-up sturdy bicycle tyres, specially

133

made to conform with the French pattern by Michelin in London, and in desperate demand in France. And much more. Mike had seen the inventory, and the load — together with his own emergency pack of civilian clothes, money, a Smith and Wesson .38 and the baby Browning— which had earlier saved his life in France — meant that they would be operating at maximum weight of 7,500 pounds. Not much opportunity for evading any flak with that lot, he recognized.

The five of them had supper in private together with the I.O. Mike went over the route in detail, partly to reassure the two agents that he had done his homework and was completely confident in the success of the mission, and partly because an alert agent could sometimes be of help in locating landmarks, so long as they were not themselves too obtrusive. Mike explained this and assured himself that they both understood the workings of the intercom.

Then, before darkness fell, they all went out to the black Lysander standing in its blast bay, fuelled and run up and passed O.K. by the ground crew Chiefy. The luggage had been taken out in a five-tonner, and Mike supervised the loading while the I.O. checked the inventory and the two agents watched where everything was stowed.

So far all had gone with routine smoothness. The met. report had improved — a thin layer of cloud at 6,000 feet, wind light north-west-by-west in target area. Moon rise at 2055. Mike returned to his room with his maps, checked that he had his gen card and its duplicate in the top pocket of his battledress blouse, and ensured that his contingency diversion airfields were prepared in case the weather closed down unexpectedly.

The Commander came out with Mike to his machine and watched him stow his emergency civilian clothes and guns in the starting handle locker, and his little parcel of escape kit, French money and Thermos flask of coffee in the cockpit.

'Your clothes all come from Baker Street?' Bowman, the Squadron Commander, asked.

'Oh sure. Genuine French, and no tabs. But plenty of French carbolic soap. My batwoman gives the shirt and underclothes a good wash in it once a fortnight. "Ooo, you Americans *are* hygienic!"'

The Commander laughed and said, 'Good luck, Mike. Your

lot'll be along in a minute. I've got work to do.'

The corporal rigger helped Mike with his 'chute and straps, and gave the screen a last wipe. The moon was coming up, casting its soft light over Southdean's long runways, the pre-fab buildings and Bessoneau hangars. A lone Typhoon took off. Mike caught a glimpse of its heavy-jawed silhouette and underslung bombs, off on a rhubarb. And he thought of Keith who loved the great brutes and had got a D.S.O. (he had heard last week) for his night work with 727 Squadron. Keith blowing things up, Mike dropping people to blow things up. He smiled at the contrast and similarity; and reminded himself too, and with a touch of bitterness, of the contrast between the steadiness of Keith's relationship with Jenny and his own continuing anxiety and unease about Eileen.

Then he glanced at the luminous clock on the instrument-panel. His passengers were five minutes later. Unusual, and irritating. He was going to have to sit long enough in this cockpit without wasting time on the ground.

He called down to the corporal, 'See what's going on, Sammy, will you?'

A car drew up alongside at that moment. It was not the big black limousine, driven by a F.A.N.Y. driver, the passengers usually arrived in. It was the Commander again. He climbed onto the step and put his head into the cockpit.

'There's a bit of a flap on, Mike. The Irishman's gone U/S.'

'You mean he's gone yellow?' Mike asked angrily.

'Maybe. I don't know. The doc's with him now. Cramps and vomiting. And dead useless for tonight.'

'Are we scrubbed, then?' Mike asked, starting to undo his straps.

Bowman told him that it was too late for that. The message had gone out on the BBC, for all Europe to hear. Mike had not listened, but it would have been something like, 'Aunt Mildred and her sister are off to the seaside,' and the local *réseau* close to the target would have known then that the op was on.

'The reserve's taking over,' the Commander said. 'They'll be along in a couple of minutes.'

'Oh, Christ!' Mike exclaimed. It very rarely happened, but it had to happen to him! On high priority missions, a back-up team was sometimes made available at short notice — unbriefed by the pilot, unbriefed on the route, ignorant of how the luggage was packed. 'Sure and begorrah, that goddam Irishman has chickened out!'

'It'll be O.K.' The Commander turned and added, 'Here they come. Better get cracking, you're going to be late. But don't let that rattle you, and don't rush your navigation or you won't get there at all.'

Mike could do without the advice. He had already given himself the message — 'Take it easy, son. Keep it steady' — as he used to warn himself in combat when in a tight corner.

'Switches on!' he shouted into the night to the engine fitter. Chiefy was beside him, supervising as usual on an op.

'Switches on, came back the voice.

'Contact!'

The heavy nine-cylinder Mercury radial blasted into life, gouts of smoke pouring from the exhausts, the prop already a blur. Mike settled the engine to a steady, full-rich tickover and turned and looked down. Four figures had stepped out of the Packard, and the Commander led two of them, heavily shrouded in their flying gear with parachute harness and helmets, to the Lysander. With the help of the controls they were soon packed into the passenger compartment, and in less than a minute, Bowman, standing under the port wing, gave the thumbs-up.

Mike answered with a wave, and then indicated chocks away. Yeah, it'd be O.K., he told himself. Give the Baker Street people their due, the training was marvellously thorough, and as back-ups, like stand-ins on the stage, they would know their parts. He glanced back into the compartment before opening the throttle and could just make out the figures strapped into the passenger seats.

'O.K. you two?' he said into the intercom, and was reassured by an immediate response, in a French accent, 'All O.K. Pardon that we are late.' At least they seemed to be genned up....

The Lysander lifted off with her usual eagerness to be in the air, in spite of her heavy load. And who wouldn't want to get up closer to the stars on a night like this, Mike reflected in a passing moment of romanticism? There were a few widely scattered cumulus clouds over the Sussex countryside to add a touch of pale decoration. Otherwise the sky was wide open, the stars dimmed to faint, far-distant crystals by the brilliant light of the

136

moon. The countryside below, the undulating spine of the South Downs, the darker shape of Worthing and Littlehampton and other coastal towns, the sparkling sea — all were seen as if through faintly smoked glass on a clear midsummer's day.

At 7,000 feet, Mike bent down to set his compass course. He could do with a bit more cloud for cover when he reached the French coast. But for the present and for the next thirty minutes, there was nothing for him to do except maintain his course steadily and watch out for his pinpoints ahead and for any stray nightfighter the radar might fail to identify.

He switched over the intercom. 'I guess we haven't been introduced,' he said. 'I'm Chicago. What about you?'

The French voice came back at once. '"Ow do you do, Chicago. I am Watermelon, and my partner is Dorothée.'

So he had a woman on board again! There were a lot of women in S.O.E. now, mostly Norwegians and French and Belgians, and a few English, largely recruited from the F.A.N.Y.s. He had had one on his first trip, and had brought another back from his second.

'Swell luck to you both. I guess we won't have any trouble tonight.'

Oh, you darn fool, Michael Browning! he snapped at himself. His superstitiousness grew with the years of the war, and like Keith who had worn Jenny's dented W.A.A.F. hat badge round his neck for nearly four years, Mike had taken to wearing a lucky charm. Only his batwoman knew about it. He had also developed little self-assuring routines. And he did one now: three taps on his compass, which also had a marginal practical advantage, ensuring that there was no hesitancy in its movement.

Old Mother Fortune didn't receive my message loud and clear, Mike reflected twenty minutes later. He had found the point on the coastline where he intended to cross in, but a new flak battery must have been set up there. Or maybe it was several concentrated mobile units. He was at 6,500 feet and he had not expected to get through without being flakked. But nor had he expected it on this scale. The heavies got their range with the first salvo, and when he dropped the Lysander, the 3.7 cm. joined in, all the colours of the rainbow filling the sky about them with curving patterns of false innocence.

Twice a heavy shell exploded close enough to toss the Lysander onto its side, sending splinters rattling against the wings and fuselage and filling the cockpit with cordite fumes. Mike was already blinded before the searchlights picked them up, bringing a renewal of intensity from the guns, like hounds closing in when all the pack has sighted the quarry.

There was nothing more he could do but rudder wildly and climb and dive — but not get too low or the goddam machine-guns would get at them, and their chances of survival then would be nil. Cold air was streaming in through a hole in the cockpit floor when they were wonderfully clear, a solitary heavy — a 105 Mike guessed — pursuing them angrily until they were far beyond range.

'You O.K. back there? Sorry about that.'

Male and female voices answered in turn. Yes, they were O.K. 'Eh dis-donc, ça se passe comme ça tous les soirs?'

'Jeez no. I guess you ought to feel flattered,' Mike replied. 'They must know how important you are.' He was, in fact, thoroughly shaken by the going over they had experienced. He was already feeling the cold from the hole in the floor and was not hopeful about their immediate future. He was off his course, and, fore-warned of a vulnerable Lysander on the way south, there was every chance of a swarm of night fighters being scrambled. The predicted cloud cover had not materialized either, and as soon as Mike had picked up the River Seine and recovered his bearings, he went down to 500 feet and asked his passengers to keep a sharp look-out astern.

It was a miserable journey all the way. The draught whistling up from the flak hole made map reading difficult and was speedily freezing his right leg. He twice lost his turning point and had to climb up to 2,000 feet to recover his position. The flak surprised them again, too, light flak squirting up suddenly from a train in a siding. Five minutes later, Mike found himself on the outskirts of Beaumont and could not turn before more flak came up from two sites by the river. Whaam! Whaam! Whaam! The arching tracer, slow at first, faster, faster still, a streaking curve of death ending in a yellow spark — yellow sparks on all sides, above and below.

Mike was angry with the implacable gunners and angry with himself. His passengers had enough to face in the coming weeks without being threatened with the firing squad before they had reached their destination. And now, for the first time, he wished he had never got onto this Special Duties work. At least he had always before been able to fire back, and had been alone in the machine without the responsibility of defenceless passengers. He had been the only one to suffer from his own ineptitude.

Five minutes later, Mike picked up the big octagonal forest, one of his two target landmarks, swung onto a 90-degree magnetic course and in five seconds, there was the Oise, the big loop in the river, the little village of Poissy with its tall church spire. Mike turned again onto a northerly heading, and almost at once picked up the target field, rectangular, on rising ground and surrounded by forest land. The shadows of the trees made it appear even smaller than it was, and with this very light wind, it was not going to be easy getting in.

Mike went rapidly through the cockpit drill: on with the fuselage tank, switch signalling lamp to Morse, mixture control full back, armrests down to allow greater freedom, perspex sliding windows set open. The code letters were the first detail he had briefed himself on that morning, and now he circled the field anti-clockwise at 300 feet waiting for a light to shine out.

'Tighten your straps back there,' he said into the intercom, 'and one of you stay on board to unload and reload if there's anything to take back.'

The light flashed half-way round on his second circuit. Letters O.K., and he tapped out his own letters. A minute later the three dim lights of the inverted 'L' came on, torches not always held steadily, the tension down there being very severe at this point. Who else could see the lights in this blacked-out land? they would be wondering. Was this black machine the real thing? Or a disguised Boche? Were there Boches in the forest biding their time? Mike knew that men's fingers would be clutching Stens more tightly, that the tension would remain fierce until he was safely airborne again and they could busy themselves with unpacking the arms and supplies.

Full flaps, slots fully extended, engine just ticking over in the final approach, almost a gliding approach. A touch of side slip, a blip of throttle. Mike never used his landing lights, preferring to retain his night vision; and from the high-set cockpit, he had an excellent view forward.

He was coming down to short grass, well-drained, he hoped. They had helpfully laid out sheets longitudinally on the left-hand side parallel with his strip. He pulled the throttle right back, brushed the tops of the pines with his undercarriage, and held off the Lysander at 50 A.S.I., maybe 40 m.p.h. true speed, and let her sink.

There was, he reckoned, less than fifty yards left when he came to a standstill, turned right between the upwind lights and opened up the throttle to taxi fast back again to the base downwind light. There were men running alongside, ghost figures in the moonlight, Stens over their shoulders, berets on their heads, guiding him. Then he turned sharp through 170 degrees beside the touch-down light ready for take-off, and locked his brakes, leaving the engine running.

'Bonsoir!' 'Eh bien, vite, vite!' There was a jostling throng beside them, arms waving. He heard the rear cockpit canopy slide open, and one of his passengers jumped down, caught and held by two of these men of the Resistance. A tall man seemed to be in command, bald and unarmed, calling out for order. No gestures from him. And they were getting organized, one group of half a dozen standing ready beside the passenger compartment, arms raised to receive, another group standing by to carry them to the forest verge.

Mike unstrapped himself and climbed out. 'Est-ce-que je peux prendre un de vos draps? On a été bien reçu et il y a un trou à boucher.'

He rolled the coarse fabric into a tight ball, thinking of the number of times the sheet would have been beaten clean on the banks of the Oise, and of the housewife's dismay at this enforced sacrifice 'pour la patrie'. 'Ah, mon Dieu, Henri ...' He forced it between the rough edges of the splinter hole, tearing his gauntlets on the folded-back alloy. By the cockpit light, he could see that another inch to the left and it would have severed his rudder cable.

The bald *réseau* commandant appeared to have lost control of the situation again. When Mike had completed his repair, the sound of the voices rose above the tick-over of his engine. There were twenty or thirty young men, and several women, crowding under the starboard wing, and four figures appeared to be the centre of attention, Watermelon and Dorothée who were explaining about the Pole and the Irishman being unable to fly.

They were all speaking French, and Mike forced his way

140

through saying firmly, in his execrable accent, 'Pardon, il faut que nous partions immédiatement.' He held the arms of the two passengers he was to take home, and tried to lead them towards the steps. Before he could do so and amidst all the shouting and confusion, his attention was drawn, as if by some spontaneous chemical fusion, to a figure beside him in the half light.

He knew at once that it was the woman passenger, the Dorothée he had just flown here. He knew, too, from her stance, from the tilt of her head, the configuration of her shoulders, her whole bearing, that it was someone he knew; and, as fast as a reflection from a mirror, the face was there, close beside him, looking straight at him from no more than two feet away.

Eileen's hair had been cut short, shorter than when she had briefly been a Wren, and died black. She was looking at him steadily, face caught in an expression of wonderment, frozen just for the tenth of a second that seemed like ten minutes while recognition swept over them both, excluding them from the turmoil and noise about them, leaving them in a vacuum of mutual joy and anxiety.

Whatever was said would sound stupid, or at the best inadequate, later. By any reckoning, it would have been better to have broken the spell, severed the visual line of communication, and gone about their urgent tasks. But the words inevitably came, Mike first: 'Eileen, for God's sake — not you, not here!'

And then her face crumpled and she started to laugh, and broke into her mock cockney, 'Well, fancy meetin' you 'ere — ain't that nice now!'

It would have been better, too, if they had not embraced, though that alone lifted the morale of the *réseau* 100 per cent, and, temporarily at least, satisfied the romantic appetite of these good people of Aisne. It also brought silence and order as Mike and Eileen briefly held each other and even more briefly kissed.

In her own voice now, Eileen whispered, 'Happy landings, Mike darling.'

And all he could say before turning and climbing back up into the cockpit was, 'This is crazy — this can't be happening ... I'm going to ...'

They were cheering now, holding their berets down against the Lysander's slipstream, and scattering to give him space for take-off. He waved once but could not distinguish one figure from another. The torches had been switched on again. He had no need of them, and the Lysander was off in less than 100 yards, with full emergency boost to take him over the trees, the winding Oise below intermittently reflecting the full light of the moon like a heliograph signal.

* * *

It had not been easy to get to the Major, and when he did he was not at first reassured. He was a big man with a small head with very close-cut — almost Prussian cut — grey hair. Mike had time to study him at leisure because he did not look up from his papers for some time. Small, spatulate fingers with too long, too obviously manicured nails, defaced by nicotine stain. There was a cigarette between the first and second fingers of his right hand, and another, only half smoked, burned in the ashtray.

'Well,' he said, still without looking up. And when he did, Mike saw grey eyes. There was great depth in them, and he recognized now that he was in the presence of man of unusual intelligence. Those eyes now fell to Mike's wings and decoration ribbons. 'Well, as we pongos say, this is all very irregular. You're only half in this game, Squadron Leader. And even if you were one of our Baker Street regulars, we wouldn't be saying anything.'

'O.K., but I just wanted to put a few facts before you.' He took the proffered cigarette and sat down without being invited. 'I took my fiancée over the night before last, unknowingly of course. She was a back up — Dorothée. You know something about her background, well-born, fluent French of course, personable. But I know a bit more.'

Mike explained briefly about the breakdown, without mentioning its cause, told him about the parents' deaths. 'She's much better now, I guess. But I don't reckon she's stable enough to take on this job — or anything like it. It's not the first time she has disappeared as she did three months ago again — not a word to anyone ...'

'Including you?' The grey face under the grey hair was set in a smile for the first time.

'Sure.'

'I'm not suggesting you're a cocky Yank,' the Major said slowly. 'I know your record. But you don't know everything about S.O.E. just because you've done a crash course in sabotage and defence and taken our Joes in and out.' His cigarette joined the earlier one, still smoking, in the ashtray, and he lit another. 'Just listen to this. Eileen Barrett came to us at our invitation in October. She was screened with our usual thoroughness. We know everything about her. And she passed out well. She has been through the Army Physical Training Corps course, crawling about under real fire. She has done drops at night from b. loons and aircraft. She has been 'captured' and interrogated for hours on end, as if she had been picked up by the Gestapo, to try to break her cover. She came through it all exceptionally well. She is a skilful and dedicated young lady, and we have every confidence that she will succeed in her task.'

The Major got up and strolled over to the window, a hard man who was at first dismaying, and then provoked an interest into the mysteries of his mind. Mike realized that he would gladly have worked for him, and at the same time wondered how many people he had been responsible, however indirectly, for sending to Avenue Foch and then — what was left of them — to Dachau concentration camp.

'Who knows,' the Major continued, peering out at a wet April morning, low clouds scudding above the Marylebone rooftops, 'who knows — you might be ordered to bring her home.'

He turned to Mike again. 'Now, get back to Southdean, and don't fret about your admirable fiancée.' His smile was wide, the smoke from the cigarette in the corner of his mouth rising to a watery eye. 'Or I shall inform the U.S.A.A.F. authorities that we have an officer deserter on our hands.'

'Gee, you really do know everything,' exclaimed Mike, laughing. 'O.K., Major.' They shook hands, and Mike left feeling a great deal better, but still with a hot shaft of fear for Eileen thrusting through his stomach.

Then he went and saw Jack Hulbert and Cicely Courtneidge in *Something in the Air*, got mildly drunk at the Flying Club, and took the last train to Worthing, reading in the evening newspaper excited speculation about the opening of the Second Front.

7

Pilotless Enemies

In his own style, Range Powell could get things just right. They were over the beaches at 0800 hours 6 June, 1944. Through drifting smoke over a wide area of the Normandy countryside, and from numerous ships off the coast, they could see landing craft like scattered matchsticks thrown into the sea, some touching the shore at an angle, others drifting and blazing, more and more coming in from the north in haphazard groups, untidily arranged. Warships — sloops, frigates, corvettes, lean destroyers, bigger cruisers — sped about the grey sea without seeming purpose, scrawling the ocean white with their bow waves and stern wakes.

Farther out in the Channel the yellow muzzle flashes from heavy guns drew the eye to near invisible bulky shapes, slow-moving battleships bombarding shore targets. There were men down there, tens of thousands of fighting men, and frightened, huddled French civilians. Their own Typhoons were too high, the visibility too poor, for the pilots to distinguish any detail of the fighting. Inland, among the fields and hedgerows and woodlands, along narrow winding roads, they could make out the shapes of military transports: the Germans bringing up reinforcements, their own Typhoons' target for today....

Range Powell surveying all this, the culminating moment of the greatest war of all time, the smoke and flames of battle where men were dying and fear and glory and pain were all playing their

144

parts at full stretch — Range Powell switched on and transmitted, 'Sufferin' snakes, someone's having a bloody difference of opinion down there.'

More solemnly, Keith in his new Typhoon with the latest improvements and bubble hood, was thinking, 'I can tell my grandchildren, "I've seen history being made. I helped fight them back when they tried to invade us, and I saw us invading them."'

Two huge formations of American Marauders above them, on a slightly different course, were cutting in and out of cloud. 2nd T.A.F. medium bombers would be over, too, and B17 Fortresses and Liberators by the hundred, and Bomber Command Lancasters and Halifaxes, and scores of fighter-bombers like themselves. Keith had seen the orders, knew that there were hundreds of Spitfires and Mustangs on protective patrol. But he had not yet heard a single report, a single alarm, of German counter-attack in the sky. Control in the air, control of the seas, appeared to be total. If the Allies could crash their way through the defences down there (Keith had seen them from nought feet — cliffs riddled with concrete emplacements and gun muzzles, barbed wire like head-high brambles, thousands of steel and concrete obstructions in the sea, hundreds of cupolas concealing gun muzzles, unseen minefields everywhere) then surely nothing could prevent these great armies from liberating Europe.

Range Powell, Polo Satterthwaite and Keith had pored over the Top Secret P.R.U. map of the road system south of Caen the night before, an irregular spider's web of main roads, minor roads and tracks, and identified the area 2nd T.A.F.'s Intelligence had selected for them as a likely route for the columns of reinforcing 12th S.S. Panzer Division. Their bombing technique had been worked out in the smallest detail over the past months, and constant practice against target vehicles on the bombing range had given them a high rate of accuracy.

Keith, with a 250,000 map strapped to one knee and a photograph to the other, turned his squadron 90 degrees to starboard just west of Caen, and reduced height. He had managed to scrape together fourteen aircraft by bullying Chiefy to work through the night on two machines due for an engine change. That had meant leaving behind only three pilots, disappointed new members of the squadron who would get their chance later in the day.

Polo called up, 'Champion line of heavy stuff (he pronounced it "stoof") coming up that road ten o'clock almost below.'

Keith had seen it. The rising dust from the wheels of tank transporters had revealed the Panzer reinforcements; and 3.7 cm. tracer flak and 20 mm. from a *Flakvierling 38* confirmed that there were prime targets about.

'Fuse your babies. A Flight follow me, B Flight in ninety seconds, from — now!'

Long shapes, well spaced for safety, spread out on this winding, narrow road, mottle-painted, newly-cut branches over the tanks. At a standstill now, crews scattering into hedges; black and white cows scattering, too, reflecting the sudden panic about them. Horses running across a field as another four-barrel *Flakvierling 38* opened up. Two black figures pausing, then running from hoeing their vegetable patch to the shelter of their cottage. (*They were Claude and Marie-Louise Despont, childless and aged fifty-seven and fifty-two, who had lived here since their marriage in 1909. They survived the fighting, though they had to live in their cellar for four days and nights when the breakthrough passed by. Both their cows died in the shellfire after suffering great distress from not being milked, and all but one of their pigs were looted. The Desponts died in the same year, 1968. The newer stone of the repaired east wall of their cottage from shell damage is still visible.*)

All this detail enlarged in Keith's screen like a focusing telescope, until he could identify individual soldiers, some lying on their backs in the fields, firing their rifles just as British Tommies and French Poilus had defiantly used their rifles on the sands of Dunkirk; the Desponts' collie dog with head raised, no doubt adding his own note of defiance to the din; a German motorcyclist with sidecar racing across a meadow on a zig-zag course instead of halting to use his machine-gun against them — and he would be in trouble later, Keith reckoned.

But the picture in its entirety was short-lived, a quick-flashed impression only, which blurred again as the target loomed up. They had learned by experience that a shallow dive was best against traffic, no more than 45 degrees, like the rocket Typhoons, firing their cannon as a discouragement to the opposition once steady on the target, and bombs released at no more than 200 feet.

This was what Keith did now, taking the brunt as usual, steady

146

at 500 feet with no more evasive action, centre dot on one of the trailers: big trailers, multi-wheeled, long slug-like trailers, his prime target and the trailer behind with the tank tarpaulin-covered as well as with branches spread over — a forest of branches like the Forest of Burnham Wood. They could only be Tigers, most feared of German tanks, Dr Ferdinand Porsche's massive masterpiece.

Tiger tanks laughed off 20 mm. cannon fire, and Keith concentrated on the trailer's cab, squeezed the bomb-release button at the end of the throttle handle, floated up like a labourer relieved of his load, and continued his fire against the next trailer, and the one behind it, where there was a curve in the track and a spinney of tall trees above another cottage. He had to pull back hard on the stick, tree tops now seen flittingly below him, very close.

A sharp turn to port, kicking rudder left, right. The new bubble canopy gave him marvellous visibility, and he was able to watch proprietorially all but his number two and Red Section behind him complete their run. That was Range in what he insisted on calling B- Bloody, a new Typhoon with bubble hood like his own. He was to succeed Keith as C.O. in forty-eight hours and did not yet know it. Range, back in France, where they had fought together until the government fell to their knees and begged for mercy from an army smaller than their own.

Range and Keith — what a lot of fighting they had shared! Down the Aussie came now, leading B Flight, seemingly impervious to the flak. A Flight's bombs had all exploded. Too soon to judge the effect. Range and his Flight touched the tip of the smoke cloud and went for the tanks farther west, bombs falling to conform with the angle of the aircraft, with scarcely time for gravity to shape a curved path — two bombs, two more, two, a pilot late and a pause, then two more....

The last of B Flight was only just clear when Range's bombs sent gouts of earth and stone and black fragments high into the sky; and Keith at 2,000 feet on the west side of the road now, guessed the black fragments were from Range's direct hit. That veteran Aussie never seemed to miss.

Range was to reform and rendezvous the squadron five miles north of Omaha Beach while Keith ran over the target area with the P.R.U. camera he had had fixed. They continued to fire at him, but it was ragged stuff. The bombing had been all right.

There were half a dozen craters well off into the fields, but at least ten right down the centre of the track which had hurled transporters and tanks into the ditches, one direct hit by a 500-pounder scattering debris like blood from a fatal wound, slashing off the treetops in the nearby wood. Even the 185 mm. armour of a Tiger could not resist the power of a bomb on its turret.

Keith clicked the shutter once, twice and a third time. He was doubtful of the results in these misty, smoke-laden conditions. But he could report seven or eight Tiger tanks destroyed, damaged, or at least delayed on their way to the fighting front.

* * *

Twilight, 18 June 1944. Almost the longest day of the year, and at ten minutes to eleven there was still light enough to make out the silhouette of the French coast to the south, and the coast of Kent and Sussex to the north. Keith Stewart, Wing Commander R.A.F., with a D.S.O. and two D.F.C.s, was flying east in mid-Channel at 5,000 feet, awaiting a visual or a radar report on one of Hitler's new *Vergeltungswaffe* — the much-heralded terror weapons.

They would come. As night would follow this twilight, the V1s would come, pulsing up from their sites in northern France, racing across the Channel for London, their rocket motors gyroscopically cutting out, sending them — momentarily silent — plunging down to detonate their ton of high explosive. Maybe a dozen houses wiped out, another dozen made uninhabitable, a hundred people — men, women and children — killed or maimed. The ultimate in indiscriminate murder....

They should have first been launched months ago, and should have been coming over in waves — hundreds a day to pulverize the capital. Instead, a mere ten V1s, or flying bombs, had been launched for the first time on the night of 13 June, thanks to the combined inefficiency of the German organization, and the pulverizing effect of bombing attacks on the sites, stores, and transport — like Randall's train.

The cry of the codeword 'Diver!' that had gone out that night throughout all the defence commands had been muted. Only four V1s reached England, only one did any damage and caused casualties. No announcement had been made to the public. But two nights later, night fighter pilots patrolling the Channel,

Observer Corps officers, and radar controllers (like Squadron Officer Jenny Simpson on the T16 at Swingham) watched in dismay as the night sky seemed suddenly filled with flying bombs, some 200 of them reaching the English coast, more than seventy exploding in London, causing severe damage and casualties.

Keith turned his Tempest through 180 degrees, knowing that on the T16 tube at Swingham, his reverse course would be plotted. The voice came over the air as he levelled out. A female voice. Jenny's? There were two W.A.A.F. controllers at Swingham, and reception was not too good tonight.

'Hullo Mushroom,' it called him. 'Diver ten o'clock fifteen miles, steering 315. Vector 275.'

Keith thrust forward the throttle and at once felt the pressure of the seat against his back. The Tempest, the new, developed and refined cousin of the Typhoon, was the fastest R.A.F. fighter anyway. But in collaboration with Napiers, who made the Sabre engine, Keith had had the power of his unit uprated to run on special fuel, had stripped his aircraft of armour plate and other unnecessary weight, including the standard dull camouflage paint, leaving a smooth shiny surface on wings and fuselage. The Mark V Tempest really was a flyer.

He could see a distant blob of flame far to the south on his port quarter, but that was not his. That was for one of the other patrolling Tempests or Mosquitoes, and Swingham was already vectoring another fighter onto it. His came into sight, almost dead ahead, at the same moment — slim, torpedo-shaped body all high explosive, pulse-jet motor attached to the rear end like a horizontal stove pipe, and a pair of vestigial wings. That was all. But inhuman, malignant, and a greater terror to its intended victims than any manned bomber.

Over the past days, Keith had worked up a passionate hatred for these devices that tore through the air and threatened to blast London apart. But he had seen what they did — those pathetic stains among the suburban housing estates and the tight-packed working-class homes of inner London, the exposed inner walls and fireplaces, the stairs leading to nowhere, scattered clothes, shattered furniture, and flapping curtains, privacy and life itself at once and suddenly extinguished. Blood in Honeysuckle Lane, Surbiton, and in Prince Edward tenements, Wandsworth.

This V1 was unusually low, no more than 1,400 feet above the sea, and Swingham confirmed that it was a fast one, too. 'Hullo Mushroom, your Diver twelve o'clock below, speed 390.'

It was Jenny all right, sitting in her nissen hut in the dark, stool pulled close to the tube.

390. That gave him no time for a miscalculated interception course.

'O.K. Mushroom. I have him.'

Keith banked the Tempest to starboard, and put her into a shallow dive, the speed rapidly building up to give him 50 m.p.h. superiority. He had had his guns synchronized to 250 yards. Anything less and he could blow himself up with his target. Much more than 350 yards, and it was almost impossible to make a hit. The V1 had wings half the span of a 109 fighter and just eight inches thick. The 'fuselage' gave only a three-feet wide target.

The heat glow from the rocket engine simplified sighting but even in this half light tended to distract and glare. Keith could still make out the robot's shape and bring it into his sight, drawing the dot through the body for a 10-degree deflection burst.

Once, he had despaired of his aim. So many years of reluctant shooting at live game as a boy when he had subconsciously shot badly, not caring to kill; then the poor results with the towed drogue at gunnery school; and even in the earlier days of the war, he seemed to need all his ammunition to make a strike.

Now he had learned to relax and concentrate at the same time, now he was darn near as good a shot as Mike; and now, at 2254 hours on this June evening, twenty miles south of Rye, he came down on the flying bomb until its little wings filled the range bars. Then he touched, almost caressed, the gun button.

The four cannon tucked into his wings spewed their shells at the target — one second, two seconds, three seconds. No more. Any closer and he would follow the V1 down into the Channel. Then, as he eased thumb pressure on the button and began to pull away, the robot blew up in his face, an all-consuming burst of light, as if someone had hurled a pot of yellow paint at his windscreen. His Tempest rocked out of control and the heat poured through the vents like a suddenly opened furnace door. (Keith's battledress sleeves already bore the scorch marks of an earlier encounter, and he had had to draw a new Mae West from stores.)

Then he felt the controls respond again, and pulled up for height. Jenny would have seen the two blips blend together as one on her screen. Now, as he turned sharply east again to resume his patrol, she would record with relief that the V1 on its steady course had disappeared from her screen, and that Keith had survived. There was no need to present that information to the enemy.

It was a bad night. 108 more flying bombs were aimed at targets in England, and seventy-eight got through the fighter defences, and then the guns and balloons, to wreck and kill and maim. Jenny directed Keith onto a second one in his patrol area, and this time he lost it in cloud at the coast after firing a single burst aimed at the brilliant glow of the exhaust in the gathering darkness. The Mosquito pilots were having the same problem of glare at night, and dark glasses were not the answer. R.A.E. at Farnborough must find it, and quickly....

June was a hectic month for everyone concerned, on the one hand with sustaining the offensive in the small toehold the Allies had gained in Normandy, and on the other hand, protecting London and other southern cities from the menace of the robot flying bombs, the V1s, or Doodlebugs as the English public named them, finding comfort in mocking what they most feared. For Keith the work seemed endless, and the pressure worse even than in the Battle of Britain, for now he had the administrative task of setting up a new Wing, as well as the personal task of fighting the flying bombs in one of the few machines that could catch them straight and level.

Two days after D-Day, Keith had handed 727 Squadron over to Range Powell. The Aussie had exclaimed, 'Stone the bloody crows!' and his batwoman had proudly added a new thin stripe between the wider stripes of a Flight Lieutenant. Then Keith had driven straight to Latchetts Green on the Kent-Sussex border to set up 338 Wing, 2nd T.A.F., consisting of 35, 40 and 178 Squadrons, an appropriate number of pilots, ground and admin personnel, stores and supplies — but no aircraft.

There was a strike at the factory building the new Tempests with which they were to be equipped — 'A bleedin' *strike* in invasion month and soddin' London bein' torn apart!' Bill Watson had exclaimed with venom. But it was true, and they were given a few early Typhoons that had mysteriously not been pranged to keep their hands in. Keith himself had taken the first Tempest, had gone to Kingston to fetch it, named it Nero, and then prepared it for its new role of Doodlebug chaser. By 20 June another half-dozen had come through, and were stripped for the task.

*   *   *

21 June. A wet and miserable morning with low, scudding cloud. They could have got off the ground, and found their way back again. But they would never have seen the V1s, and the wear-and-tear on their engines was already stretching the resources of the engine fitters without wasting flying hours. At 2.30 p.m. Keith stood outside his office, feeling the rain beating on his hat. Above the sound of the rain, he could hear the off-beat pulses, like an old single-cylinder motor cycle straining uphill, which told of the arrival of another flying bomb. It passed close overhead, causing the windows of his office to rattle. The radar-directed guns would pick it up later, but they were not having much success so far, the height being awkward for the 3.7s and too much for the light guns. The chances were that it would explode somewhere in the Greater London area, with the usual terrible consequences.

As soon as its sound had faded, it was replaced by another — no, two more, one far to the east and another closer to the west. The launching sites were busy, taking advantage of the bad weather.

Bill Watson joined Keith in the drizzle. To Watson's consternation, he had been selected as C.O. of 35 Squadron — the ex-Halton boy who had only wanted to fly and fight, had later been bullied into accepting a commission after getting a D.F.M. and Bar in the Battle of Britain, and was now a senior officer with the responsibilities of command. But as Keith had expected, he had slotted into the role well (even if his language remained as lurid as ever) and his pilots admired him for his experience and skill.

Now Watson said, 'What're we going to do about these buggers, Boss?'

'Nothing — not in this.' He put his face up into the rain, shook out his hat and climbed into his car standing beside them. 'Let's go over to Swingham and get the gen.'

'The trouble is, Bill,' Keith said as he drove out of the station gates, acknowledging the guard's salute, 'we've got to get organized. Met. says it'll be fine tomorrow, maybe later today — scattered cloud and a clear night. So we'll scramble as soon as the first wave comes in, and so will every Tom, Dick and Harry hereabouts — you've seen them. Old Mark V Spits, Typhoons, American Thunderbolts, I even saw a Hurricane the other day over Dymchurch. They're all out to have a go.'

'And they're all getting in the sodding way.' Watson had been deprived of a V1 two days earlier by the intervention of a pair of Spitfire IXs that got in his line of sight, had a go themselves, found they were too slow, and the Doodlebug had got away. At night it was even worse, with German intruders infiltrating the patrols with the latest Mark 109s and 190s, adding to the chaos and having some success, too.

The fact was that, apart from the Mustang, and a handful of the new Meteor jets (the first in the R.A.F. but having a lot of teething troubles), the Tempest was the only effective fighter against V1s.

'I'm going up to Group tonight,' Keith said. 'And try to sort things out.' He adapted one of Churchill's famous appeals. ' "give us the sky, and we'll finish the job." '

Swingham's T16 was high up above the old C.H. Station where Jenny had served as a junior officer four years earlier. The site consisted of two aerials, one a vertical half moon in shape for recording the height, and the big rectangular aerial that rotated day and night searching the Channel for intruders, manned and unmanned.

Jenny, telephoned by the guard on the gate, welcomed them into the control room, saluting Keith solemnly and disregarding his wink. It was nearly three months since they had married at Caxton Hall, Tom and Moira — sworn to secrecy — the only witnesses, and Keith could still not accustom himself to the comforting and scarcely believable sense of possession — now, under these circumstances, temporarily irrelevant.

A new wave of V1s was just beginning to come over, and Jenny led them up the length of the dark hut so that they could watch events from the ground end. Her number two, a Flying Officer, was bending over the table, drawing lines with a chinagraph pencil and a ruler, and marking the course of two flying bombs on

153

the tube. A third blip, very faint and over the French coast, told of another.

'You can almost see the devils take off,' Keith noted. 'How high is that one?' he asked the senior controller, Squadron Leader Miles.

'Too early to say,' he replied. 'But they climb very fast, and we get a better reading the nearer they come.'

A pair of Mosquitoes were patrolling in weather that was suddenly clearing, and the controller brought them both south on an interception course.

'Hullo Household, vector 210 — two, one, zero. Diver nine o'clock, twenty-two miles. Over.'

They heard the pilot's answering voice, crackling, hollow-sounding in the dark hut. 'Roger, Blackbird.'

The V1's blips marched across the Channel in great strides matching the aerial's rotations, and they could see the Mosquito on its interception course, striving to close the gap before the coast was reached.

Then other blips appeared, coming out from the English coast. 'Oh Lord!' Jenny exclaimed. 'Here we go again. Every blessed pilot in A.D.G.B. and 2nd T.A.F. thinks they're ripe game.'

The drama of this V1 engagement was presented to them in its entirety on the small rectangle of glass, and from the loudspeaker beside it, a drama as fast-moving as the robot itself. The Mosquito, with the initial advantage of height, got within range of its prey, and the two blips blended into one for almost a minute. Keith could imagine the pilot firing from as close as he dared from astern. Then other blips blended in, too, from both sides, and the pilot's angry voice came over the air, 'For Christ's sake clear off, you in the bloody Spitfire.' Then, 'Hullo Blackbird, this is a bloody shambles. Can you get these other kites clear? I've just nearly shot one down.'

The controller transmitted, 'All aircraft in the Rye area after Diver, please return to base.' Then, 'Household, what's the gen?'

There was silence for a moment. The V1 had crossed the coast just west of Rye, pulsing its way implacably towards London — in and out of the scattered cloud, while below, people working in the fields, people in the villages, in Hawkhurst and Tonbridge, and then in the outer suburbs, would hear the approaching sound, the dreaded beat, and would look up and pray that it would continue on its way — just a bit farther, so that someone else would get it....

Then the Mosquito pilot: 'Hullo Blackbird. The guns are having a go now. Mostly at me. Oh Christ — that was close!' Those clueless Pongos ...'

It was the last they heard from Household until the Mosquito resumed its patrol out in the Channel; while according to Observer Corps plots, this V1 continued on its course towards the capital.

Another Tempest Wing had lost two aircraft to defending gunfire in the first week, others had been damaged. While the rate of launchings steadily increased, no sort of co-ordination of the defences appeared to have been worked out.

Keith said to Jenny, 'I think you should come along to the meeting at Group. This business has got to be sorted out, and you know the picture as well as anyone.' She was not looking well, and Keith longed to have her (his *wife*, for heaven's sake!) alone for a few minutes, but there was no opportunity in this busy Ops Room. Instead, Jenny agreed to attend if she could get away, and took the place of the Flying Officer in front of the screen, slipping on the headset and at once picking up the scene: the total professional.

As Keith and Watson left, he could hear her transmitting, 'Hullo Mainstay, hullo Mainstay, this is Blackbird. I have a Diver for you ...'

'Bloody tough grind,' Watson commented as they got back into the car. 'They also serve, who only sit and bloody well control . . .'

On 338 Wing they became more and more skilful and destructive in dealing with the flying bombs. Bill Watson became the top scorer, once getting three on one patrol. 'Get under the buggers,' he would say over a pint. 'Dead astern, get your nose up, open fire at 300, close to 250, and then out of the way, whether you've got him or not.'

A wild Pole, Flight Lieutenant Wrynkowski, who had served with Keith on 151 Squadron in the full heat of the Battle of Britain, perfected an economical method of destroying V1s. 'I teep zem into ze zea. Eazy!' he told Keith one day. And Keith, half-impressed, half-disbelieving, went up and watched the Pole in action. They caught one close to Folkestone. The Pole ripped

155

up alongside the chugging robot in Hendon-style close formation, slipped in closer still, until his starboard wing was no more than a foot under the V1's port wing. This caused such turbulence in the air around the wing that the gyro was thrown off balance, and as the robot began to sway Wrynkowski rapidly withdrew.

For a second the flying bomb wavered on its course as if flown by a drunkard, then it went over onto its back, and plunged into the sea, sending a 300-feet spray gout up into the air....

'You zee, zir. Eazy!' the Pole transmitted cockily.

It did not always work, but was useful when you were out of ammunition.

Then a sergeant-pilot on 178 Squadron one day tried flying ahead of a V1, throttled back so that the machine gained on him, was caught in the Tempest's slipstream, lost control, and again dived in.

Unfortunately, this flying bomb landed in the transport park of a gun battery, destroying most of their lorries and cars but causing no casualties. As the ack-ack gunners were highly unpopular with 338 Wing, this was regarded as the greatest triumph of the campaign. Keith thought it diplomatic to drive over and apologize.

Keith shot down five flying bombs, but as the campaign intensified, he had so much work to do on the ground that he could fly only once or twice a week. The first problem was keeping his Wing's machines flying at all. The Sabre engine was much more reliable than it had been, but it was being subjected to very high boost levels in order to pursue the V1s and this was telling on maintenance. Everyone on the engine side was having a hard time, from the senior Engineering Officer down to the humblest engine fitter.

All the ground staff were under heavy pressure. Over and above the routine servicing and engine changes, the Tempests were frequently damaged by flying debris, and several times the rudder canvas was burned right through by the heat of an exploding bomb.

But Keith managed to keep the patrols going day and night — at night fitted with a new optical gunsight which gave good results, aided by searchlights which were dipped and pointed in the direction of approaching V1s.

Keith tried out this sight on the last night patrol on 12 July. Two images were superimposed on the sight, aimed at the exhaust flame of the flying bomb, and their coincidence one on top of the other, indicated the point at which to open fire. Again the searing ball of fire, the blast of heat — and Keith resumed his patrol in the early dawn light.

Jenny had been controlling, and that always brought Keith luck and satisfaction. Ten minutes later, she called up again. 'Hullo Mushroom, this is Blackbird. More trade for you at 6 o'clock.' There was a pause, then, urgently, 'Not Diver, Mushroom. Repeat not Diver. Suspect Bandit at angels 6, repeat suspect Bandit angels 6 at 6 o'clock. Course 270, speed 380.'

In a split second, the experienced Jenny had distinguished this manned machine from a V1 by its height and course, recognized that it was hostile from the absence of an I.F.F. (Identification Friend or Foe) signal, and had warned Keith just in time.

How close it had been, how narrowly she had saved him, Keith saw as he wrenched the control column to port and back, threw open the throttle, and went into a tight spiral climb, pursued by lines of slashing tracer. In less than two minutes he was at 9,000 feet. There was a touch of dawn light up here, but he could see nothing of his attacker.

'Hullo Blackbird, any sign of that Bandit?'

Jenny came back crisply, 'I've lost him, Mushroom.' Then, 'Stand by'. A pause. 'Blackbird calling. I have him at ten miles south-east Folkestone, steering 090.' Another pause as she made rapid calculations. 'Angels three, speed 375.'

Keith pushed the Tempest's nose hard down and aileroned onto an approximate intersecting course, based on the dim outline of the English coastline.

'Steer zero three zero.'

'Roger.'

'Zero four zero, Mushroom.'

'Roger.'

The T16 must be getting clear blips now, and Jenny vectored him confidently.

'Zero four five, Mushroom. Bandit one o'clock, slightly below you. Bandit turning starboard now ...'

At that moment, Keith saw a faint flicker of exhaust flame. He was overshooting and had to throttle back as he went into a dive to get below.

'Tally ho, Blackbird.'

He momentarily lost sight of the flame but was close enough to pick up the dark silhouette against the lighter sky above. A long-nosed 190 intruder, a fitting adversary for his Tempest in a day contest. But now ... like Keith a few minutes earlier, jumped and helpless.

Keith pulled up very close and right below. Almost nil deflection. Straight shooting. With total confidence in the result, he pressed the button for a two-second burst. His cannon shells tore into the underbelly of the Focke-Wulf. Every shell, it seemed, was striking home, like a clip from *Hell's Angels*. Too good, too horrible, to be true; a killing burst if ever there was, and as near to murder as that first Stuka he had tumbled back in '40.

The intruder did not blow up. With the pilot dead at the controls, and the controls themselves shot to pieces, the 190 was taken over by the vagaries of balance and gravity, turned slowly onto its back, and was lost to Keith's sight.

Then, five seconds later while Keith banked in a tight turn over the sea, the slate grey below was broken by a spread of white. It was a brief stain, gone before he could pinpoint it: one German pilot's grave, so hastily marked and so close to what could have been Keith's.

'Blackbird, Bandit destroyed.' Keith's voice sounded flat to his own ears.

'Wizard show, Mushroom.'

There was silence between them for four more minutes. There was a steady glow of dawn over the Straits of Dover now, and the swift-moving lights of distant V1s grew dimmer with the approach of sunrise.

Then a tiny pinprick of light racing out from the Pas de Calais. This one was for him — for sure — and seconds later, Jenny's voice:

'Steer zero eight five, Mushroom, steer zero eight five ...' There was a pause, then, in a voice that was now clearly halting, 'Mushroom, steer ...'

Keith, already on the course, and closing in fast on the V1, listened with concern as a male voice broke in, the transmission switch being inadvertently left on. 'That's all right,' the voice said. And then there was inaudible muttering, a click, silence.

158

Keith brought his Tempest onto the same course as the flying bomb, his mind confused and anxious. Without thinking, he lost height and made his calculations while the robot thundered on towards Folkestone,.its exhaust trailing continuous flame. He did not need his special night sight, steadied the centre dot on the tiny body of the bomb, both hands on the stick and told himself to relax.

He opened fire, failed to hit, fired again, too close, throttled back, lost his advantage. 'I'm cocking this up!' he told himself. 'But what the hell's going on down there?'

The second time, he blew the bomb up with the first few rounds, and turned sharply away from the flame and smoke in the sky. Blackbird was calling him, 'Any joy, Mushroom?' It was the voice of the Flying Officer controller he had seen at work when he had visited Swingham.

Keith did not answer. He was heading fast towards the Romney Marshes. There were the tall C.H. masts, and five miles north, the rising ground. The T16 station was more difficult to find in the dawn light, but in less than a minute, he was circling low above the aerials and camouflaged nissen huts.

'Hullo Blackbird, what's the gen?'

The Controller's voice came back crisply. 'No more trade for you at present, Mushroom.'

'I mean, what's going on at your place?' Keith could see lights below, contravening the blackout regulations. The door of the ops hut appeared to be open and there were figures standing in the light blazing out from it. A 5 cwt Commer with canvas top had drawn up close to the door. There was a big red cross painted on its roof.

'Fully operational, Mushroom,' said the Controller. 'But I have nothing for you. Are you returning to base?'

Keith was already heading for Latchetts Green, where he landed just before the sun rose, and taxied in fast.

The I.O. met Keith at the door but was brushed aside. 'Give me Ops One, and make it quick.' He had the telephone in one hand and was trying to get out a cigarette with the other. Jerry Owen gave him a hand, and lit a match. Keith, drawing heavily on the cigarette, was saying, 'What's going on at Blackbird...? No, I know it's fully operational, but the Controller suddenly broke off.'

A voice at the other end told him that he would try to find out. 'Was it a W.A.A.F. on duty?'

Keith said sharply. 'Yes, it was. Squadron Officer Simpson. Please let me know what happened at once.' He drew deeply on the cigarette, fingernails tapping the telephone's mouthpiece. Keith's mind flashed back to 1940, the Heinkel diving out of the mist and cloud to drop a stick clear across the C.H. Station. Jenny in the debris, dreadfully wounded. Ambulances at Swingham. And now?

'The Controller was unwell, sir, I understand.'

Keith barked, 'Put me onto Squadron Leader Miles there. Yes, direct. Don't bother to scramble.'

A minute later, Keith was listening to the voice at the other end, and himself breaking in. 'Yes, I see ... Yes, I'm sorry ... Oh, that's all right, then ... It was just rather odd, breaking off like that, especially as she's usually so steady ... No, no flap, old boy.' And Keith, becoming increasingly embarrassed, ended lamely, 'Thanks very much. Just concerned, you know. Very good Controller. I'm sorry. I hope it'll be all right.'

Jerry Owen was eyeing him curiously when he replaced the receiver. 'Anything the matter, sir?'

'No, nothing at all. I'll give you my report now.' Keith crushed out his cigarette and began to dictate to his I.O., relieved at his tact and calmness.

Then he ordered breakfast in his bedroom, and lay back reflecting on the odd shape of his life; reflecting that while he had been destroying one life, his Jenny, with a new life in her womb, had collapsed over the set and had had to be carried away unconscious. How had Jerry Miles put it? 'It seems all the W.A.A.F.s knew she was pregnant except Squadron Officer Simpson herself. Ah well, you never know with W.A.A.F.s — specially officers. Her husband'll be pleased.'

* * *

London was to suffer the ordeal of the flying bombs for many more weeks. Twelve thousand civilians were to die or be dreadfully injured, sometimes several hundred at a time, as at a Woolworth's store in Lewisham, or when the Guards' Chapel was struck during a packed service.

When 338 Wing scored their first century of V1s destroyed, a

160

number of the successful pilots organized a celebratory party at a local hotel. Keith did not go. Not only was he piled up with administrative work, but he felt no reason for celebrating while so many of 'the malignant robots' were getting through to their target. The next morning, he sent a pilot from each squadron up to Charing Cross station by train with orders to report to him on their return with an account of what they saw. They were chastened by the experience. 'I didn't know it was as bad as that, sir,' a Flight Sergeant from 40 Squadron confessed. And he went on to describe one incident, which had only taken place the night before, with the Heavy Rescue workers and firemen still bringing out the bodies from the rubble of a dozen houses in South Norwood....

All through July and well into August, the battle continued with unabated fury, with the Germans launching their robots from the easily concealed mobile sites as fast as they could be brought up from the supply depots, and the Allies answering by bombing these depots, the sites when they could be located, and shooting more and more of them down as they perfected their skills.

Keith's pilots became dead-eye shots and learned to shoot them down over the sea at precisely the right range, near enough to hit, distant enough to escape damage themselves. To their fury, they were deprived of their best zone close to the English coast when the gun batteries, equipped now with proximity fuse shells and S.C.R. 584 and B.T.L. predictors, were moved south from their sites inland. The guns had got the measure of the enemy now, and began shooting them out of the sky like clay pigeons, whether in the dark, in cloud or in good visibility.

Then, with the armies at last released from the Wehrmacht's grip that had held them close to the Normandy beaches for so long, the launching sites were slowly forced to retreat or were overwhelmed by the advancing tanks and infantry. The Germans took to launching them from bombers off the Dutch coast, and much more damage was done to London. But by the beginning of September the worst was over.

On 4 September 1944, Keith received a long signal from 2nd T.A.F. H.Q., and asked his squadron commanders to come to his office for a drink before luncheon.

Young Ron Easton was the first to arrive. Keith told him to sit down, and poured him a whisky. Since the Dieppe raid in August '42, he had earned a commission and rapid promotion, at length (and on Keith's recommendation) to Squadron Commander: a steady, tough fighter-pilot who had survived two hard years of ops. Now, though he did not know it, Keith had put him in for a D.F.C.

'How's your serviceability?' Keith asked him. The number of machines ready to fly had been a daily anxiety all through the Battle of the Doodlebugs.

'Ten O.K., three U/S, two engine changes, sir.'

'Good. You've got a clear week to get up to maximum.' Keith nodded to Watson and Walters as they came in together, and told them to help themselves from the bottle on the table.

'I've just heard we're back in business,' Keith told them, walking up and down with a cigarette. 'As we all expected. But it's good to get confirmation.'

'How's that, sir?' Easton asked.

'Finished with damn bugs. You can undo your top buttons, flash your silk scarves and wear flying boots in the mess again.' His commanders laughed, and Watson said, 'You mean we're sodding fighter pilots again, boss?'

Keith held up the signal. 'France next week. Long range tanks. But no rockets or bombs. We're pure pukka fighters. Antoise, on the Somme. That's our base. And the mesdemoiselles from Armentières are as lovely as ever — so I'm told. Have another drink to celebrate. I'm taking a week's leave ...'

* * *

Jenny had settled down to the quiet life of an expectant mother philosophically and with a good deal of self-mockery.

'Oh Keith, you should see me at the clinic,' she told him on the first evening of his leave. '*The* most obscene exercises, all in giggling rows on the floor. And then relaxation talks and dreadful things about dilation. I don't know what life's coming to. But I do get lovely extra rations. My dear, *piles* of milk and butter to make lovely new cannon fodder.'

They were back in Half Moon Street, which now felt properly lived in again, redecorated after years of neglect and with new curtains. Keith had done a quick recce to Antoise in his Tempest and had succeeded in smuggling back some French cheese and three bottles of champagne.

He poured her another glass and told her it was well known as being vital for pregnant ex-W.A.A.F. officers. 'Are you very cross, darling?' he asked.

'Not really. I was getting a bit stale as an officer. Bit above myself, too. Thought I could do anything. And then who did I pass out on, in mid-op?'

'I've never been so terrified. Far more terrifying than almost being bounced by that 190. I'm glad you waited until you spotted him before passing out.'

Keith smiled over the glass at Jenny, who was stretched out comfortably on a sofa in her luscious pre-war white dressing-gown. 'Thanks for that bit of live-saving drill, too,' he said. And then he decided to get up and kiss her, which he did for a long time, their champagne-tasting lips close together then wide apart.

* * *

Keith's trip to Antoise had been a strange and moving experience. Spread out beneath him was the historical evidence of victory, of the turning of the tide after five years of war. Smoke streamed from burning farmhouses, villages and towns. The roads were packed with the traffic of the advancing Allied armies jammed here and there at bridges blown by the fleeing Germans. Over the Channel ports — Boulogne, Calais, Dunkirk — it was like a film of 1940 played back in reverse, with the Germans struggling to maintain a toehold against hopeless odds.

All over the world, the pace of counter-attack was gaining momentum. In carrier warfare and island hopping, the Pacific Ocean was being reconquered by the Americans; new heart and new strength were behind the advance into Burma; the Russians were advancing into Europe, from Esthonia, through East Prussia and Poland to Bulgaria; armies from another Allied landing, this time in the south of France, were marching north and had already reached Lyons. In Italy Rome had long ago fallen.

Would the war be over by Christmas? On his return from Antoise, Keith saw the writing in the sky that told him that there were many query marks at the end of that question. Far away to the north-east, from somewhere over Holland, there hung an uneven line, like a giant vertical vapour trail. It was not the first he had seen, and he knew what it meant. That white scar in the sky was the trail of one more high explosive rocket aimed at London, the second of the German *Vergeltung* (or retaliation) weapons.

The first had landed on 8 September, silently, without warning. The V2s killed about twice as many people as a V1 flying bomb, and no fighter nor anti-aircraft gun could shoot them down; and their launching sites were very difficult to locate.

Jerry Owen had said only that morning, before Keith had taken off, 'We've been expecting the Hun to be sending these over for months, and still nobody knows what to do about them.'

'How many a day?' Keith had asked.

'Who's to tell, sir? Might be hundreds.'

Could one weapon, at this late hour, reverse again the course of the war and force the Allies to sue for peace? Only the advance of the armies, from east and west, to overrun the sites from which these rockets were launched could end the threat of destruction by rocket.

Then, just one week later, Keith led his Wing on an escort operation that seemed to suggest that the end of the war was not, after all, far away.

At Antoise they were under canvas for the first time. All about them, the timeless French rural life was pursued as if there had been no invasion in 1940, nor liberation in 1944. The stout women, in uniform black, and their husbands, toiled in the fields all day, working horse-drawn or oxen-drawn ploughs, hoeing between the rows of late vegetables, helped by their children when school was over.

The nearest village was untouched by shell or bomb. There was food in the shops, the bread coarse perhaps, the coffee ersatz, but no evidence of hunger or deprivation was reflected in the expressionless wrinkled brown faces of the local people.

Only on the airfield was there the evidence of war. It had been a peace-time base of the Armée de l'Air, and Keith remembered visiting it when he had been flying Hurricanes from Lens-La Bassée in 1940. The three great hangars had been gutted, and were now heaped piles of rusting girders and sheet steel in which could be identified fragments of Arados, Ju.52s and Heinkel 111s, like disturbed corpses in a smashed graveyard. All the brick buildings had also been razed to the ground, by a combination of Allied bombing and German self-destruction. Around the dispersals were the wrecks of 109G fighters and the latest Mark of Ju.88 bombers, stranded by lack of fuel and blown up by their crews before the retreat — just as the R.A.F. had left behind hundreds of Hurricanes in 1940.

338 Wing's junior officers slept two to a tent, while Keith and his three squadron commanders and senior officers had tents of their own, with three batmen between them. The Officers' Mess was a large marquee with folding tables and chairs, and a bar at one end, now well stocked with champagne and local wines. With the fine weather, and the scent of victory as well as the scent of the French countryside in the nostrils, there was a feeling of satisfaction in the Wing that Keith had not encountered in all these years of war.

'Big flap tomorrow,' Jerry Owen told Keith on the evening of 16 September. 'Bags of airborne boys going out.'

'And we're to escort?' asked Keith.

'Here, sir.' Owen clanked over to his desk and handed Keith a buff envelope marked 'Top Secret' in red. Keith pulled out a thick wad of papers. The top one was headed 'Operation Market Garden'. The following morning, the First Airborne Army, composed of the 1st and 6th British Airborne Divisions, three American divisions, and a Polish Brigade, were to seize three bridges across the Lower Rhine, thus opening the doors to Germany itself.

'Looks promising,' Keith commented.

'It's Monty's baby, and the luck seems to go with him.'

With the Wing at maximum strength, Keith led them off at ten o'clock in the morning. As they formed up, he reflected momentarily on the long and complex pattern of his flying life, from his first solo at Eldergrove back in 1938, through the disastrous campaign in France, the ordeal of the Battle of Britain, and the long years of patrols and balbos, shipping strikes and rhubarbs by day and by night, of escort ops like this one: this one, to help plunge in the first dagger thrust at Germany. From very junior officer, rebuked for beating up the airfield after his first victory with Mike on his twenty-first birthday, to commander of a Wing of the finest, fastest R.A.F. fighters.

'I've been lucky, all right, all right!' he told himself. 178 Squadron, fourteen aircraft in three fours and a pair, had formed up now, to port and five hundred yards behind. 'My God I've been lucky! And now I'd like just one more — just one to bring up my score to sixteen.'

But they saw no German fighters that day. Instead, they saw the biggest aerial armada of all time. It appeared out of the misty September sky from the west, over the Dutch islands from East Anglia — countless Dakotas full of supplies and paratroopers, countless towed gliders holding steady formation in a stream that seemed to stretch back clear across the North Sea to England.

There were Spitfire XIVs escorting them, and American 8th Air Force Mustangs, glittering like silver gems high above. Keith took up station on the starboard side of the stream at 7,000 feet. He did not have to give R/T orders. Every one of his pilots knew exactly what to do, every one would be scanning the sky for a sign of enemy fighters swooping down on the fattest, juiciest target they would ever see....

For the following half-hour, it was as if they had come only for the spectacle, as if the war were over, and the spread of transports and gliders were a part of the victory parade. Then, as they approached the German lines, the flak started to come up, ragged at first, then with greater venom and concentration.

The transports were almost as helpless as the gliders. Keith saw several keel over and go down, one in flames, and one after an enormous explosion that could only have meant the destruction of ammunition.

'Mushroom, will you take your Wing down and see if you can do anything about it? Over.'

It was Group Captain 'Pepper' Arnold, the Station Commander at Savile Farm who could not be kept on the ground and was in command of the escort.

'Roger. Mushroom aircraft, operate in pairs and rendezvous Ploughman at 11.40 hours. Out.'

Keith put the nose of his Tempest down, and now tore past the suffering Dakotas at the van of the stream. There was a heavy haze over the Dutch countryside which blurred definition so that it seemed as if he was looking at the flat fenland, the geometrical dykes and roads, through smoked glass.

Against an occasional protest from 2nd T.A.F., he had kept his Tempest in the form he had flown it against the V1s, without armour plate or camouflage paint, and with the much higher-rated engine. He was doing almost 500 m.p.h. when he levelled off, gently aileroning right and left in his search for flak posts. Ahead of him was the Nijmegen railway bridge. He recognized it from photographs contained in the Top Secret packet — three arching spans, the centre one larger than the other two. There was bound to be flak there, at one of the three prime targets, and Keith could see the flash of 3.7 cm. medium guns firing at low elevation at the head of the glider stream above.

It would, he reflected, be stupid to get shot down now, a married man with a child expected, after five years of fighting. Beating up flak batteries was generally regarded as one of the more unpleasant and ridiculously dangerous tasks of ground attack. And he went at them.

He picked a battery packed behind sandbags beside the road leading to the bridge. He went in so low that the telephone posts on the road verge were above him, kicking hard left-right rudder and with the throttle wide open.

Keith lifted the nose at 1,000 yards, found the air suddenly full of 20 mm. tracer, steadied the dot on the stacked sandbags, and went in....

At 500 yards the detail was suddenly vivid. He could even see that one of the sandbags had burst, and spilled out on the grass of the road verge to make a small sand pyramid. He could also see the steel helmets of the gun crew. They were in shirt-sleeves, one blonde Aryan stripped to the waist.

Keith opened fire, a long burst, until the gun emplacement filled his sight, then his screen, and he would have plunged into the holocaust of bodies, flying sand and steel if he had lifted a fifth of a second later.

'Keith's luck!' That's what he used to say, what the others used to say, back on 140. It still held, miraculously held, as he vertically banked, belly at the steel girders of the bridge, and spiral climbed with the Sabre supercharger screaming, the four 20 mm. guns of the *Flakvierling 38* following him round very closely but failing to make a fatal strike. Then he was too high for them, and he caught a glimpse of the first released gliders going down through the mist, very steeply, hellbent on reaching the ground quickly.

Well, they had a better chance of making it than ten seconds earlier...

'Mushroom aircraft. Steer 250, and keep your mixture lean. Long way to go.'

* * *

It had seemed as if it were all over, bar the tidying up, the sorting out of prisoners of war, the cleaning up of a few last centres of resistance. The Rhine had been crossed at its most vulnerable point, the bridges were intact; the American generals, Patton and Hodges, were driving all before them; the Russian steam-roller was crushing its way through eastern Europe; the V1 had been defeated. How could Germany last out, with this over-whelming pressure on every frontier? people were asking. Her short-lived empire lost, her surface navy annihilated, the sting of her U-boats pulled?

Six days after the Arnhem drop, Keith overheard two of 40 Squadron's pilots talking over pints of beer in the officers' mess bar. They were not only full of optimism, they were presuming the war was over....

'I thought of going up to University — a year's crash course, and you can get a teacher's diploma.' His name was Outwood — Jerry Outwood, a particularly promising young pilot who had been with the Wing no more than a month. Keith had watched him beat up a column of trucks only the day before, setting a dozen of them blazing, jinking his way out of the flak and then coming in again. What would young Jerry Outwood make of the tranquillity and uneventfulness of peace-time living, teaching Geography to twelve-year-olds?

His companion said, 'I was going to have a crack at the law. Wizard money to be made — solicitor you know, not barrister. Too chancy being a barrister.' Too chancy? His number two had been shot down by flak on Tuesday. Keith had seen it. But Flying Officer Tim Baldwin had accepted it philosophically and was quite cheerful in the mess that evening. Chancy, eh, the life of a barrister?

They caught sight of Keith at that moment, and straightened up, putting down their drinks.

'Would you care for a noggin, sir?' Baldwin asked deferen-tially. Keith had never accustomed himself to being judged a hero and a veteran in the eyes of junior officers. The elevated rank was different. Trained for so long in the disciplines and rank

168

gradations of the service, the number of rings on a sleeve was no more than a material reflection of seniority to which one adjusted automatically.

Keith accepted the pint and raised it to the young Flying Officer. 'So you two think the flap's over?'

'Well, as good as, sir. I mean, we'll be home by Christmas, won't we?'

'That's what they were saying thirty years ago, in September 1914. "We'll have the boys home for Christmas." Only it was Christmas 1918 — ten million lives later, with half Europe starved and in ruins ...'

'Wasn't that rather different? Now we've got ...'

Keith interrupted him gently. 'You're right. It's not the same. But don't bank on Christmas. Or Easter.'

They talked of tomorrow's early op instead, for which Keith had recently supervised the briefing. Then he bought them both a drink, and went to his office.

He had not wanted to depress those young pilots. But Keith knew more than they did. He and Jerry Owen were privy to a lot of highly confidential intelligence, as well as some authoritative hearsay at H.Q. Like the Arnhem drop had stalled. Thick autumn fog had delayed the sending in of reinforcements and supplies, and it seemed they had landed in a mare's nest of German armour insteady of elderly reservists. Like all the armies stretched beyond their limit for supplies, still coming up all the way from Normandy, with no sign of Antwerp being usable as a port for a long time. Like the Germans digging in very determinedly, morale unimpaired, with short supply lines and plenty of armour left.

And ominous pointers, too, as far as they were concerned. The Luftwaffe had developed an astonishing rocket fighter, the Me163, as far a cry from the 109 as from the Wright Brothers' 'Flyer'. And there was very persuasive gen that the Luftwaffe's first jet fighter, another product of the fertile mind of Willy Messerschmitt, was now in large-scale production, in spite of the constant bombing of German industrial plants. The Me262. Bill Watson had encountered one at low level, photographing Allied armour coming up towards Brussels. He had dived down on it, but it had just opened its throttles and soared up into the sky. 'I felt like a sodding cripple saying "come back" to Jesse Owens,' he had commented.

By November, there were few people talking about being home by Christmas. Arnhem had been an expensive catastrophe. The Allied armies had been halted, bogged down by winter mud and German defiance as in 1918, the commanders full of discord, frustrated after the smashing advances of the late summer when General Patton was convinced he could have broken clean through to Berlin.

Keith read in a two-day-old copy of a newspaper, 'Crushing Offensive Opened. The invasion armies are smashing down the matchwood doors leading into the once invulnerable Greater German Reich. It is no longer great. It is rotten to the core, and nothing can halt or even delay the advance of our brave ...'

Did anybody, after more than five years of war and propaganda, believe that sort of hogwash he wondered? In his pocket he had a letter from Jenny, now seven months pregnant and looking like a barrage balloon (or so she claimed), telling of the disillusionment in London after the triumphs and hopes of only two months back. The V2s were still falling on the capital, dull thuds heard for miles and committing fearful carnage, the object of rumours worse than the reality until at last, on 10 November, the Prime Minister made an announcement.

Keith begged Jenny to get out of London and stay for a while with friends or at Market Rising but her letters still came from Half Moon Street....

338 Wing was moved up to Raachen, deep inside Holland, where they could support the army more closely. The airfield buildings had long since been wrecked, and it was too cold to live under canvas. Keith ordered the commandeering of some local empty houses, trim little Dutch suburban homes, still half furnished with the contents the owners had been unable to carry when the Germans had driven them out. There was no coal or other fuel, and foraging parties spread out and came back with railway sleepers, demolished sheds — anything that would burn in the grates of the houses.

Keith suffered from the cold like everyone else, and slept in his uniform and rarely changed. The water pipes were frozen solid, and they began to burn the wood of the houses in which they lived, leaving a mere skeleton of floorboards and stairs without banisters. The engine fitters had the worst time, having to start up the Sabre engines several times every night to prevent the oil from freezing.

250 miles south, in the heart of the Ardennes, von Runstedt's armies struck at a weakened point on the American front on 16 December. In appalling weather, the offensive drove deep into the Ardennes and there was even talk of Paris being retaken. At one time the Panzers were only four miles from the Meuse. Winston Churchill commented, 'A crisis burst upon us ... The Fifth Panzer Army drove through the centre of the VIIIth U.S. Corps, by-passed St Vith and Bartogne, penetrating deeply ...'

* * *

At early dawn on 1 January 1945, Hans and Millie Schvengen, both in their fifties, of Huisberden 23, Snippeling on the outskirts of Deventer, heard the sound of low flying aircraft approaching. It woke them both up but they were not afraid, nor did they bother to go to the blacked-out window. The sound, rapidly reaching a climax and shaking the house as the planes travelled very low overhead, did not alarm the Schvengens. Like so many citizens of the Netherlands, they had for long accustomed themselves to the din of low flying Allied aircraft. Like hunger, and the longing for a cup of real coffee and new tyres for their bicycles, it was something they had to put up with.

At about the same time, Jean-Claude Billistre, who had a small-holding outside a little village called St Augustine south-west of Bassenet, heard the faint rumble of a raid, rapidly increasing in volume. He was engaged in harnessing up his horse at the time, and cursed. Marie could react violently to low aircraft, and only a month ago had broken her traces and bolted. Jean-Claude held the big mare's head close to his head and talked soothingly into her ear, patting her neck at the same time. The planes went overhead at scarcely a hundred feet, and while he muttered, 'Calm down, calm down my Marie, soon over, soon gone!' he swore at the thoughtlessness of the Allied pilots. 'They do not have to be so low!'

When at last he looked up, feeling the mare shivering, the planes were out of sight.

Thousands more in north-west Germany and the Low Countries heard the dawn raid. Among them were two Dutch boys of eleven and twelve, going out fishing in the canal, their breath like

171

smoke on the freezing air. They lay down flat in the grass that was white and crisp from the frost, as they had been instructed at school in case they were fired on in error. These two boys, after half a childhood of war, knew as much about aircraft recognition as a veteran British Observer Corps officer. They were also canny on the destination and likely purpose of raids, from American Eighth Air Force B17s heading for ball-bearing factories through the spattered dots of heavy flak, to 2nd T.A.F. Mosquitoes on some pinpoint mission at fifty feet.

But these machines were single-engine fighters flying from east to west in great numbers in the half light. Which meant, surely, they were returning from an op? But it was not the full moon period, and single-engined fighters did not usually fly out en masse in the dark and return to their bases at down....

Both boys turned their heads at the same time as the machines were racing overhead. The explanation was simple yet surprising. These were not Allied fighter-bombers or fighters. They were Luftwaffe machines, black cross and swastika clearly identifiable even in this light, and in greater numbers than either of these boys had seen for months.

'190As.'

'No — 190D9s.'

They walked on through the frosty grass, swinging their rods and arguing....

Very few of those who heard the thunderous sound as 900 Luftwaffe fighters and fighter-bombers raced towards their targets even knew that they were German. And only those two Dutch boys disputed whether they were long-nosed Focke-Wulfs or the earlier short-nosed breed.

* * *

At 338 wing H.Q. at Raachen, Keith Stewart was alerted to the sound of the machines approaching while he was shaving at 0925 precisely, and had no doubt at all that they were hostile. He cursed and leapt for the door. 'The buggers, the crafty buggers!'

The explosive sound of their engines was at once, and even before Keith had thrust his feet into his boots, succeeded by the chatter of multiple cannon and machine-gun fire. And there would be delayed action bombs, too, of that he had no doubt.

There had been a party at Raachen last night, as there had

been in every 2nd T.A.F. mess. The ack-ack boys had had a party, too. And why not? Life was dull and cold in liberated Belgium and Holland.

As the Germans had once again calculated, there were plenty of New Year hangovers among the pilots of 35, 40 and 178 Squadrons, and the Bofors gunners, too. But the gunners were already replying, and when the second wave came in (Keith was out by then, arms half into his Irvine) the Bofors were thud-thud-thudding, a deeper sound in the chorus of gunfire. And men were running fast.

Keith was into his car and away towards the dispersal, hand on horn. He recognized two pilots by their boots and opened the rear doors for them, racing off before they could shut it behind them. There were fires down at the dispersal, a big fire over by the store of jerrycans, each with five gallons of 100 octane aviation fuel.

A late 109G, flames spitting from wing cannons, came straight down the east-west runway, right on the deck. Keith swerved violently to the left and back again onto course. The fighter's slipstream set the car rocking. The Bofors, barrels depressed right down, were firing tracer which criss-crossed and raced away in pursuit of the enemy.

'Christ, sir!' One of the pilots— Keith had not recognized him — had caught sight of the shambles ahead. Through the windscreen they could see their Tempests looking like Dinky Toys smashed about by a bad-tempered boy— wings severed and crushed, a naked fuselage with the engine half out, two more burning, blue fuel flames beating up into the sky. One appeared intact but was on its back, neatly turned over. Some of the temporary huts were crushed and blazing, too. A fire engine was on its side, half cocooned in its own foam like a dying animal lying in its intestines. And there were sprawled figures, and others running, some sharp-silhouetted against the flames.

Keith leapt out while the car was still moving and ran towards the blast bay where he kept Nero. She looked all right, and his engine fitter was there, tearing at the ropes securing the canvas engine cover. Without helmet or goggles Keith climbed up into the cockpit. Someone had slid open the hood, and his 'chute was in the seat. There was time. Nero could do it. Off in ninety seconds, nine pounds boost, 450 ASI in no time. Get them on the way home, the sneak, cowardly sods!

'Look out!' Keith shouted. 'Stand clear!'

The Coffman started the engine first time, and he released the brakes. Someone else had removed the chocks, and he taxied straight out of the bay. There were D.A. bombs going off now and one went up fifty yards away, throwing dirt at him. He opened the throttle wide, accelerated over the grass, ignoring the runways and perimeter track.

The Tempest was travelling fast, close to take-off speed at around 90 m.p.h. when the jet Me262 lifted up over the trees at the east end of Raachen, dipped down its nose, and opened fire with its 30 mm. cannon.

The burst of shells caught the rear of Keith's Tempest, thudding in high explosive and incendiary shells— a dozen, two dozen and more. It was expert shooting, lacking only in variety. Because, by a freak chance of fate — the fate which had placed him once again in the position of greatest hazard— not one of the shells struck forward of the unarmoured cockpit seat.

With his hood still open, Keith heard the unfamiliar high-pitched whine of the twin-engined jet tearing above his head at a straight-and-level speed he had never approached, even in his stripped once-beautiful Nero.

Its passing was the briefest shadow, free of the Bofors fire which could not predict such speed. And the remains of Nero, rudder, tailplane, half the fuselage gone, skidded and skated to a halt in the middle of the blasted runway and amidst a shower of sparks.

Keith's situation was as ridiculous as the new configuration of Nero, a mere half-Tempest, nose high in the air, the cross members of the fuselage two feet behind the cockpit, bent and on the ground.

The crew of a surviving ambulance, and 178 Squadron's Chiefy himself, helped Keith out of the cockpit.

'Yes, I'm O.K.,' he told the ambulance corporal. 'But get clear of this lot — it could still go up.'

And the ridiculous and confused phrase raced through his mind — 'Fiddling while Nero burns!'

Poor old Nero! Finished off by something even faster.

Five minutes later he knew the worst.

'Not good, sir,' the Chief Engineer Officer told him. He had a greatcoat over his pyjamas and was still wearing slippers below his white ankles.

'How bad?'

'I'm afraid none. None at all.'

Keith asked, 'You mean nil availability?'

The Squadron Leader nodded. 'Same everywhere. Hardly a serviceable single-engined kite left in 2nd T.A.F. That's the gen I've heard.'

8

The Truth

The Lysander's engine died on Mike as he opened the throttle to take off from the small grass clearing in the forest, and the silence was stunning. Then the voices rose in a chorus of dismay and speculation from the reception party running from the trees.

'Nom de Dieu, qu'est-ce-qui arrive?'

'Oh merde, ils sont en panne.'

'Mais non, ils ont oublié quelquechose.'

From the passenger compartment Duclos called out anxiously, 'Nom de Dieu — what's the matter?'

'Je ne comprends pas,' Mike said.

But he did understand. The engine had died almost immediately after switching tanks; and there was a finality about the cut out that confirmed Mike's diagnosis. Water in the tank, a great deal of it. Almost certainly sabotage, and at Southdean, not here. There had been no time nor opportunity to interfere with the fuel tanks here, at this target.

'Il y a de l'eau dans l'essence,' he called out to Duclos. 'Je regrette, mais nous restons en France...'

The politician was outraged. 'Mais c'est très important, pour moi, pour la France, que ...'

'It's no goddam use, buddy. The Lizzie's U/S and that's that,' Mike shouted in English, and climbed out of the cockpit and jumped down.

The firing began at once, as if triggered by the impact of his feet on the grass. It came from two points in the forest verge, one to the east and very close; the second point a quarter mile away and clearly intended to halt the Lysander if it escaped the other fire. It was standard Schmeisser fire, so fast that you could not distinguish the individual explosions, like a multi-cylinder racing bike with open exhaust. The Germans had lights, too, thin pencil beams that ranged over the field, mercilessly freezing crouching figures for the killing.

The first few seconds of firing must have killed or wounded half the Reception Party. Mike saw a group of four struck down together, limbs twisting, torsos thrown into violent and unnatural postures before being hurled to the ground. If there were cries of warning or screams, Mike heard nothing — only the multiple overlapping bursts of Schmeisser fire.

The Lysander saved Mike. Duclos had begun to run with the pace and panic of any politician who recognizes danger, but in the wrong direction, straight towards the fire, and had been cut down, cut almost in half, by the fusillade of bullets. But they did not want to harm the Lysander. They wanted Duclos and the pilot alive, and the Lysander intact. Instead, they had shot Duclos in error, and Mike had been quick to recognize his advantage — a slim advantage, razor slim. He could not remain here, beneath the Lysander's wing, crouching, shocked, yet so well tempered by war and danger that he could still work things out in his mind.

It was 200 yards to the cover of the forest, he guessed, and he started out at a crouching trot, keeping the plane between the Germans and himself, trusting that he might not be detected by the second more distant party.

The firing was less intense now, and he could hear voices shouting, in French and German. One or two of the reception party were firing back with Stens, lying in the grass at a hopeless disadvantage. Most of these resistance men would prefer to die, with a Boche or two to his credit, than be captured. Mike was about fifteen yards from the pine trees when the Schmeisser fire began to cut the air about him, and thud into the ground, sending up spouts of earth through which he ran and hurled himself to the grass, rolling over and over for the last few yards.

He rose to his feet the moment he felt the twigs and pine needles and recognized the darkness of moon shadow, and began running fast between the trees. The fire was intermittent now, blasting out distantly in short bursts like the tired end of an orgy. The Sten fire had ceased entirely, and Mike felt sure the Reception Party were now all dead or captured. Twenty of them. Not fewer.

He halted and leant against a tree. The sweat was stinging his eyes and he had to flex his knees consciously to prevent their giving way. His chest ached, and he realized how unfit he had become since the training course in Wales months ago. The chances of getting out of this alive, he realized, were virtually non-existent. He was in uniform. His civilian clothes, emergency pack, maps and arms were all in the Lizzie. He could remember the shape and approximate size of this forest from his study of the target area before take-off; and that was about all. They knew that he had escaped from the ambush, and with the coming of daylight they would certainly make every effort to hunt him down.

Mike was still recovering his breath and strength, back leaning against the rough bark, when two new sounds reached his ears, from one side the unmistakable whine of dogs, from the other, a low-pitched, rising and falling groan. A vehicle of some sort? Mike began to run towards it, saw nothing, paused. The sound was steady as if the vehicle was temporarily stationary. Then he saw it between the trees, the low outline of a *traction avant*, a Citroën, with a charcoal-gas bag on its roof. Dimly in the moon shadow, he made out two figures. They were smoking and talking as if taking a break on an arduous journey.

Mike called out, 'Je suis l'aviateur anglais — le R.A.F.'

The taller of the two men turned and said, with little expression in his voice, 'Eh bien, tu t'es évadé. Maintenant, donne-nous un coup de main.'

Mike recognized the tall man as the officer in charge of the Reception Party, wearing the usual black beret and a short jacket tied at the waist with a length of rope. He had introduced himself briefly as Carlos. Like the smaller man, who turned out to be his son, he had a Sten slung over his right shoulder, and there was a naked Smith and Wesson stuffed brigand-like into the rope belt. They appeared to be taking their critical situation with unusual calmness.

'Va aider Pierre à l'arrière de la voiture.' Carlos said, and climbed into the driver's seat.

The rear wheels had sunk deep into a shallow drainage ditch, and the front wheels merely raced and dug deeper into the pine-needle surface when Carlos put his foot on the accelerator, in spite of all their efforts.

Mike could see the cause of the trouble. Besides the wireless operator, he had flown in a container of 9 mm. Parabellum Sten ammunition, Mills grenades, detonators, some P.E. explosive and much-needed field dressings. The contents had been spread out on the rear seats and in the small boot of the Citroën. They would not get out of this ditch until their weight was discarded.

'But it is essential for our *réseau*,' Carlos protested when Mike told him they would have to leave it behind or allow both the supplies and themselves to fall into the hands of the Boche.

But some renewed firing, and a louder cry and more barking decided the argument in Mike's favour. Suddenly swift and decisive, Carlos and his son threw everything out. The front wheels at once gripped, and the Citroën accelerated away with Mike in the front seat and the boy behind, window lowered and Sten at the ready like a Chicago gangster.

The light varied with the density of the foliage and Carlos flashed the hooded headlamps from time to time. He struck a tree only once, and that a glancing blow — crossed a track — 'Cette fois on n'y coupera pas!' — and plunged into the forest again as if he knew every square metre, every tree.

They emerged at last on a dirt track that led them between open fields where harvesting had already begun. The moon set behind a low hill before they reached a road. Mike, feeling more secure in the darkness and the increasing distance between them and the Germans, asked Carlos if he thought anyone else had escaped.

'If they have, the Boche will get them in the morning,' he replied. 'This is the only car. I tried to persuade two to jump in, but they were shot before they could reach it. Une sale nuit!'

In ten more minutes they reached a village. Mike could just make out the shape of a tall house, a track running up one side of it. Carlos drove up this track without lights, turned round the back of the house and straight into an old stable block.

Mike followed father and son into a dimly-lit kitchen. There was oilcloth on the table, a litre bottle of unlabelled wine, some chunks of cheese and sausage. Carlos's fat wife rose from the table where she had been patching a sheet, and greeted him as if he had just returned from a day's work at the office.

'Comment ça s'est passé?' she asked.

And Carlos replied, reporting an unsuccessful day's business with calm regret, 'Les Fritz nous attendaient au tournant. On nous a choppé.' And he shook his head when she asked if there were any survivors.

Later, they gave Mike a bed in the attic above the stables. With the help of the wine, he went to sleep at once. It was not until he awoke in the strange surroundings, looking up at the cobweb-strewn tiles with chinks of daylight showing through, that he appreciated fully his situation. 'Old Browning on the run again,' he told himself philosophically. It was three years since he had bailed out, not far from here, and had worked his way across France with the help of the Resistance. This time it was different. The Allies were now in France — that was true. But this had only made the Germans more desperate and more savage in their treatment of Resistance fighters. And this time, Mike was impli-cated in clandestine work and could expect nothing but torture and the firing squad if he were caught.

* * *

Mike recalled Eileen as a girl of nineteen, long-legged in shorts, striding through the Black Forest; at Rising Hall as the daughter of the house, emulating her mother as hostess; at his bedside in the Inverness hospital when he was recovering from that major prang; in W.R.N.S. uniform, as near to being self-conscious as he had ever seen her; Eileen dignified in her bereavement — in all these situations, the first thing to be said of her was that she was stylish. Self-confident, authoritative, even rather dashing, but above all, stylish. Coming himself from a family that was con-scious of breeding, Mike knew that it was the authority her class gave her that contributed most to Eileen's style.

He looked at her now, her short hair unbrushed, and with its natural colour showing at the roots, her hands dirty, fingernails black, squatting over a box of detonators, counting them out and packing them up with P.E. Yes, Eileen Barrett, stylish as ever as she prepared for the raid with brisk efficiency.

180

'You know I'm coming with you,' Mike said again.

'Don't be silly. They don't want you. And I'm in charge, and don't forget it.' She looked up from her work and smiled at him. 'Don't forget it — Wing Commander Browning.'

Mike was aware of the others watching them, not liking it. And Jean-Pierre said sharply. 'Eh l'Américain, parlez français!'

Mike had been in the Dorothée *réseau* for only twenty-four hours, and was still regarded with deep suspicion. There were several reasons for this. This was an F.F.I. organization, at loggerheads with the F.T.P., the communist resistance movement to which Carlos's *réseau* belonged. (Duclos had been a prominent and ambitious communist politican who had convinced Baker Street of the necessity of his coming to London.) Then, how was it that Carlos and his son and this American pilot had neatly got away when the rest of the reception committee had been massacred? And how had this American known of the location of the Dorothée *réseau*, and how had he got here?

Mike's explanation that he had flown Eileen in and therefore knew the geography, that he had borrowed a bicycle to get here, were both treated with suspicion; and they listened to Eileen's confirmation of Mike's explanation with equally bleak doubt.

In fact, Mike had been extremely fortunate to discover Eileen. Since D-Day, she had had to move three times, once closing everything down when both the *réseau* commandant Mike had seen at the target, and Watermelon had been captured and taken to Paris. Now, like so many of the *Maquis*, they had taken to the woods and become nomadic, praying that the Allied armies would break through before they were located, although very much aware that with every kilometre of retreat the Germans were becoming more ruthless with the civilian population, and more determined to avenge the humiliations and damage from sabotage for which the Resistance had been responsible.

Soon after his arrival (Eileen clearly pleased but anxious for him with his appalling American-accented French, and inexperience and inadequate training for the field), he was taken to the edge of the wood on the hill where they had been for five days.

Eileen, in much-washed, faded and stained cotton skirt, a man's old jacket which was too big for her, and wooden-soled shoes, pointed out the lie of the land. The small town of Dreux-sur-Oise could be seen through the heat shimmer a mile away, huddled in the river valley, church spire, the tall hôtel de ville, and the railway station most prominent.

Mike remembered hunting with her back in the winter of '37-'38 — eager, enthusiastic, passionately keen to be in at the kill. Seven years ago she had been secure, safe in her own environment, her loving parents alive, devoted servants about her.

Now she stood, dishevelled, in critical danger day and night, far from a home that no longer existed. And as keen as ever to be in at the kill. Not a fox, either. 'You can see the line, running north-east south-west,' she said matter-of-factly. 'Double track, and very important. Half a mile beyond the river, it divides, one line going to Rheims, the other to Paris.'

'Doesn't it get bombed?'

'Oh heavens, yes. Thunderbolts had another go a few days back. They hit the track but they didn't get the points. And, of course, the Boche is very quick at repairing lines now — they've had plenty of experience.'

Mike could see the triple cantilever bridge carrying the railway line over the Oise. There were craters flanking the approach on both banks of the river from unsuccessful bombing attacks.

'Some target,' he commented.

'And the Boche knows it. There are day and night patrols and four light flak batteries and a dozen 3.7s guarding it. That's one reason why the Thunderbolts missed. They had three shot down, too.'

Eileen had turned to the young Frenchman who had accompanied them and ordered him to return to the site to see if there had been any messages. Listening to her crisp instructions in impeccable French, he could not help contrasting again this unwashed, tough, intrepid saboteur, Dorothée, with the Eileen who had lain about Rising Hall slowly recovering from her breakdown over idle, unproductive months. If only her parents could have known what their violent death had done to their own beloved daughter! Mike guessed that old Sir Richard would have been proud of her, risking her life carrying out effectively one of the most dangerous of all tasks open to women in this war — destroying with a few pounds of precision-placed explosive, communications, power cables and stations, vital parts of factory machinery, and so much else that might take many bombers, with

182

many losses, to accomplish.

Now, as the heat of the day faded with the light, Eileen completed with Jean-Pierre the preparation of the plastic explosive they would carry down to the railway intersection, shape the P.E. to the rails at the points, link them together and blow them....

'There is good news of the advance.' The little French W/T operator who had been working with the *réseau* long before Eileen arrived, came and sat down beside them. 'General Patton has reached Fontainebleau,' he announced excitedly in French. 'They are saying that Paris must fall any day now. I heard that on the BBC so it is true. But I have also heard by code from London. It is a general message to all the Resistance in France.'

'What has London to say?' Eileen asked, diving briefly into her little camouflaged tent for a pair of wire cutters.

'Il faut à tout prix faire sauter tous les ponts ferroviaires dans le nord-est et immobiliser l'ennemi.'

Eileen remarked, as if deciding to shop at Harrods instead of Harvey Nichols: 'Then we will blow the bridge tonight, Jean-Pierre, instead of the points. And we will need bigger charges.'

'Goddam it, woman, that's plain nutty suicide.' Mike looked at her in horror. 'You can't do that.'

Eileen turned on him, green eyes blazing. 'Will you stop interfering with my orders and decisions. I have work to do and will not have my authority undermined.'

Mike flinched back from this attack, recognizing for the first time the invidiousness of his position among these tough Resistance workers. She had been at this game for weeks in the field, had acquired the respect of these Frenchmen and had twice his knowledge of sabotage and fighting behind the lines.

He was starting to apologize when she spoke again, less savagely now. 'Look Mike, imagine me turning up at your dispersal just before you were going out on an op, and saying,' (she broke into cockney) "Oh no, you carn't do that, you carn't do that there 'ere. Don't want him to taike no charnces"...'

'O.K., I get it. Sorry.'

Later, as darkness closed in and it started to drizzle, Mike became very depressed and decided that he hated this place and longed to get Eileen out of it. He hated the rough civilian clothes Carlos's family had given him, these suspicious, dirty, unshaven

Frenchmen who seemed already to be thinking more of political advantage than of France and the outcome of the war, the vile food that was brought to them twice a day in containers from local sympathizers— tepid, greasy, garlic-laden, and the smell of this site where all Eileen's efforts had failed to persuade the men to use a distant latrine she had arranged to be built.

It was raining hard when the party set out — Eileen, Jean-Pierre, an elderly, fanatical little man ('he scares the pants off me,' Mike had confided to Eileen), and three others Mike had not spoken to. They had three waterproof bags of P.E., and the plan was to strip to underclothes and enter the river at a point 300 metres upstream from the bridge, where a plantation of saplings grew down to the bank. They would float down with the current, the P.E. and detonators on a small raft two members of the *réseau* had built that evening. After placing the charges with delayed action fuses, they would continue downriver, to be met by a second party of three with dry clothes. Then they would make best speed cross-country, over the railway lines and back up the hill to the camp.

The whole *réseau* would then spend the rest of the night in retreating to a friendly barn they knew five kilometres north-east, on the reasonable assumption that there would be an almighty hue and cry if the charges blew satisfactorily.

Their first enemies were the guards on the bridge, the lights that they switched on intermittently to scan the bridge's approaches, the river banks and the river itself, and the tracker dogs, who might well catch their scent as they floated down towards the bridge, although Mike noted with relief that at least the wind was from the west.

It was after ten o'clock when the first party left, heavily laden, dim and already sodden figures in the torchlight. Mike was at the entrance to a tent he shared with the W/T operator, and he simply called out, 'Good luck, kid!' to Eileen.

She turned and said, 'Ta, Ta. I don't know why we don't strip now and save time. Still, it's my first wash for a week or two.'

He watched the figures moving off, talking quietly in French, at once swallowed by the darkness and sheeting rain. Mike could not bring himself to believe any of them would return. They had given him a Sten gun and three clips of ammunition and there was a precious last remaining Bren with about 200 rounds. But he, and the other four who remained at the camp, had been instructed by Eileen to retreat at the slightest sign of the Germans closing in on the wood. 'And no stupid heroics from you, either,' she had added in English to Mike.

* * *

Mike's illuminated watch showed ten minutes after midnight when the first sounds of shooting reached them in the wood. The nature of the shooting was predictable, with brief bursts of Sten and Schmeisser broken by individual rifle shots.

Mike told himself angrily, 'It's only what you knew would happen — how could they possibly hope to get away with it?'

The Frenchmen had a small fire burning under the shelter of a canvas sheet stretched between four posts, and he could see from his tent that they had turned in the direction of the firing. They had the Bren ready on its tripod mounting, and had loosened their Stens.

Mike called out to them in French, 'Put out that fire.'

There was rainwater pouring off the canvas, and one of the men held a bucket under it and then threw it hissing onto the fire. The rain had eased, and there was a hint of light in the sky above the trees. The firing continued intermittently, and Mike tried to console himself with the conclusion that at least someone was left alive while the sound of Stens was part of the chorus.

'You remain here,' he told the Frenchmen. 'And wait for the pass phrase before firing. I'm going to meet them.'

He shone his torch on them briefly, and he saw them nod but none of them spoke. He ran off into the night, the Sten cocked in his right hand, in his left trouser pocket the little Browning he took with him everywhere. He was soaked through almost at once by the drops from the branches which came down in a torrent when the wind gusted.

Mike broke out of the wood at the point where Eileen had led him to view the landscape. It had stopped raining and the skies were clearing fast on a fresh westerly wind. No moon, thank God for that, but clear stars seen between the clouds scudding east and breaking up. The firing seemed to be closer, or was it only that the trees no longer muffled it? It came from the direction he expected, due south-east, but he could see nothing — nothing at all until a flare shot up, illuminating wheat fields that fell away

185

down to the river below, the main road winding down through them, a farmhouse and outbuildings, and another farm farther away, the line of the railway marked by telegraph posts, the level crossing, and beyond — but only dimly — the outskirts of Dreux, the tower of the church dominant.

At once the firing was intensified, and Mike could no longer distinguish the sound of a Sten. Then, while the flare fell slowly on its parachute, both its lights and the sound of the guns were overwhelmed by the explosion from the bridge.

Mike, feeling the blast in his face like a sharp gust of wind, was forced to a sudden standstill. The glare was a sharp blow at his eyes and he dropped his gun as he put his arms to his face. It seemed impossible that they could have carried so much explosive; and it seemed just as impossible that the bridge remained intact. When he next looked, a second flare confirmed it. A cloud still hung over the two bridge piers but the wind was blowing it rapidly clear, and the centre arch was no longer there. At first he was not certain, and he searched for evidence of steel girders, bent, twisted, half hanging in the water or protruding from it, like some of the blown bridges he had flown over on moonlight ops recently. But there was nothing, nothing at all. 'A goddam clean sweep!' The charge had lifted the whole of the centre span, and thrown it away, out of sight, just like that.

Then it was mortar fire, rapid light mortar fire — one, another, a third. Heavy thuds, throwing up fountains of brown earth from the nearest wheatfield, not a hundred yards from him. Out of black confusion, there came illuminated order, a neat panorama of combat, as neat as the clean-snapped bridge.

There were figures moving through the corn, waist high like wading swimmers on the last yards of the shore, a long line of them, some firing rifles, others with Schmeisser machine pistols firing short bursts ahead. Marching before them were the exploding mortar shells, one, two, three, four — wet brown soil spilling back, killing splinters splaying out: a cold, deadly efficient, flushing-out job that could not fail.

Mike was on a track which ran dead straight down the side of the hill, roughly at right angles to the advancing troops. There was no cover, not even the precarious part-concealment offered by the wheat. But they had not seen him, and could not expect him to be here. The flares that were guiding them in their hunt

186

made them easy targets, like a shooting gallery line-up. And many a gallery in Atlantic City, Philadelphia and New York had reluctantly paid out the prizes to Mike in his 'teens.

Now Mike simply raised the Sten, curved steel plate to his right shoulder, centred the primitive sight, and squeezed the trigger, running from end to end of the line, the nearest only twenty yards distant. New clip in, which took about three seconds; then back again, a less satisfactory target now because most of the Germans were dead, wounded or flattened for cover. (They were, in fact, elderly reservists, brave enough but slow in their reactions at forty-five and fifty-five.)

He was able to slip in the third clip of twenty-eight 9 mm. bullets before the firing came back at him, and he was shouting now in French, 'Run for it!' Then he fell back into the corn on the other side of the track, tucking himself deeply in before raising his head.

The mortar fire had ceased, the gunners no doubt confused and anxious not to kill their own men. But another flare broke out, making a new daylight of the cornfields.

No one had emerged, the infantrymen were still concealed, but a burst of fire came in his direction and he fired back blind, just to keep his spirits up and their heads down.

And he kept his own head up just long enough to glimpse a shape — a fast-moving shadow it seemed.

At once Mike called out the code phrase, 'La porte est fermée!' and it stopped in its tracks like an animal catching the scent of danger.

'Venez ici,' Mike called. 'C'est moi, l'Américain.'

It was Jean-Pierre, panting, soaking, mud-covered, without his gun. He tumbled at Mike's feet, crushing the wheat stalks, like a child in despair.

'Où sont les autres?' Mike asked, and knew he was wasting his time and breath. For at first the Frenchman made no reply, and when he could speak, softly and in a shaking voice, he said that they were all dead— 'Ils sont tous morts, je crois, à part Henri. Il est gravement blessé, et les Boches l'abbatront. Peut-être Richard et Claude ont pu se sauver — je n'en sais rien.'

They had been caught at the worst place, down on the river bank just as the demolition party came out of the water. Two guards had seen them, had opened fire. 'D'autres se sont amenés tout de suite.' They had been pursued up the hill, had held out for five minutes in a pigsty. Two had been with him when he had plunged into the corn. A chance burst had got them both. Both dead — Emile and Robert, good men, married with children....

The firing had started again, the mortars, too. Mike and Jean-Pierre lay flat on the wet, strong-smelling soil while the search moved past on the other side of the track, like a trawl for herring. The ground shook again and again. Jean-Pierre was shivering, from the cold or fear or both. 'Quelle nuit, quelle nuit!' he kept moaning. 'On a eu le pont, hein? On a eu le pont.'

'Yes, you got the bridge,' Mike said in English. 'You got the goddam bridge all right, O.K. A good clean break. No goddam retreating Krauts will get over that bridge.'

He was surprised to find himself shivering, too. Yes, quelle nuit O.K.

Did he want to know? Yes, he decided, he did. And this shivering Frenchman beside him was the only person who could tell him. And they would be separated or dead soon.

Yes, said Jean-Pierre, she had died in the river, the first to be killed. She was wading in almost naked when the first burst of fire blasted out and had caught her in the leg. He was not sure it was the leg, but she was hit. But she had reached the cache of guns the rendezvous party had laid down while they helped the demolition party ashore, and had cut down the first two of the Boches as they closed in firing their Schmeisser pistols from the hip. Yes, she had killed them, with rifle fire, of that he was sure. A good shot. A good woman.

'Et puis ...?'

'Et puis — They had got her — inevitably, and she had fallen on the shelving bank and rolled over. She would have died instantly, of course. Elle n'a pas souffert. No, I am not sure whether the current carried her away. She may have been in shallow enough water to remain there. I did not see — we were very busy, you understand.'

Mike understood. But he hoped the current had taken her away and that the Boches had not found her, bullet-riddled on the bank of the River Oise. He preferred to think of her drifting down that beautiful river, safely, quietly through the noise and fury of the front-line fighting near Beaumont, and then, still unseen, down the Seine and into the Channel, where she could

188

sink in peace....

So Eileen had fulfilled her old promise to do 'something really useful'— at a price. 'I want to know the truth,' she had said softly in the garden of the Rising Hall lodge when Rising Hall itself was no more. She had wanted to know what it was like to kill someone, and she had found out for herself, as she had been determined to do. Yes, she had avenged the killing of her parents, and had— for a second or two of pain— experienced the knowledge of the truth.

Mike said, 'I think we should separate. They will be coming back through this field. And I don't want to return to the camp.'

'O.K., American. Bonne chance. I shall go into hiding in the town where I have friends. If I can get there.'

He seemed to have recovered his purposefulness and courage, and Mike said, 'Good luck, Jean-Pierre.'

'That Dorothée, she was good — for a woman she was good. We all thought so....'

When Mike stood up, it was quite dark, and the only sound was the rustling of the ripe wheat in the wind. A brief silence of honour to Eileen? Then another flare went up, and Mike began to run, north-east, crouching, throwing away the Sten.

*   *   *

The mortar fire awoke Mike at five o'clock, deep c-r-u-m-ps that shook the ground, followed by the unmistakable shriek of Mauser fire — like calico being ripped angrily into small pieces. He had slept for less than an hour, and the pain of realization hit him a blow in the stomach. He turned and lay still, his face buried in the peat-smelling sacks.

During the night, he had forced his way to the south-west, parallel to the Oise, skirting villages, avoiding roads and keeping as far as possible to standing corn fields or stubble, and then becoming swallowed in a seemingly endless forest. In the first hour of flight he had felt a strong sense of light-headed carelessness, as if nothing mattered, least of all his own safety. The last time he had experienced this feeling it had been caused by Eileen's defection at the height of the Battle of Britain, and then only a series of miracles had preserved him. Now it was her death. But as he hurried on, skirting a field of barley, up a gentle slope, past a small farm — the inevitable dog inevitably barking

189

— he had increasingly felt the need to survive.

'What the hell for, for Christ's sake?' one voice asked. And another answered, telling him first that Eileen would have wanted him to live, and next that he must survive in order to recount the events of her last days and hours, to tell of her courage, and of the admiration she had attracted among the Resistance fighters who had died with her.

This filled him with a sudden new optimism that he would make it, and when he descended to a crossroads, he was able to reach the etched lettering, like Braille, which spelt out 'Senlis 10'. He calculated that he had already covered about twenty-five miles. He thought that he could hear the rumble of artillery from the west, but it died at once.

Then by four o'clock he could go on no more, drained of power like the run-down spring of a toy car. Above a smashed bridge over the Oise, he had found a farmhouse demolished no doubt by a stray bomb, and in the garden a stone shed that had somehow survived, though there was broken glass on the floor. And there he had collapsed on the pile of sacks.

More sounds of battle joined the chorus as the dawn light increased. Heavy guns began shelling in the west, the sounds running together and growing into a continuous ripple of thunder. Then from close by came the answering fire, the air torn apart like trains emerging from a tunnel in rapid succession, very fast, followed by whipcracks that stung the ear. There were planes about, too, and when Mike emerged cautiously from the shed, he saw to the north at 3,000 feet Thunderbolts circling like carrion crows.

A target for the fighter-bombers was not far distant from Mike, beyond the ruined farmhouse and on the other side of a small field. There was a rising wood of willow, eucalyptus, chestnut and beech, and beside it a dirt road with an obelisk war memorial at the verge carrying six names of French dead at Verdun. He had followed it during the night, and now it carried a convoy of trucks — Citroëns and Berliets mostly — camouflage painted on their metal bodies and canvas tops and strewn with branches. To the right of the wood, half tucked in among the trees, he could just make out the long barrels of 88s protruding from the turrets of four Panther tanks. Every few seconds, one of the barrels would spout flame and recoil, tearing more leaves and twigs from the trees, and almost at once Mike felt the shock and heard the percussive blast.

Later, several platoons of infantry marched past raggedly, interspersed with B.M.W. motorcycle combinations, and once a single Mustang in R.A.F. colours flashed past at very low level, as steady as if under automatic pilot control, firing short bursts from its six .5s, scattering a group of infantry and setting a truck on fire farther down the road. But it was no more than a matter-of-fact *entre-acte*.

No one came near the farmhouse, and when the sun got up and the Panthers rumbled away, leaving one of their number with its crew struggling with an unserviceable track, Mike crept back into the shed, and in spite of the steadily increasing sound of mortars, medium artillery and automatic fire, he fell into a deep sleep.

When he awoke again, he felt hungry and thirsty. The sound of battle had died, as if the armies were resting in the heat of the day, and there was only the steady drone of aircraft high in the clear blue August sky, and the rumble of traffic, this time from the north-west.

The single Panther still lay with its rear end in the verge of the wood, its barrel at 30 degrees and silent, abandoned by its crew. The dirt road was empty, except for a single elderly French farm labourer clanking past on an old bicycle, as if stupid old war did not figure in his considerations. The activity now was on the far side of the Oise. In the shimmering heat, and between the willows, Mike could make out mixed heavy traffic, from jeeps through heavy G.M.C. trucks to Sherman tanks, all carrying the white star of the Allied armies. There were military police in white helmets on motor cycles directing the traffic, urging it on, and as Mike watched, suddenly excited and moved by this sight of so many of his countrymen and such evidence of American power, a big truck halted on the verge and the crew began handing out jerricans of petrol to every passing jeep.

While he had slept, the Battle of France had swept over him, and he had been liberated.

Farther downstream, a shirtless group was already starting work on erecting a Bailey bridge alongside the wrecked remains of the steel cantilever bridge which had been bombed or blown up by German demolition.

'I'm sure not waiting for you to get over here!' Mike said aloud, and walked the hundred yards to the southern bank of the Oise between willow saplings and through heavy damp soil. Even in this heat, the river looked singularly unattractive, muddy brown-grey and eighty yards wide. But Mike paused only to take off the wooden-soled agricultural boots Pedro's family had given him, and tie them round his neck. Then he waded through the mud and weeds, and launched himself into the water.

No-one appeared to see him swim across, or climb up the steep bank on the other side. Even when he sat by the roadside under a poplar to put on his boots, leaning against a stone indicating 14 km. to Creil, he attracted no more than passing glances from the dusty, tired-looking American infantrymen in the open trucks, most of them chewing gum, all with their steel helmets off or thrust onto the back of their heads.

'I'm Colonel Michael Browning of the U.S. Army Air Force.'

The corporal in the dirty white helmet raised his eyes from the map he had been studying and looked Mike up and down evincing interest only in the drips masking the dust at his feet.

'Oh yeah? Posing as a French peasant.' He pronouced 'peasant' as it is spelt. 'I guess you'd better tell that tale to General Bradley.'

Mike became angry then, and threw his rank at the M.P. hard. A jeep pulled up while he was dressing down the corporal, who was now at attention and had saluted Mike twice.

'What the shit's goin' on?' And when Mike explained, he was asked — half-suspiciously, half-deferentially — 'Do you carry any papers, Colonel?'

'Only French ones. Goddam it, you don't carry U.S. Air Force identification when you're fighting with the Resistance.'

The lieutenant indicated the empty seat beside him. He was a Southerner, and had a dead cigar slotted into the corner of his mouth. He took it out to say, 'You'd better come along with us, Colonel Browning. No good fighting to get back through this fuckin' mob. We'll be stoppin' for chow in 30 minutes, I guess.'

They ate K-rations and someone brewed up some coffee on the porch of a little château, deserted and shuttered, outside Compiegne. A dozen Shermans were refuelling from a stack of cans on the far side of the lawn, which their tracks had torn up in careless patterns, and the smell of gas lay heavily on the hot midday air.

One of the Sherman crews sauntered over to Mike's jeep. He was wearing regulation tank-crew overalls, buttons undone against the heat, and carried the insignia of a Major. He was twirling his helmet, which had some twigs thrust through the netting, the leaves now dead.

The Major looked down quizzically at Mike, who was sitting on the lowest of the steps leading to the porch of the château. There was a smile on his oil-smeared face, which he had not shaved for days. 'It's Mike Browning, isn't it? For Christ's sake what're you doing here, and in that crazy get-up?'

Mike leapt to his feet and the two men, the Colonel in the U.S.A.A.F. and the Major in the armoured division of General Omar Bradley's First U.S. Army, embraced like a couple of Frenchmen, to the astonishment of the tank crews.

Jo Forrester had been at Andover with Mike until '36 when they had both left Bartlet Hall, and the families had been friends for years. Jo had even met Eileen, briefly, back on that walking tour. And now, here in France, close to the banks of the River Oise and 1½ kilometres west of the little village of St Muerdelin, they held each others' shoulders and launched into a torrent of reminiscences.

'To think,' began Jo, handing Mike a Lucky Strike, 'I've been chasing that damned 58th Panzer Corps for five days, and all I've caught is one Andover boy.'

Briefly, in that mid-day heat, Mike felt the grief and weariness of the past twenty-four hours slip away. He was back home, and he had not realized until this moment how much he had missed it in almost six years of fighting.

9

The Last Battle

The voice was unmistakable. 'Hi! What's doing?'

'For God's sake, Mike, where are you?'

'I'm at B70 — Antwerp. Not so far from you.'

Keith asked, 'Have you got a squadron there?' It was a bad line, thick with static, but Keith thought he said, 'No — liaison.' Then was it 'Swell job'? And he seemed to add, 'Be right with you'.

For the next two hours, Keith had to concentrate all his mind on his job. The Canadians had opened a massive offensive into the Reichswald Forest where the Waffen S.S. had been holding out all through the winter in spite of heavy bombing and shelling. 338 Wing's task was to act as top cover to the rocket-firing and dive bomber Typhoons which were busy on cab-rank work, directing their ferocious offensive power at pin-point targets to which they were directed by Army and R.A.F. officers in forward posts.

From 10,000 feet, Keith in his new 'Nero' and with his three squadrons fanned out behind in sections of four, could see the field of battle laid out in smoke-strewn miniature. The defeat of Germany, in the greatest war in history, must be imminent. The Russians were at the gates of Berlin, their massive armies rolling implacably into the Greater German Reich. The Allied armies in the west, foiled of victory in the late summer, and now stronger than ever, morale high, well led, short of nothing (2nd T.A.F.'s fighter losses on that memorable and damaging 1 January had been made up from England within a few days) must soon break across the Rhine and sweep over the flat plains of northern Germany to meet the Russians.

Yet still the Germans fought on — fought for every metre of the gateway to the Fatherland, calling on boys and middle-aged men to fill the thinning ranks in the front line. It was like 1918 over again, with the big difference that this time German morale seemed unaffected by the desperate odds against them.

The scene below was surely unchanged from 1918: Keith might have been on patrol in a S.E.5a instead of a Mark V Tempest, the zig-zag lines of trenches, the devastated landscape of tree stumps, ruined burning buildings, torn roads, the pock-marking from countless shells and bomb craters, all half seen through the smoke of destruction.

On this clear February morning, Keith could hear nothing but the steady rumble of his Sabre. Two miles below, the sound would be a cacophonous chorus of German Schmeissers, Mausers and Nebelwerfers, 37s and 88s, 105s and 150s, Allied 25-pounders, 5.5-inch, Brens, howitzers and w-h-o-o-s-h-i-n-g flame-throwers.

Nor was the Luftwaffe dead yet. The days, five years earlier, when the skies were dominated by Heinkel, Dornier and Junkers bombers, when the Stuka was the terror of Western Europe and Messerschmitt fighters swept all before them during the invasion of France and the Low Countries, were now only history. The skies were Allied skies. British, American, Canadian, Australian, New Zealand, Rhodesian, French, Norwegian and Belgian air crews dominated the air. A thousand Lancasters, Halifaxes, American Liberators and Flying Fortresses, could be turned onto a target at a few hours' notice, dropping a greater weight of high explosive than the whole of the German bomber force could carry in 1940.

But the Luftwaffe still had a sting in its tail, as it had demonstrated in the Ardennes offensive in December, and again on 1 January. Me262 jets still ranged the battle front, harassing Allied columns on the ground, photographing their progress, capable — at the touch of the throttles — to outpace anything the British or Americans could put into the air.

It was still necessary to protect the ground attack aircraft, as 338 Wing were now protecting 146 Wing Typhoons, although no

262s or long-nose Focke-Wulf 190s appeared on this first day of the Reichswald Forest offensive.

'Mushroom aircraft — drop tanks,' Keith called, and turned the Wing once more onto an easterly heading above the smoke and fury of the battle, and the sinuous River Rhine still barring the way into Germany.

Two thousand feet below, the dive bombers were flicking over onto their backs, revealing black and white identity stripes, and disappearing vertically into the smoke of battle. The pilots would be holding their sights onto the artillery positions, the concentrations of transport, perhaps a shattered building still acting as Panzer H.Q., the 3.7 and 20 mm. flak racing up to meet them.

But up here all was serenely quiet.

Keith called, 'This is Mushroom Leader — any trade?'

Control at Raachen came back at once: 'Mushroom Leader — sorry, no trade. Give it another fifteen minutes and return to base.'

'Roger.'

Yes, different from 1940.

* * *

The Mustang was parked by the little watch office at Raachen, at once identifiable as American by its unpainted alloy shine and camouflage markings, by contrast with the dead matt camouflage paint of the 338 Wing Tempests. On his circuit before coming in, Keith noted the five-pointed star on the fuselage, the scarlet rudder, black-and-white checker-board nose, the mark of one of the Duxford-based 8th Air Force machines.

'Be right with you.' Is that what Mike had said? It looked now as though he had arrived.

Keith touched down, his Nero still running fast as it passed the watch office. He caught a glimpse of Mike's short, stocky figure standing with some officers close to his machine, cap off, overalls discarded, in khaki U.S.A.A.F. uniform. He gave Keith a wave, and then turned back to the R.A.F. officers beside him.

Keith disregarded his rigger who was waving him into his hardstanding, and taxied on to the watch office, swinging round his Tempest to park it alongside the Mustang. Mike was looking up at him, just as he used to come out and greet him if they were not flying together on the same op in 1940: the same ruffled-up hair, the same lines of anxiety on his forehead belied by the broad smile.

'Hi, buddy.'

'Mike — what're you doing here?' Keith took in the Colonel's insignia, the American D.F.C. ribbon in addition to the British D.F.C. and bar. 'I never know whether you're going to be a Yank or a Limey.'

'I'm having a special uniform made — half and half — Wing Commander Colonel Browning of the mid-Atlantic, Anglo-American bastard squadron.'

They walked towards the mess, their breath steaming in the cold February air, exchanging news. Yes, Keith's Richard (named after his adopted father, and born Christmas Day) was fine. Jenny was in Half Moon Street, but looking for a house. Tom Mathers was M.O. at a new airstrip only ten miles away. Moira had had a girl and loved being a mother. Buffer was coming out to 2nd T.A.F. as a Squadron-Leader I.O., was engaged to a W.A.A.F. officer — 'Well that's swell, really swell!' Polo Satterthwaite had got a Spitfire Wing — but that hadn't affected his style or dress, apparently.

Keith looked at Mike over a pint mug of bitter in the bar. Yes, he was thinking — swell about Buffer. She must be some girl. But what about Mike? How had he recovered? Keith's mind went back to 19 September, the previous Autumn, when the Arnhem operation still looked as if it might succeed, as if the war might really be over by Christmas. He had just landed from an escort show, Lancasters and Halifaxes, the usual frowsty feeling after over two hours in the cockpit breathing oxygen, the first draw on the cigarette like nectar, and relaxing him as he talked things over with Bill Watson.

A corporal had come at the double. 'Excuse me, sir, telephone.'

'Ask who it is and say I'll ring back.'

'It's direct from London, sir. Personal.'

Then Keith had run to his office, suddenly desperate. It could only be about Jenny. She had miscarried ... had had an accident.

It was her voice. 'Yes, yes, I'm all right. Fine. But, darling — oh Lord, I hate this, this telling, especially when you've got so much to worry about ...'

'Come on, Jenny.' If *she* was all right, then it could be nothing,

nothing at all.

'It's Eileen, darling. She was killed in France, nearly a month ago. Mike was with her, but he's O.K. ...'

Jenny's voice faded and came back, faded again so that he could only just hear her, and the commercial G.P.O. pips sounded out every few minutes, and once the operator asked impatiently if they had finished.

All Keith had been able to say, angrily, was, 'Why didn't she tell us? S.O.E.? It's incredible. She wasn't fit for that sort of thing.'

'No, you're wrong, Keith. She was doing marvellously, Mike said. Was killed blowing up a bridge somewhere near Paris. She's been given a posthumous George Cross.'

Nothing at all indeed! Eileen dead. Eileen, half-sister or so it had seemed, for years, for almost all his boyhood. His last link severed. First his own parents, then Eileen's, and now Eileen herself. Now it was as if his childhood had never happened, and his life had been only war and fear and killing. Nothing else at all.

Then Jenny's voice again: 'I can't tell you how sorry I am, darling. You've got me, though. Don't forget that, and don't forget how much I love you, and don't forget our child. Moving about now.'

And then the voice had been cut off, as if the impatient operator had decided enough was enough.

Now here was Mike, seen for the first time since that tragedy, though they had written and spoken. What about him? How was he getting over it? Was there not a certain gravity in the set of his face, in the timbre of his voice, which had never been there before? Certainly not in 1937, in the Black Forest.

'How're things, Mike?'

'O.K. Swell. I've made myself a new post. S.F.L.O. 8 A.F. 2 T.A.F.'

'What does that gobbledygook mean?'

' "Senior Fighter Liaison Officer American 8th Air Force and 2nd Tactical Air Force R.A.F." No guy in high command seems to recognize it, but it allows me to get around, like this. Fly the ops I want. Berlin with Forts one day, looking for V2 sites the next.'

'Lies. All lies. Colonel Browning line-shooting again.'

'God's truth.' Mike ordered another pint, and sat Keith down

198

at a folding table in the corner of the bar. 'But what I really want — and this journey really is necessary — what I really want is a 262.'

'You're nuts. No one catches 262s. Even a stripped Tempest. And certainly not that old tortoise you've got out there.'

'D'you want a bet, old buddy of my youth?'

'What on, you being faster than my Nero? Or on who's going to get a jet 262 first?'

Mike laughed. Perhaps he really was O.K., Keith mused. Perhaps he had got over Eileen's death. 'Both,' he said decisively. 'A crate of Mumms Extra Dry on both. And to celebrate the end of the war.'

The Wing was stood down at 3 p.m. and Keith asked Mike if he would like a drive round to see how the other half lived. Wrapped up against the cold with balaclava helmets and Irvine jackets, Keith drove his jeep out of the camp and through the Dutch village of Schaijk. The little single storey houses lacked paint but everything was trim and immaculately tidy. There were hollow-cheeked, severe-looking men on bicycles without tyres, and the women in their worn and austere dresses showed the gaunt evidence of four years of German occupation and semi-starvation. There were several little shops in the village, all with nothing for sale and with no more than a patterned paper decoration on the window-display counter.

It was Mike's first time in liberated Holland. He had seen pictures of the wild welcome given to the advancing Allied troops — garlands of flowers, laughing children held up, catching bars of chocolate they had not seen for years. This dour little village seemed in strange contrast.

'They look as starved and miserable as under the Krauts,' he commented. 'Don't we give them enough to eat?'

Keith said, 'They're still on pretty short rations. Supply's the problem. And the Dutch are feeling a bit let down. Five months ago they thought they had seen the last of the Germans. Freedom for the whole country. And then Arnhem. And now most of the country's still in German hands, and things are pretty rough in The Hague and Amsterdam. It's hard on them.'

The main Nijmegen road was thick with military traffic of trucks and tankers, transporters with tanks, mobile artillery, staff cars, jeeps and motor cycles. Keeping several million men supplied with fuel and food, arms and ammunition, in the middle of a great offensive, was a major logistical operation, and that was the reason why there was little more than subsistence rations for the local people.

Keith took the jeep half up onto the verge, and they bumped past the long convoy like this, with military police signalling them through and saluting them as they passed. They ran over the famous Nijmegen road bridge, past fields littered with the carcasses of gliders from the September airborne landing which had secured this vital link, and then turned right towards German-occupied Cleves. They were nearing the front line now, and there was a less relaxed, more business-like atmosphere. The road had been heavily shelled, the craters roughly filled in. Knocked-out tanks, some carrying the white star of the Allies, others the black cross of Germany, lay in the ditches or in the fields, blackened and holed by direct hits, tracks cast off — like the gliders, more of the vast detritus of war.

A battery of Canadian 25-pounders was firing from a camouflaged site in a nearby copse. Keith felt the percussive crack as if his cheek and ear were being smacked with the back of a hand.

A Canadian M.P. signalled the jeep to a halt. 'I guess that's far enough, sir. They're mortaring up the road and there're still a few mines about.'

'How's it going?'

'Tough.' As confirmation, am ambulance pounded down a track, joined the road, and headed fast for Nijmegen. Half a dozen trucks full of troops and two mobile Bofors trucks pulled into the side of the road to let it through. Suddenly the air was rent with a mixed chorus of machine-gun and mortar fire. The nearby 25-pounders added to the onslaught of sound, and from farther away came the threatening moan of German Nebelwerfers.

Keith and Mike crouched down beside the jeep. Their soft flat-topped hats, which they held down over their heads, felt inadequate as a heavy mortar shell exploded a hundred yards away, sending a spray of dirt in their direction.

'I guess we'll leave this to the pros,' Mike suggested. In a brief lull, they got back into the jeep and drove fast down the road towards Nijmegen again.

'At least the flak doesn't last.' Keith drew the jeep into the side of the road when they were well away from the sound and fury. He offered Mike a cigarette. 'Now we know what it's like down there.'

'Gee, we were a mile *behind* the front line!'

* * *

The next morning, the entire Wing was despatched to strafe the front-line trenches in the sector they had visited. The flak and small arms fire was ferocious, but Keith went back a third time after ordering the Wing back to base, using up the remainder of his ammunition: The Reichswald Forest like an ill-shaven face, tortured stumps by the thousand, water-filled craters by the hundred, glimpses of wicked barbed wire striding across the mud, deep trenches zig-zagging, a flash of S.S. helmets and field grey.

Keith spotted a gunpost a shade to the right, pine branches over the camouflage netting, kicked rudder, and poured his last shells into it. There was not much he would be able to tell the I.O. A 105 mm. probably. The crew were bunched together, caught by surprise. He had seen only a whipped up cloud from his two-second burst. A thousand shells a minute from four Hispanos. Yes, he guessed he had killed some, left behind a desperate confusion of blood and flesh and bone.

Not for the I.O.: *Yes, I do mind. I have always minded. No, I do not enjoy killing men, singly or* en masse *like that. By any rational calculation, I should long ago have added my body to the pile of corpses I have accumulatively been responsible for over the years.* No, not for the I.O., not even for Jenny, ever: *Yes, I have hated it from the beginning, as I knew I would. But then does anyone actually enjoy it? Only a sick mind could relish the agony and death caused by fighting in the air, from that 11 November 1939, my twenty-first birthday (Oh God, how young and innocent!) to this 10 February 1945 over the Waffen S.S. trenches, figures tumbling in the mud, smashed by me.*

* * *

Mike greeted Keith the next morning at breakfast. 'What about my 262? Good day for hunting.'

It had snowed or sleeted all night, and the cloud was low. Mike was right. These were the conditions the Luftwaffe recce pilots enjoyed, when they could come over very low, below the radar, and nip up into cloud if there was any trouble. The Army hated them, and the information they brought back in their cameras was often very damaging to the Allied campaign.

'O.K. keen type,' Keith said. 'We'll take off at nine.'

It was good to have Mike lined up on the runway beside him. The American looked small in the cockpit of the heavy-bellied silver Mustang, and Keith watched him slip on his old, much battered early type R.A.F. helmet, mask and goggles. Mike lifted his thumb to indicate that he was ready, and Keith raised a hand and thrust it forward in the old gesture they had learned at flying school a million years ago.

It was a faultless, flying-display formation take-off, with Mike's starboard wingtip almost brushing the Tempest's port tailplane, and they were airborne exactly simultaneously — undercarriage up together, flaps up together, identical canopies slid shut together, two vintage veterans who knew each other's flying as a long-married couple can read thoughts and anticipate every gesture.

Already at 500 feet they were brushing the base of the grey clouds. Keith headed down the S-Hertogenbosch road, planning to patrol just off the line of the main supply routes of the 2nd British Army. There was a measures of risk of mis-identification by trigger-happy ack-ack gunners, but it was where they were most likely to pick up the odd recce machine.

South-west down to Tilburg, south of Crockzijde, then east again on the dead straight road pointing like a lance towards Germany. Keith and Mike flew in loose line abreast, five hundred yards apart, turning their heads constantly from side to side, experienced eyes searching the winter sky. There was scattered snow on the ground, obscuring the identity of the winter crops, and the long, straight drainage ditches were dull-grey with ice. Once some tracer came up from a group of parked trucks, but stopped almost at once as the gunners recognized their mistake. A section of four rocket Typhoons swept past in the opposite direction, the rails beneath their wings carrying their eight missiles — doubtless off on some pinpoint mission.

They were far south of Tilburg when Mike called up. 'Nine o'clock'. That's all. But he had kicked his Mustang round through 90 degrees, white streamers from his wingtips, and Keith conformed. It looked like a long-nose 190. Yes, it was. Travelling very fast on a southerly course, a bomb under its belly.

They had both opened up to maximum boost, Rolls-Royce Merlin against Napier Sabre, and Keith was in and out of cloud in an attempt to conceal his approach. Then suddenly, at 1,000 yards range, the 190 put up its nose, and disappeared. That was all.

Keith cut his way through 1,500 feet of cloud on instruments and broke out into blinding sun but saw only Mike emerging half a mile ahead. Keith transmitted: 'Steer 170 below, I'll stay up for two minutes'.

But the Focke-Wulf was clearly staying within the comfortable concealment of the thick cloud, and when they slipped alongside one another again, there was no sign of it.

They picked up the Me262 five minutes later. They were steering due south over Beckaaut. Keith said, 'Tally ho!' But they had spotted the unfamiliar sleek shape of the twin-engined jet simultaneously. It was flying fast, but no faster than they were, aileroning from side to side as if lost or in search of prey.

'There's my baby.'

'We'll see,' said Keith. 'I'm going upstairs again. You see what you can do down here.'

Back in the sun, endless rolling white hillocks in every direction. High above, the vapour trails from a formation of American heavies, too high to identify as Forts or B24s.

Mike's voice, urgently, 'He's coming up, heading about 170 when I lost him.'

Keith with throttle lever full forward, then through the gate, weaving his Tempest gently, button to fire. A quick sweeping glance over the instrument panel, left to right, ending with fuel gauge and radiator temperature.

The jet came up like a rocket from the white sea of cloud, almost vertically and at a climbing speed Keith had never seen before. 'I have him, he's up here. Christ, he goes!'

Mike broke out of the cloud, a shade to the east of the 262. The jet turned as if to make a diving attack on him, then the pilot changed his mind and continued his climb, with Keith hard astern. The Tempest was flat out and there was nothing more he could do. 390 on the clock, 3,000 feet per minute on the rate of climb, and he was dropping behind.

The 262 would have got clean away. Neither Mustang nor Tempest could hope to catch it. But Mike was between him and his base, and with the Tempest behind, the pilot appeared to lose his nerve. The Messerschmitt went over onto its back, black crosses, scarlet tailplane, clearly visible, and pulled into a vertical dive that shallowed out as he dropped into the cloud again on a due east course, the sun on his starboard quarter.

Mike was in the better position to follow him. Keith watched the silver machine — diminutive and suddenly outdated — flick into the cloud, and seconds later, Keith himself was swallowed in damp grey vapour, over 500 showing on his A.S.I.

He came out smack above the 262, dark against the white snow. It was jinking and slewing, and thus losing speed. Mike was dead astern, 500 yards Keith reckoned, opening fire to keep the German pilot worried and evading.

Keith came in on the port side, just matching Mike's speed, and lined up for a ten-degree deflection shot. A three-second burst, some hits, he believed. Then Mike. They both climbed, manoeuvring in long-practiced co-ordination, the 262 gaining ground fast, but losing it again when the two fighters came down, one from each side, and the pilot began to kick rudder and throw the stick to and fro.

He did not make an easy target. Keith's next burst was wild, but he got in a second before having to break, and this time he saw strikes along the fuselage. And Mike got the port engine, which gouted black smoke.

They were no more than fifty feet above the flat white landscape. Then the Messerschmitt's nose went up as if kicked from below, and the sleek dark shape was swallowed by cloud again.

'Hold it!' Keith said. 'I think we're going to see him again.'

They circled, one behind the other, over a farmhouse, a track, a field of mottled snow, a wide ditch that might have been a canal, a road with some light military traffic. And waited, watching.

Keith was right. Still swinging heavily, the pilot came out of the cloud under his chute, a suddenly vulnerable little figure deprived of his lethal and mighty Messerschmitt. He was still swinging when he made a bad landing, tumbling over and over, and failing to release his chute which dragged him along for a dozen yards before collapsing.

A truck had halted and Keith saw figures running across the

field, marking their footsteps in the snow.

'That's that!'

'What did I say, goddamit!' Mike was laughing triumphantly. 'Now for the Mumms.' He had made his point, and it was an equal share, just as their first had been on that distant day in that distant place five years and three months ago.

They were only five miles from base, and Mike tucked in close again, canopy open, helmet off to cool his head in the old style. There was nothing left to prove. They had shot down a jet, and the combat had shown that there was nothing to choose between 'Nero' and Mike's sleek silver Mustang as far as speed was concerned.

* * *

The reason why the Luftwaffe pilot had made the disastrous tactical error of diving for cover close to the ground became clear after luncheon. It had begun to snow again, and the Wing was stood down. Keith and Mike and a dozen others were in the mess bar drinking beer (no Mumms available — 'Bad show, ol' boy!') when an orderly came in with a message. The Army had dumped their victim on them. They did not know what else to do with him. And he needed some attention to a sprained ankle.

Keith told the orderly to inform the police that he wanted him brought to the mess. He arrived ten minutes later, a woebegone Feldwebel in loose flight blouse and supported by a stick some-one had lent him. Keith answered his salute and asked him to sit and gave him a beer. The German took it reluctantly, defiantly— but he took it, and then suddenly drank it thirstily.

'I am sorry to have caused you this inconvenience,' Keith said in German, introducing Mike. 'It was two against one. But I don't think you will be our prisoner for long.'

The Feldwebel was reluctant to speak at first, but mellowed under the influence of another pint. He had nothing to hide, he said. He was eighteen (he looked more like sixteen), had soloed in a Henschel in December in Bavaria, had done four hours on 262s, and admitted to finding them intimidating. Yes, he had fired the guns once — 'Mein Gott, the power ...!'

Looking at this inexperienced boy, with the acne of youth on his young face, thrown into battle without proper training or experience, Keith reflected on the decline of the once great

Luftwaffe. Leaving behind orders that he should be given something to eat before being taken to the guard-house, Keith shook
the pilot's hand, thankful that he had not killed this boy who was
so ill-equipped for war. At least *he* had been spared.

'Guess I'll make it back to Duxford before dark.'

'Had enough of Holland, Mike?'

'I've got what I came for. Seen you, got me half a 262. See you
at the Club on Victory Day. O.K.?'

The snow had eased but visibility was still poor. Mike would be
O.K., and it would be no use warning him anyway. Mike Browning always got his way, winning right along the line. Then Keith
corrected himself as he watched his old friend slip into the
Mustang's cockpit — corrected himself harshly, recalling that
Mike would say he had lost the most important battle of them all,
the battle for Eileen. And he had never mentioned her.

The Merlin roared into life, the slipstream sending back a
cloud of snow. Mike made a single economical gesture to cover
'Chocks away!' and 'Be seeing you!' and taxied out fast, swinging
the sleek silver machine's tail....

10

M for Mumms

A warm, drowsy evening in May. Victory in Europe night. V.E. night, the streets in Central London already filling, and they had been *en fête* all day, flags and drunks everywhere, embracing couples, every uniform and every nationality in the world, from Burmese nurses to Czech S.A.S. colonels, privates from Delaware, submariners from New Zealand, Warrant Officer rear-gunners with two D.F.M.s (miracles of survival) to Pioneer Corps corporals who had never left the country. Allies, every one. Especially tonight.

At the Flying Club in Pall Mall it was not all blue uniforms, and women had been allowed in for the evening (they would have come anyway). Mike was not the only U.S.A.A.F. officer, but he was the only American with British and American D.F.C.s, and that turned even the most blasé, most senior, head. He had four friends from the American Embassy, Jo Forrester and a girl he called Mabel-Lu ('ol' love of my youth'). He was already very considerably and very cheerfully high, but only Mabel-Lu was actually on his knee, with her arms round his neck from time to time. At other times she drew out another bottle of Mumms from the crate at their side and gave it to one of the aged (and shocked) servants to open.

Keith, inevitably, was not far away, in about the same condition. More demurely, Jenny was at his side on the sofa, though very close to him, and absent-mindedly kissing him every so often. Buffer Davies with his enchanting W.A.A.F. wife, at the other end of the sofa, was doing most of the champagne bottle withdrawing from the other crate. Buffer was singing a dreadful song dreadfully out of tune about Garbo, who stood outside in Pall Mall in all her pre-war glory, and with her tank filled to the brim with 110 octane aviation fuel.

Somewhere in the milling mob of R.A.F. officers and W.A.A.F.s (with a strong contingent of W.R.N.S. officers) they had caught sight of Polo Satterthwaite (Wing Commander D.S.O., D.F.C.), very plastered, Bill Watson, unconscious in a corner, and more sober old-timers like Skewer Daniel (Group Captain with two D.S.O.s), Bull Rowbotham, and Willy Williams the Spy, unstable in his seeming craftiness but with an unspilt brimming tankard of Guinness in each hand.

Jenny, complaining that her Richard would be dying of hunger if she did not return home, and would certainly get drunk on her milk in her present state if she did, announced that it was time to go to the Palace.

So they did, in Garbo, Mike and Mabul-Lu, Keith and Jenny, all clinging onto the tail, Buffer's wife in the only passenger seat. They travelled very slowly, edging through the packed crowds in the Mall, the object of much cheering, arriving with streamers criss-crossed over the Bentley Special like cobwebs, and Buffer now driving standing up, supported by his wife, and using the hand throttle on the wheel.

By the Victoria Memorial, they came to a halt. Tom and Moira were already there, by arrangement, Moira carrying her baby. It was still difficult to get used to the street lamps being on, and to lights streaming from windows and doorways. Buffer got a huge torch out of the glove locker and shone it towards Buckingham Palace and the balcony on which the Royal Family were due to appear.

Someone shouted, 'Put that light out!' mimicking an outraged Air Raid Warden, and laughter rippled round Garbo. At the same moment the lights went on over the balcony, drowning Buffer's beam, and the Royal party came out, answering the tremendous cheers.

Mike and Keith both stood up unsteadily on Garbo's tail, waving empty bottles of champagne. Then, with the cheers and clapping sounding as loudly as ever, they bent down in unison and withdrew the last two bottles from the crates jammed between the car's seats.

For a fleeting moment their eyes met as their heads almost cracked together.

'Here's cheers ol' boy ol' top,' said Mike in his execrable mock posh English.

'And here's mud in your goddam eye,' said Keith, in his equally appalling American accent.

'We made it.'

'Yeah, we made it.'

The noise was so awful, and they were so drunk anyway, that it was not until the next morning when they woke up at about 11 a.m., with the room going round (quite pleasantly because Mumms Extra Dry is a very good champagne) that the images began to project themselves upon their minds, forming a summary of their war that had been won at such cost: sombre images, terrifying images, as well as happy and triumphant images: For Mike, Sammy Crow in his makeshift Hurri-bomber diving to his death at the Norwegian tunnel-mouth, Sergeant Walker dying in his arms on that raft of frozen despair and death, a B17 going down in a spiral so fast that no one got out, an engine, a wing, then the second wing, stripping off to leave only a fuselage, a bomb with a human charge. And Eileen, shy and blushing and heart-rendingly vulnerable, in her W.R.N.S. uniform for the first time.

For Keith there remained memories of shock and guilt-ridden ecstasy when he had blown up a Ju.88 over Ashford way back in '40, of grief and anger surging up in him as he tried to talk life back into Sergeant-Pilot Henry, shallow diving into cloud in his blood-smeared cockpit, and that loner, fearless Randall, the most skilful pilot he had ever known, blowing up a hundred — it might have been two hundred — flying bombs, and himself.

There were memories of mess parties and beat-ups as well as the early retirement after dinner to write letters to next-of-kin — 'He was a grand pilot and a grand officer to have in the mess, and I hope it will be some consolation for you to know that ...'

The sounds and smells — the ripple of German cannon fire high in the summer sky, the roar of a Merlin on test at the dispersal, the discordant singing of drunk airmen in the black-out, the heart-freezing cries and shrieks of terror-filled airmen trapped in a direct-hit air raid shelter. The whiff of gunk and glycol and high octane petrol pumping from bowser to wing tank, clinging about a refuelling Hurricane. The cigarette smoke staleness in the air of a blacked-out ready room, the heavenly flavour of the first inhale after an arduous show. The stench of blood and German dope and lingering cordite fumes in a crashed Heinkel. For Mike, the sweet scent of Eileen dancing in his arms, by contrast with the latrine stink of that encampment in the woods above the Oise from which she had walked off into the rain and darkness to her death.

So many sights and sounds and scents, the flotsam, the gleaning, the tragic detritus, the precious panned gold-dust of this long war.